PRANKZz

PRANKZz

Harish Sharma

RUPA

First published in 2012 by
Rupa Publications India Pvt. Ltd.
7/16, Ansari Road, Daryaganj,
New Delhi 110 002

Sales Centres:

Allahabad Bengaluru Chennai
Hyderabad Jaipur Kathmandu
Kolkata Mumbai

10 9 8 7 6 5 4 3 2 1

Printed in India by
Nutech Photolithographers
B-240, Okhla Industrial Area, Phase-I,
New Delhi-110 020

Especially for Sanjay and Ajay.

Also for all those in the medical profession who save and prolong lives.

I think, therefore I am.

Rene Descartes

The body is a big sagacity, a plurality with one sense,
a war and a peace, a flock and a shepherd.

Friedrich Nietzsche

Acknowledgements

First and foremost, my thanks are due to Rupa Publications for not only accepting the proposal for this book but also for the thoroughly professional and efficient manner the book was produced in. In particular, Suzanne, who edited the book, bringing out the best out of it with her incisive suggestions.

Thanks also to Chinta Kallie, Dee Kallie, and Professor Krish Bharuth-Ram in Oxford for providing support and shelter when I needed it most.

In Bangalore, my adopted home, Joe and Susan Varghese, Sarita and Anmol Vellani, BC Lingappa and Narayana Narasappa – for being there and helping me settle down; as well as Neha Sharma in Delhi.

And dear reader if you're still there, many thanks for picking up this book. I hope the harmless little prank I played on you with this story was enthralling and entertaining. Do hit back.

Prologue

DARKness.

Total darkness is oppressive enough, given its unquestionable might and mystery. It can be seen and not. All that human eyes can do is to note the darkness and let a lazy brain register it with the arrogance it deserves. In a windowless morgue at the dead of night, darkness is an unexpected comfort to its occupants, not that they need it, being dead to everything for every possible purpose. Almost. Even the air, still and heavy with formaldehyde that pricked sensitive nostrils, discouraged any activity, in particular at this exact midnight hour. Sounds, if there were any, were magnified in the echo laden folds of the room.

A key rattled in the door with the urgency of a speeding ambulance, yet disturbing no one. The door of the morgue creaked inwards, widening a triangular shaft of yellow light on the granite floor. A hand swept a wall, feeling for light switches. Click after click energized the neon strip of lights into long awaited life.

The morgue assumed a different atmosphere as Kamal stepped in, closing the door softly behind him. At almost six feet and in his usual black turban, the ever present black necktie, and with his sharply trimmed beard, the first-year Sikh medical student cut an impressive figure as he approached the large metal drawers that ran along one side of a wall, each one chilled so that the occupant remained of some use. Kamal ignored everything else that resided in the morgue – three spotless white marble like 'prep' or 'preparation' slabs with gullies on the edges for fluids to drain away, accompanied by dead sound recording mikes, spotlights and a water spigot, all suspended from the ceiling on twirled extendable cables. Behind the idle slabs were rows of sturdy shelves on which rested labelled glass jars containing human embryos of all sizes, curtailed at various stages and preserved in faded yellowish formaldehyde as if still resting in the warm comfort of a womb, except for the eerie silence and stillness. Internal human organs – brains, livers, hearts and many others, some sliced in cross sections and others intact were similarly confined. Miracles of evolution over millennia, once aflutter with a seamless coordination of activity, keeping their owners intact and above all, alive, had different uses now. Below the shelves, on the floor were wooden crates with neatly arranged human bones in them, small ones, long ones and skulls too; each one dignified with old, tattered labels that gave them some form of identity, no matter how feeble. Yes, even a morgue has its hierarchy but Kamal was not interested in this section. At the beginning of the academic year, like all first-year students he had been inducted to all the functional, educational, social and recreational facilities of the academy and his group had already spent a whole afternoon familiarising themselves with what the morgue had to offer. There was some unease at first but by the end of the session, under some expert guidance, all the students had relaxed and even cracked some questionable jokes and witticisms about dead bodies. Since that time, some ten months ago, Kamal like the other students had gone in and out of the morgue countless times, and by then had handled, dissected and studied so many cadavers that this became second nature and he no longer felt the slightest trepidation. The difference this time was that it was midnight and he was on his own, and his mission was different although it did concern the kings and queens of the morgue – the cadavers.

He pulled open the first drawer of the top row in the left corner. Steady and expressionless, he looked down at the top half of a clean-shaven middle-aged male cadaver which was pale yellow and waxen in its stillness, the unseeing eyes wide open, which no one had bothered to close. Kamal extracted a packet of small red sweets from his pocket and placed it on the cadaver's chest. He bent over and attempted to open the cadaver's mouth by pulling the chin downwards, but the stubborn chin refused to budge even when he tried with both hands. He realized in an instant that the jaws were locked and stiff and then looked around wondering what to do. It was a simple matter of unlocking the jawbone from the joint just beneath the earlobe, which is where he placed the base of his palms, pressing hard till the head jerked upwards. This was the first time he had done this but sure enough he felt and heard the telltale 'clack' of bones disengaging, just like knuckle joints when pulled. The slack mouth sagged open easily and Kamal reached for a sweet and dropped it into the gaping mouth. He collected the sweets and tried to close the mouth but found that the lower jaw had jammed. Curling his hand into a fist, he tapped the chin. The second tap was slightly harder and the mouth snapped shut with the loud sound of gnashing teeth, not unlike an angry crocodile's. Kamal was jolted by a momentary stab of fright and the packet of sweets nearly fell out of his hand. He took a deep breath and recovered quickly; sliding the drawer shut and opening the one below it, smiling at his own unnecessary reflex action. The next one was an older male cadaver and Kamal repeated the same procedure with him. He was getting better at feeding sweets to the cadavers, old ones, young ones, males and females, one after the other. Composure regained, Kamal smiled to himself again as his mission was turning out to be much easier than he had anticipated.

A small fright and a smile or not, this was not how or where it had started but it was here that it began to get serious.

Before this it was just silly supposedly harmless mischief to
which almost all first-year medical students were prone.
All the same, everything has to start somewhere
and it was here that the mischief
got beyond itself...

At the beginning it was all very different at 'RAMS'.

PART ONE

1

The Rajiv Gandhi Academy of Medicinal Sciences or 'RAMS' was one of the two best academies in the whole country in terms of location, structure, facilities and most importantly, results. Over the years it had grown from a single, old building to a widespread campus in keeping with the growth of its reputation and the generous donations received from highly reputable and well placed alumni, some of whom worked in rich countries around the globe. Each year the academy accepted only thirty of the ablest and brightest domestic students and only six foreign exchange students, and after five years of rigorous practical, theoretical, and personal training, accompanied by examinations of the toughest kind, turned them into motivated and efficient young doctors, who, in the years to come would go on to become leading specialists, consultants, registrars and professors in their chosen areas of medicine.

The students came from different states and backgrounds as having wealthy parents was not a criterion for selection, though the academy did have a handful of very rich students. Situated beyond a leafy suburb on the northern periphery of Bangalore, the academy was everything and more that any aspiring student could wish for. As expected, the students, especially the new ones, valued and extensively used the social and recreational facilities in and around the academy grounds as soon as the much awaited Friday evening crept around. Weekdays were taken up by the sheer hard work of studying and keeping up-to-date with the various subjects that became more deeply complex as weeks went by. Hardly any student socialized due to the need to be up fresh and early for the next day's lecture or 'practical' which would start promptly at eight in the morning, with the last class ending at seven in the evening and often even later into the night. Starting Friday evening, through most of Saturday and half of Sunday, it was different. The tiredness and the stress of the week needed to be dealt and dispensed with, and just about every student forgot or tried to forget their textbooks, the lecture theatres and the labs in favour of much high-spirited partying with hollering, singing, card sessions, abundant beer drinking and general horsing around with each other, either individually or in groups. Many of these steam releasing sessions began in the common room, which was everything to everyone, where beer and snacks vied with each other. There wasn't much mingling across the batches as the first-year 'freshers' kept to themselves and the seniors to their own classmates. Friday or not, the final-year students were hardly ever seen, so steeped were they in preparing for their final exams. Year after year without fail, everyone passed their 'finals' because the one or two who were not going to pass were invited by the dean to leave the academy, and no one dared to refuse his invitation. In some batches, there would always be the odd one out who would succumb to pressure and the stress of competing, to eventually leave on health grounds, usually of a psychological nature.

It was the start of the second week for the year's new intake and already friendships and groups had been forged, usually on the basis of being from the same state or city, rooming next to each other, or sharing the same floor in the accommodation block, or all three as was the case with Kamal and Sanjay. Back in Chandigarh, they not only lived on the same street but had attended the same elite school and now, naturally, they had managed to acquire study-bedrooms next to each other on the top floor in block 'A', which was solely for the first-year students. Thus their long friendship and companionship would continue. This despite Kamal's persistent teasing of the muscular Sanjay's pride and joy, which was cultivated with such tenderness – shiny, shoulder-length silken hair.

Young men were assigned the two upper floors of the accommodation block and young women were assigned the bottom two, with each floor having its own basic washing and cooking facilities. These were kept spotlessly clean by two eager Tamil ladies who were supervised by the caretaker, who ruled from his ground floor office and wore the thickest possible lenses in his spectacles.

As was customary, the thirty-six students were split into study groups of six for their practicals and other 'lab' work, both of which required extremely close attention and supervision. Walking a step or two ahead were the three other members of Kamal and Sanjay's study group. Uma, Shivani, and Rosie had rooms next to each other on the floor below. The tall and slender, hardly modest Uma, had already assumed leadership of this group, which was in keeping with her rich and arrogant outlook on life. Compared to her, Shivani was distinctly the original Ms Average and in the week they had known each other, had accepted this station without knowing it. As for the ever so slightly plump Rosie with her tape-repaired spectacles, she too had accepted herself as a lesser being and walked accordingly, half a step behind the other two, speaking only when she was spoken to. No one knew that both her parents had died and only a bursary had enabled her admission at RAMS. She was one of the financially poor ones but she did not want that to be known.

The sixth member of this study group, Krish, did not live on campus as his parents were rich enough to rent a separate flat for their son, keep him clothed in all the latest designer outfits as well as gift him a BMW motorbike to ride. They themselves lived in an amazingly quiet square next to a golf course, right in the middle of Bangalore. With a background similar to Uma's, Krish was naturally drawn to her and it was to her that he was crashing towards, pushing past Kamal and Sanjay without acknowledgement, let alone an apology.

'What's the hurry, dude!'

A clearly annoyed Sanjay didn't bother to disguise his dislike but Krish was more interested in the girls for the moment. All of them had 'bumped' into each other during the various induction activities, but so far, this study group had not had any meaningful conversations that would give their group any identity or cohesion. If anything, there seemed to be a north-south rift emerging between the northern boys and the southern girls, with Krish gravitating towards Uma within days of having met her and her entourage of Shivani and Rosie.

Kamal and Sanjay hurried to catch up with their study group and tried to exchange inane 'good mornings' but were only met with cold, dead stares, particularly from Uma and Krish. Only Rosie murmured a reluctant greeting from beneath her broken spectacles. They were outside the old red building with a signboard proclaiming 'ANATOMY' in faded lettering, which appropriately seemed to suggest dying. All of them placed their packs on the steps and struggled into their starched and spotless white lab coats, which had to be buttoned from top to bottom with the name badges situated at the exact designated place on top of the left breast pocket. The protocol – more than sacrosanct – was that no one, not even the teaching staff could go into ANATOMY without a super-clean lab coat. The other first-year students went past them. They were chattering with some excitement as they had the less nerve-tingling task of being observers in the oval upper gallery while the six below would perform – that's right – perform their first ever dissection of a real human cadaver. None of them had ever come across a dead body apart from the induction, during which they exchanged brief, nervous glances from a distance, while pretending to be shockproof, throwing jokes about.

Waiting on the stairs of the anatomy building, the tension became palpable and even the coolest of them, Kamal, felt his heart quickening just that little bit. He decided that all the unfriendliness within his study group was due to the occasion and for no other reason; knowing what lay ahead in the immediate future – the cadaver waiting to be cut open and studied, which was its only use now. Kamal knew there were five years of blood, sweat, and tears ahead but he retained his composure best of all, and uncaringly adopted a deadpan expression. Context re-established, he waited with the other five for a lab assistant who would usher them into the theatre of life and death, where the cadaver, useful for the living, waited with the patience of an unforgiving statue.

Gleaming, pristine, and shameless silver surgical instruments that were imbued with the essence of sharpness, sawing, hammering, and gripping were arranged neatly by the side of an operating table upon which rested a white sheet with small hilly protrusions on either end. The group of six had ample time to look at and take in what awaited them. After that they even looked at each other and some false smiles were exchanged here and there, possibly in an impossible effort to relax. Apart from the anticipation of what lay beneath the unforgiving white sheet, they were tense as they were about to encounter the formidable dean of the academy, Professor Verma, whose reputation extended thousands of miles beyond his cherished academy. Having absorbed their surroundings and acknowledged what lay ahead, the group of six had ample time to dwell on Professor Verma while the lab assistant sat in his corner, filing his nails at this early hour of a crisp, sunny morning. Prof V, as the students referred to him in his absence, only taught anatomy and that too, only to first-year students. The rest of his eighty-hour week was taken up by matters of administration, discipline, meeting foreign dignitaries, and travelling abroad. Once a month he delivered a lecture for about four hours on a chosen medical subject open to the whole academy in the main hall, which would be packed. This was the teaching highlight of the month and its reputation had spread far and wide within and outside the academy. The lecture would take place on the fourth Sunday of every month so that students, teaching and technical staff, and any other interested outsiders had the time to attend.

Prof V firmly believed that the first year of studies for a medical student was the most important because this was where the foundations for correctly channelled zest, zeal, and passion for medicine were laid and it was his job to provide it. Despite that, he was already ten minutes late and the attention of the study group was beginning to wander as they looked up at the oval observers gallery above them, where increasingly loud murmurs were replacing the initial silence. None of the students above or below knew that the delay was deliberate and was meant to enable them to get used to their surroundings and to understand what the training to be a doctor was going to be like.

The dean had selected this particular study group to be the very first to carry out the very many dissections because he had adjudged them to be the brightest of the first-year batch at the interview stage. He expected these six to set learning and behavioural benchmarks for the rest.

The door flew open and Prof V strode in, nodding at the lab assistant, Pralad, who rose slowly to his feet, having been part of this long running drama for a number of years.

Prof V's lab coat was shorter and the buttons undone. He was the dean, after all, and the white hair and full grey beard were impressive enough despite his short, slightly rotund figure. After casting a quick and silencing glance at the gallery above, he turned to the group of six but addressed all the students in general.

'I trust everyone's had a good breakfast because some of you won't feel like having lunch. Others might see their breakfast again. In which case vomit bags are over there.' He pointed and Pralad held up a few brown bags.

'You'll get used to all this very quickly. Just remember, if you've gotten into this academy, then you're good, very good. Believe that and believe in yourselves.'

Prof V looked at each of the six as he strolled past them. Uma, Shivani, and Rosie stood together with Krish just behind Uma. On the other side of the operating table, Kamal and Sanjay stood together, elbow to elbow, eyes fixed on the formidable Prof V.

'All of you can choose to be the best in whichever field of medicine you want and you'll get there. But...but, you'll have to work hard. You'll have to work your hearts and minds out. Then, you'll become gifted. You'll have it in you to save lives, to prolong lives. Thereby enriching your own lives. That long road starts here.'

Prof V gestured at Pralad, who removed the white sheet with a practised flourish to reveal a naked middle-aged male cadaver, hands by its sides and eyes wide open. A collective gasp arose in the oval gallery and Shivani stepped back in revulsion while Uma rocked on her feet, needing Krish to steady her. Prof V continued his stroll, hardly caring for the prone cadaver or for the students' reactions.

'This man had a name, a history, a past, but for your purposes it – not "he" – is what you're looking at. Bone and tissue, dead meat, a corpse, a cadaver. You will cut it open bit by bit. You will look, you will feel and you will learn till you know the inside of a human body better than the back of your own hand.'

Prof V looked from the six students to the cadaver with satisfaction and to their astonishment, lowered his face to the cadaver's, till his very much alive, free breathing nostrils almost touched the very much dead ones, which were no longer bothered with the traffic of air. He elicited gasps from the gallery as he inhaled deeply and rose up, smiling.

'Get used to it and its beautiful scent. Nothing like it. Now, to business. There's an old belief in this academy, that the first incision carries an honour that leads to many more, greater ones in the future. True. It's tried and tested. Any offers before I point to someone?'

He was not given to lies but this was half of a white one, and the pure purpose of it was to get the dissection underway. An honour it certainly was but what or where it led to was far from certain. None of the six felt compelled to seek the honour at first, then three hands shot up almost at the same time with Rosie beating Kamal and Uma by a fraction of a second. Prof V checked her name badge.

'Step forward Ms Rosie Braganza and a rosy future you shall have.'

While Pralad helped Rosie's stubby fingers into skintight latex surgical gloves, Prof V put a marker pen to the middle of the lower lip of the cadaver and drew a straight line over the chin and throat contours, down the sternum and all the way to the well of the belly button. He looked up to see Rosie examining the tip of the scalpel grasped in her gloved right hand. She knew its sharpness warranted serious attention unlike the old ones she had used at her school in Goa to dissect frogs and rabbits, and suddenly she was reminded of her childhood home in a poor part of Panjim, when her parents were still alive. Prof V disturbed her untimely reverie.

'Above all, I want precision. Rosie Braganza, straight incision, half an inch deep to the second layer and always remember, the steadier the hand, the more control you have over it. Begin.'

Rosie steadied herself, thought a brief silent prayer in a silence that ghosts in graveyards would fear, and placed the tip of the scalpel where the marked line began. With a concentration that made her tongue protrude a little, she applied some pressure and pulled the scalpel along the line. The ease with which the scalpel slid through the dead tissue surprised her as did the absence of blood. The tension lifted and ease settled in. The very first incision told Prof V that Rosie's first incision was several cuts above average.

By the end of the fifth day, all thirty-six students had had their close encounters with the cadaver. Some sessions were shorter than others and some messier, but the purpose had been achieved. Now that handling surgical instruments and understanding their functions and learning dissection techniques was well underway, more practice would make them recede into the subconscious and simply become second nature. Then the real learning would begin. But not just now, as Friday evening had arrived at last.

∽

The common room was full before seven and just about every first-year student was present, standing, sitting, playing and talking. Each one was in the best of their 'casuals', mostly jeans and T-shirts. Kamal and Sanjay were at one of the four pool tables and nearing the end of a game but their attention was focused on a table around which Uma, Shivani and Rosie were sprawled on large easy chairs, drinking beer from small bottles and crunching crisps. Sanjay let Kamal win the game and quickly pulled out a quarter bottle of whisky from his pocket, emptying it into their half-full beer glasses. The small empty bottle was tossed into a nearby bin. The recreation committee had agreed to allow the sale of beer in the common room some years ago but spirits were still banned, although those who wanted them knew where to get them from and how. Kamal and Sanjay drained their glasses and looked at each other. They were still smarting from the girls keeping their distance from them even though they were all in the same study group. Seeing a suave and very urbane Krish saunter to the bar and food counter in his snakeskin loafers made them make up their minds simultaneously, as if they were one. If they didn't socialize and take their chances on a Friday or Saturday then when would they? A lot remained unspoken between them yet each knew what the other one was thinking most of the time.

'Kam, you go for Uma. I'll try Shivani.'

'No. You go for Uma. The prettier they are, the harder they play to get. Big heads, you know.'

Sanjay shrugged his considerably strong shoulders and both headed for the girls' table. He was game and smiled warmly at each girl when they reached them.

'Hi, you all. Thank God it's Friday. Interesting week, hey?'

Uma and Shivani rolled their eyes upwards and at each other. This did not go unnoticed by Kamal, who pulled a stool and sat next to Shivani. He was determined to be friendly despite the open snub.

'Hey, we're in this together. We're in the same study group after all so we might as well be a bit more sociable. Shivani?'

Kamal put his hand on Shivani's knee, which she jerked away almost as a reflex. Sanjay took a bold step and perched on the armrest of Uma's chair, taking her by surprise.

'We have five years of solid hard work ahead. We could help each other along the way. At least we could smile, occasionally, be a bit sociable, right Uma? Specially as your rooms are directly below us. So we're neighbours too.'

In response, Uma recoiled like a spoiled child and exchanged looks with Shivani while Rosie looked from one to the other and then at the boys. Rosie had a perpetual smile on her face and even a spark in her eyes but no one noticed, though Kamal threw a glance or two at her, at times. Standing at the bar counter, sipping a small glass of beer, Krish watched his study group with interest and considered joining them but decided to wait till Kamal and Sanjay left, which he knew they would. Instead, Kamal edged his stool closer to Shivani and the ever bold Sanjay placed his arm around Uma, who flinched and spoke through clenched teeth.

'Get off me, you creep!'

The arm was pushed off but it returned to the backrest of the chair. At the bar counter, Krish thought it intelligent to join his study group, after all. He finished the last of his beer, strode to them and calmly lifted Sanjay's offending arm and let it drop, then rubbed his hands as if to clear away dirt. He addressed the boys.

'Around here, chaps, no means no. Understand?'

His hostility was unmistakable and not lost on anyone, least of all by Kamal, who rose to his feet.

'Oye, none of your business. Get lost!'

'No offence meant, chaps. Seems your company is not appreciated. You should know when to take a hint especially if it's staring you in the face!'

Kamal's restraint fled. He stepped forward and grabbed the lapels of Krish's denim jacket.

'Who the hell do you think you are! Tom Cruise, kya!'

Sanjay sprang up and parted the two before matters

escalated, which they often did in the common room on Friday evenings. He pulled the glowering Kamal away.

'This goat shit is not worth it, Kam. Let's go.'

He was already thinking of another bottle of whisky, a full one, as was Kamal who could not resist a parting shot at the girls.

'All right, darlings. You might hear from us soon, you lot! You're not that far away from us. So long!'

Sanjay also wanted to confirm his solidarity with his friend.

'We'll see who has the last laugh, girls. Just watch yourselves. We'll teach you some manners.'

Kamal and Sanjay strode away and out of the common room to buy whisky and some kebabs off campus. Krish, smiling, straightened his jacket and pulled the vacant stool next to Uma and settled on it.

'Don't let it worry you, guys. Our cousins from the north, subtle as sledgehammers! Different manners, you know. Good to see you, by the way. How're you all?'

Uma and Shivani rolled their eyes heavenwards and Rosie giggled as Krish flustered on.

'You guys are in the hostel. Block 'A', I gather. Actually, I've my own flat, ha.'

The opportunity for Uma to show and prove her leadership popped up and she took it.

'We are not "guys", if you haven't noticed and there is nothing wrong with where we live. Got that?'

Krish felt a little crushed but he wanted to be with the girls, especially Uma. He tried to make amends.

'Terribly sorry. Terribly. Can I get you all a drink? Beer, yea?'

The girls were not going to refuse.

2

Sunday night in block 'A' was always depressing even if the coconut trees near the end of the block waved to it in the gentle breeze and a full moon tried to cheer it. In a small car park were four small cars, including a dusty red Maruti that belonged to Uma. Of two-wheelers, there was no shortage. Almost every window in the block was open and lights were on in all of them. The first-year students were wretchedly preparing for Monday and for the inevitable ton of hard work for the rest of the week. The next Friday evening seemed months away.

The girls were gathered in Uma's room and suffering in silence, mostly. The half-hearted sporadic conversation was about anything but studies. Uma, in her pure white silk pyjama suit, was arranging textbooks on to a bookshelf, and Shivani, on the bed in her light nightgown, stared vacantly at the ceiling while Rosie, also in a nightgown, leaned back in the study chair, scribbling in a notebook. When Shivani announced her intention to have a contraceptive coil fitted, the other two perked up a little. Rosie got the giggles but as always waited for Uma to have the first retort, which she would follow. Turning around from the bookshelf, Uma duly obliged.

'Uck, how I hate that, having something interfering with my body. Best method – don't do it, Shivo, dear.'

'Can't keep your legs crossed all the time, Uma. What with all the testosterone flying around.'

Rosie immediately worried that she might have caused some offence but Uma was in her element with her favourite subject, which was herself, as she stood erect, hands on shapely hips.

'Any chap who comes near me, even an inch, has to be special, believe you me.'

Rosie decided on another barb before she left for her room.

'Special like Kamal and Sanjay, you mean.'

This one hit the mark and Uma glared at her.

'Those idiots! Honestly, Rosie, fatso, anything in trousers will do for you. Except, I don't see anyone heading your way. So there.'

Shivani, who had started this, decided to push it further.

'Uma, don't be a rot. You've got your beady eyes on that Krish, haven't you! Just 'cause he's as filthy rich as you.'

Rosie and Shivani had managed to rattle Uma, who took a quick step towards them.

'Him! Him! God! No chance, not in a million. Simply not in my league. Mind you, he's got better class than the other two clowns.'

Job done, Rosie and Shivani got up together to take their leave when a flash of something red splashed in through the window and hit Uma squarely on the face and chest, taking her breath away, drenching her and staining her pyjama top bright red. Uma stepped back, spluttering and wiping herself while several swear words escaped from her. Rosie and Shivani were staring at the open window. Uma stepped to it, leaned out, looked sideways, downwards, and finally upwards. In the moonlight tinged with the orange glow of a nearby street lamp, she saw a tall, male figure, dangling upside down and suspended by a rope tied around the ankles. The figure was holding on to a bucket near its face. Uma's shock was changing to seething anger when the figure suddenly let the upturned bucket fall to the ground, revealing an upright, grotesque mask with long black hair, dangling downwards. A loud and piercing, primitive roar filled the night. Uma reeled back into her room, screaming louder and louder. The shock had returned with a vengeance as she bumped into Shivani, who knocked down a laden flower vase from the desk and in turn bumped into Rosie, both of whom had edged closer to the window. Trying to maintain her balance, Rosie grabbed at the newly laden bookshelf. A broken vase, books, flowers, the bookshelf on its side, Rosie and Shivani lay strewn on the hard floor, while Uma's screaming had subsided and the sobs had turned to the muttering of one word over and over.

'Bastards...bastards...bastards...'

Rosie helped Shivani to her feet and both realized that Uma was still in shock, her hands trembling. Both held Uma's hands and led her to the bed but Uma stood her ground, recovering. With still trembling hands, she took out an ornate bottle of French brandy and three crystal tumblers from a desk drawer and filled them to the rim, spilling some of the amber gold on the desk. She drained one of them and refilled it. She gestured at Rosie and Shivani to help themselves as she drank half of her second tumbler. As the warmth of expensive brandy coursed down her throat and into her stomach, it calmed her so quickly that it was little short of a miracle. Her hands stopped trembling and she handed Rosie and Shivani their tumblers. While Rosie gratefully accepted hers and drank half of it, Shivani, sitting on the edge of the bed next to her, looked up at the towering Uma in whom resolve was building up. It unnerved Shivani, who looked balefully at the brimming tumbler of brandy proffered to her.

'Sorry Uma, I don't drink hard stuff, never have. Don't think I ever will. Not my scene. Please, you carry on.'

As often was the case, Rosie looked from one to the other. She saw Shivani cowering down, and a flicker go across Uma's left eye. Shivani looked at Uma, who was as still as a stone pillar, still holding the tumbler.

'I only ever offer once and don't you dare look at me as if it is poison I'm offering you. Take it or leave it!'

Behind Uma, Rosie made faces and desperately gestured at Shivani to accept the brandy, which finally, she did. Uma walked to her wardrobe, selected a fresh T-shirt and changed out of the wet and red stained silk pyjama top, watched by the other two. She joined them on the edge of the bed, the three of them sitting in a row, comrades in hardship. All three knew who was responsible for the silly prank which had given Uma a fright, not once but twice, besides ruining her best nightwear. Uma studied her long and slender fingers and the long, perfectly shaped nails and proceeded to remove one extension after the other, revealing closely cropped nails which were an essential requirement during study hours, especially so for anatomy and other lab work. She was absorbed in this task but her mind was elsewhere. Finally, she looked up, with total resolve.

'We've got to hit back. Hit back big. Teach them a lesson they'll never forget. I don't know how but I'll think of something.'

While Shivani looked ruefully at her untouched brandy, wondering how to avoid drinking it, Rosie had cheered up and the twinkle had returned to her eye.

'Right on, Umi, baby. Don't you worry about a thing. We're with you all the way. I'll drink to that.'

Rosie clinked her tumbler with Uma's and then with Shivani's. Uma and Rosie finished what was left in their tumblers and Shivani had no choice but to take a small sip. Immediately, she choked, spluttered, and launched into a raucous bout of coughing which brought tears to her eyes. Rosie and Uma made faces at each other and both patted Shivani's back. Shivani handed her tumbler to Uma, hurried to the water bottle on the desk and drank gulps from it. She joined the other two on the edge of the bed, having recovered and cleared her throat.

'Sorry, Uma, Rosie, but never again. Never, ever. I was about to ask, which one of them was it?'

Uma looked at the gaping red wounds on her pyjama and the whole episode that the brandy had distanced rushed at her just as the red water had. She raised Shivani's almost untouched tumbler of brandy and drained it all, wiping her mouth with the back of her hand.

'Who else but that moron, Sanjay, with his stupid long hair, no doubt aided and abetted by his crony, Kamal. Wish to God the bastard had dropped on his fat head.'

3

The room was painted completely black, even the ceiling and the inside of the door. The bedclothes and curtains were also black. Everything that afforded a choice of colour was black. One of the few exceptions was a creamy bleached human skeleton which was suspended on a chain from a big metal hook in one corner of the ceiling. It could have been painted black but then it would have blended with the background and it would have been difficult to study the proportions of the component bones that made it what it was. However, its purpose was more than mere 'study' as its master and owner, Kamal, treated it as a companion, if not as a pet. Sometimes it was even spoken to, but Mr Bones, as it had been named, never had any answer to anything, which was fine by its owner, who poured a fresh steaming cup of black – what else – coffee from a flask. Kamal glanced at the desk clock by the bright lamp and it showed that it was ten minutes past one. He had another fifty minutes of studying to do. He untied his customary black necktie and flung it aside. It landed near Mr Bones's territory. Kamal was drawing the human digestive system from a thick textbook. Later, he would turn the book upside down and label all the different parts on his drawing, then check if he had got them all correctly. On most days he would study for two hours in the morning, having arisen at six. After the day's lectures and practicals, he would rest for two hours and try his best to be at his desk by nine at night and finish at two in the morning. Some weekdays he would sleep as little as three hours, kept awake to study by coffee, two flasks of which were a standing order at the refectory, after the evening meal. On weekends, his routine was completely different, of course.

In the room next to his, his childhood friend Sanjay wasn't as strict with himself or his time or his textbooks. He slept when sleep came, which depended on how heavy and hard the day had been, and what time he woke up depended on when he had gone to sleep. The logic of this suited him as he was good at getting order out of chaos. The two diversions from studies which he welcomed happily were pumping iron at the gym every weekday at the end of studies, which is when he forgot about them; and to admire his long hair in the mirror. In his room he kept a set of dumb-bells if the need for a diversion arose or if he found it difficult to sleep. Also in the privacy of his room, he preened, protected, and styled the pride and joy of his life – shoulder-length silken hair, not one of which was allowed to be out of place. Every hour or so, he would stare at himself in the large mirror atop one side of the desk to ensure that all was well with his hair. It usually was but he would still preen and dab here and there as if to ensure his hair was still there. By the mirror was a plethora of sprays, gels, and oils as well as an abundance of combs and hairbrushes of all shapes and sizes. Every time Kamal came in for a ten minute break to chat, without fail he would either tousle Sanjay's hair or disturb the order of the hair accoutrements much to his pleasure and Sanjay's annoyance. In turn, every time Sanjay went into the black room which he could only stand for twenty minutes or so before it became oppressive, he would rattle Mr Bones, making it seem like an electrocuted, mad marionette, prancing about.

Directly below Sanjay's room was Rosie's, with a prominent black cross mounted on one of the walls and a framed print of a crucified Jesus Christ, large black nails permanently stabbed into each outspread hand and both feet. Rosie's diversion from studies was to make a matchstick model of her church back in Panjim. Every two or three hours, she would put the books aside and lovingly devote fifteen minutes to the nearly complete model, much to Shivani's annoyance. Shivani interrupted her regularly, entry to Uma's room being by invitation only most of the time. Rosie's explanation as to why she 'wasted' time on the matchstick model was that besides the love for her church she was conditioning her fingers and wrist to a steadfast steadiness, which was necessary as she was going to be the best ever neurosurgeon of her generation, and perform surgical miracles in rural hospitals. To this, Shivani responded tartly that it was as likely as herself becoming the next Mother Teresa. There was another reason why Rosie was so devoted to the matchstick model. It was a representation of her childhood, when the church and Mother Superior had taken her in after she was orphaned. Besides that, it was in this church that Rosie had confirmed her faith in God. The other diversion Rosie had was to write short stories whenever an idea struck her, which wasn't very often. While everyone knew about the matchstick model and Rosie's passion for it, no one knew of her writing efforts. On this occasion, Shivani had another reason for interrupting Rosie.

'Hey, fatso, have you got any of that brandy stuff?'

This took Rosie by surprise and the glued headless matchstick in her hand stopped midway to its destination on the church model.

'I thought you hated the stuff. Uma's always got some and good stuff it is too.'

'The other day I slept so well, even though I only had a tiny bit. I thought I'd try it with water but Uma's not in.'

Rosie returned to her model and decided to give it five more minutes.

'Lucky Uma. Got everything, hasn't she. Now she's after that Krish chap. Like attracts like, both of them filthy rich – more money than brains.'

'You sure you haven't got any brandy or something?'

'Sure I'm sure. Don't keep any. I think you should go and do some work, Shivo. Don't let it pile up.'

Very carefully and tenderly, Rosie pushed the church model to its allotted place on a corner of the desk, put away the box containing scores of headless matchsticks, the pot of glue and the small brush. She brought the open book in front of her while Shivani reluctantly rose from the bed, pulling at the tightest possible jeans, which hugged the contours of her slender hips and pertly shaped posterior, which was the envy of many a girl and an eyeful for many a boy. Shivani knew this.

'Work! Work! Work! I want fun, fun, and fun! Come on Rosie, fatso, lose some weight.'

Suddenly she broke into an enthralling dance, which was a mixture of eastern and western moves at which she was better than good. Shivani pulled Rosie to her feet, who refused to join the dance at first but then relented as Shivani persisted. Rosie was as clumsy as Shivani was elegantly accomplished, with the latter's swaying and swinging body, legs and arms, having charms of their own.

4

Three Mondays later, a dusty red Maruti, crying out to be washed, swerved dangerously past the open gate, making a couple of students take quick evasive action, and skidded carelessly to a halt in the small car park. Uma got out of the driver's seat, slamming the door shut. Shivani got out from the front passenger's side and Rosie wiggled out from the back seat. Each one collected her lab coat and pack from the back seat and led by Uma, who had an extra plastic shopping bag, strode to the entrance of block 'A', home for them for the next five years less a month, which had gone by so quickly it seemed they had been there for days only.

Halfway down the corridor along which were dotted various notices and posters was the caretaker's cubbyhole of an office, with a small desk behind which dangled bunches of various keys with small labels. Unusually, the caretaker, who got to know the quirks and demeanours of each student within days, wasn't at the desk. The girls looked at each other and waited till Uma got impatient and put on her sexy, sing-song, innocent girl voice.

'Uncle...helloooo...are you there, uncle? Yooo...hooo.'

A croaky voice emerged from an inner room, followed by its owner, who was a prematurely old man, who had spectacles which such thick lenses that they magnified his eyes manifold. He was clutching an equally thick book entitled, 'Principia Mathematica.'

'Ms Uma and her little gang. What is it that you want this time? Be very quick about it. I am very busy.'

'Please, Unclejee, I've misplaced my room key. Can I borrow your master key, just for a second?'

'Not allowed. Not allowed. I will come up and open your room.'

With that the caretaker turned to the assortment of keys behind him. Uma was lost for the moment, which did not happen often. On such rare occasions, Shivani took over while Rosie just looked from one to the other, as usual.

'Save you climbing all those stairs, uncle. Oh, that's an interesting book. Have they made a film of it yet?'

The caretaker's magnified eyes turned to the cover of the book he was carrying as if it was a baby and then glared at Shivani with such intensity that she wilted. He ignored his triumph and turned to Uma.

'Ms Uma, your esteemed father, the General Sahib, asked me to keep an eye on you. Be assured, I am keeping it and also on the rest of you.'

Uma was about to give up when the caretaker turned to the keys behind him and without looking, plucked a bunch and handed it to a relieved Uma.

'Exactly one minute, otherwise the dean shall hear of it and your father as well, for good measure. Go.'

Uma clutched the keys and the girls hurried away, but the caretaker had an afterthought which made him lean out and shout to the backs of the hurriedly departing friends.

'One of you is not going to make it. Mark my words.'

Having got what they wanted, the girls bounded up the stairs. They had arrived at block 'A' much earlier than usual, having missed the afternoon lecture on how the internal ear processed sound waves. The caretaker smiled to himself and took his seat at the small desk and addressed *Principia Mathematica.* He had been at the academy for close to seventeen years, having risen from cleaner to gardener and then to caretaker of block 'A', and over the years he had also become the caretaker of the students as well, becoming fond of each one without revealing it. Many a time, over many weekends, he had coped with several escapades of student misbehaviour that many others would have considered monstrous, but which he thought nearly normal for students who had chosen to be trained to care for humanity with all the mad, almost inhuman effort that was essential to acquire the knowledge, skill, and the will to do so. Traffic lights waiting to be embedded at a road junction had been brought in to serve as disco lights, toothpaste had been smeared in one room and into the various orifices of its drunken occupant, fire extinguishers had been set off. The cat that had taken residence unbidden had been frightened by firecrackers tied to its tail and was nowhere to be seen since. The caretaker always remained calm towards the 'children' as he considered them to be, and hardly reported any student mischief to the dean unless it was deadly serious and life threatening.

5

'Settle down, please. We haven't got all day.'

The lecturer was keen to start and waited for the buzz to quieten down as the thirty-six students settled into the tiered semicircle of wooden seating with a similarly arched writing surface in front of them. On the long table in front of the lecturer sat a large cross-sectional model of a human eye and the blue optic nerve trailed behind it as if it were a plume of smoke. The lecturer switched on a PowerPoint presentation on his laptop and a labelled diagram of the same appeared on the screen. The students were poised with their pens.

'No need to write anything down. You'll never keep up and you'll end up with strained wrists which won't be much good for your anatomy stuff. There will be a handout at the end of the lecture.'

Pens were discarded en masse. Uma, Shivani, Rosie, and Krish sat together and a couple of tiers below were Sanjay and Kamal, all of them resplendent in their smart white lab coats. The three girls were clearly unsettled, as they kept leaning forward to see the backs of Sanjay and Kamal, and would exchange hasty looks with each other. The lecturer switched on his laser pointer and was soon in full flow.

'Today, I want to concentrate on the optic nerve in some detail. In passing I'll touch upon the eye, briefly, at this stage.'

Kamal was distracted by a distinct odour of iodine and put it down to another one of Sanjay's pathetic hair improving concoctions, or 'hair manure', as he often referred to the various oily potions, yet this one was much too potent to be so. Kamal stole a quick sideways look at Sanjay and did a quick double take just as excitement was growing amongst the girls two tiers behind. The girls suppressed their giggles as they tugged at each other. As yet, the destruction was only apparent to those near it or those who had arranged it. The hasty lecturer was neither one nor the other.

'Right, basics first. The optic nerve connects the eye to the brain. That much is simple. This is one of the biggest nerves in the body and it carries up to a million nerve fibres. You'll see what these look like when we slice one this afternoon in the lab.'

Sanjay was wrapped up in attention even as Kamal nudged him urgently.

'Sanjay, your hair's gone yellow.'

Sanjay leant towards Kamal covering his mouth with one hand.

'What fellow? What fair?'

Kamal's stomach rumbled loud enough for the lecturer and those nearby to hear it, inciting a titter two higher rows behind. The lecturer could sense some disquiet but not enough to disturb his flow. He pointed at the screen behind him with the blue laser pointer.

'The optic nerve connects the sensory cells, right here at the back of the retina to the optic centre of the brain, right here. More about that later. At the embryo stage the optic nerve develops as an outgrowth of the brain. Messages from the eye...'

Kamal's stomach rumbled loudly but it was something else that caught the lecturer's eye. He stepped forward and glared at Sanjay, who was puzzled and looked behind as if the lecturer was looking past him at someone else behind. Kamal clutched at his stomach, almost doubling over. What the lecturer saw of Sanjay annoyed him enough to interrupt himself as he stepped closer to the tiers of amused students in front of him. His eyes were definitely pinned on Sanjay, temper rising.

'Unless my eyes deceive me, Mr Sanjay, your hair has metamorphosed to a lurid yellow. You, Mr Sanjay Dutt, will not turn my lecture into a fashion parade!'

Instinct made Sanjay reach for his hair, which felt like a bird's nest knitted with stubborn wire wool. Student necks craned backwards and upwards and those above leaned forward to get a better view. Amongst these, Uma, Shivani, and Rosie were beside themselves with glee while Krish tried to work out what the fuss was about. Strands of yellow starched straw came loose in Sanjay's hand much to his horror but to Kamal's oblivion, who paled and clutched at his stomach, the insides of which were threatening to implode. Sanjay felt his hair and knew, now, why his scalp felt like it was crawling away from him. The lecturer exploded in anger.

'You may wish to continue your preening outside of this lecture room, Mr Sanjay. You have permission to leave.'

Without hesitation, Sanjay gathered his writing pad and rushed down the steps and out, all eyes propelling him. A buzz arose and the lecturer tried to regain attention.

'Not my favourite colour, yellow! Specially on top of a stupid empty head!'

Everyone except Kamal laughed or giggled. The three girls exchanged gleeful thumbs up gestures while he got up in a sudden hurry and stumbled down the steps almost bent double. He left his notepad and pen and was out of the lecture theatre before a murmur arose. The girls winked and smiled at each other but the lecturer was keen to resume.

'Must be something in the air. Alright, back to the optic nerve. Yellow notwithstanding!'

In the men's toilet, standing in front of a mirror, Sanjay's horror had turned to intense anger as he looked at a wriggly mass of starchy yellow hair, some of which had uprooted easily in his hand. His shoulder silky black hair had turned into a complete tangle of yellow. The only word that echoed in his mind over and over was 'bitches'.

The door swung open so hard it seemed to fly off its hinges. Kamal rushed to the nearest cubicle and slammed the door shut. Kamal had seen Sanjay but didn't have the time or inclination to say anything and it soon became apparent why this was so. Sanjay heard a loud and long smatter of held back diarrhoea finally released and walked out, head bowed and muttering, 'bitches', over and over again. He did not hear Kamal groaning in the toilet cubicle.

6

The next day Kamal remained in his bed, groaning and moaning as his stomach and sides ached, leaping out every hour or so to rush to the men's toilets at the end of the corridor. Sanjay had come in a few times with bottles of water, a lot of sympathy and such mournful looks as if both had lost more than their dignity and poise. The commiseration was mutual and shared silently. Kamal was desperate for coffee but knew his condition would worsen if he drank any and Sanjay knew better than to bring him any food. All Kamal could do was to drink water and lots of it as he was dehydrated with the constant loss of bodily fluids. In his frame of mind, Sanjay, too, found it difficult to eat much food. He had found an old cap that ill-fitted him and he had a decision to make. He had woken up to see masses of his defunct and definitely dead yellow hair on the graveyard of his white pillow. The few wisps that were latched to his scalp gave him the appearance of a badly made up character from a second-rate horror film. The two friends had consoled each other as much as they could, given their own predicaments. Knowing and understanding the functioning of a human body more than the average person, each knew it was going to be a matter of days before Kamal regained his currently dysfunctional digestive system and a matter of weeks before

Sanjay's dried up and starved hair roots started to sprout and months before he could discard the silly cap and possibly years before his new growth of hair attained its former glory, if ever. Time had to be endured and growth had its own whimsical time scale. Today, Sanjay was not inclined to attend any of the lectures or lab work. His immediate intention was to visit his expensive hairdresser and stylist to have his head shaved clean of the few remaining ugly, curly, yellow wispy threads. Decision made, he did just that except that he was too annoyed and angry to think of some viable reason to explain the mishap. He had not made up a white lie to explain the demise of his lovely, black hair, which the stylist knew only too well. Naturally, the hairstylist was curious and Sanjay had to think fast.

'Er... Acid rain...acid rain...rain harvest. Too much chlorine...too much...in the tank...in the pool...'

Sanjay's voice trailed away and his hairstylist, sensing a hurt soul beneath his manically busy fingers, let the matter rest.

Kamal and Sanjay suffered such lofty misery that there was no room for thoughts of retaliation or revenge in their ravaged minds. Uma, Shivani, and Rosie had not seen their victims for two days as they attended the scheduled lectures and went about their hectic routines. They were ensconced in Uma's room in the evenings where Rosie wondered if they had overcooked their revenge for the water splashing on Uma, which had only caused mental damage to pride and no physical harm to the body. Uma dismissed Rosie's increasing concern with her contention that if a lesson was to be taught it was best if it was learnt well and in this instance it had been well and truly taught and learnt. Shivani was indifferent and usually concentrated on sipping watered down brandy when it was on offer, which was not often. Uma was more than satisfied with the outcome. It had been a simple matter of a few minutes for her to court the internet and coax out of it which chemical compounds would do the two jobs for her and what ratios were to be used. After that it was a matter of a visit to a nearby chemist and a small raid at the lab store and she was ready. All that needed to be done was to lace one of the two flasks of coffee on Kamal's desk and to do the same with all the different hair oil bottles on Sanjay's desk. It was as simple as that. If anything, she was beginning to feel proud of what she had achieved and she was eagerly waiting to see and savour at close hand the effects of her lesson on Kamal and Sanjay. She was not going to hesitate to rub salt in their wounds, so to speak, both mental and physical.

Having taken a day off from studies to have his head shaved, Sanjay forced himself into the ill-fitting cap the next day and turned up for the first lecture. He avoided eye contact with everyone and said not a word to anyone, least of all to his three tormentors, who looked at his slouched head from time to time from the upper tier in the lecture theatre. Rosie was beginning to feel some guilt although she did not have a direct hand in the prank. She had misgivings about ruining Sanjay's hair and the effect it would have on him. It was much more than harmless mischief and not at all fun, certainly not for Sanjay. Such was Uma's stubbornness with her plan that Rosie's protests were not only ignored but also jeered at. In the end, all she could do was hope that it would be the last of pranking for them before matters got out of hand. Perhaps it was the devout practising Catholic in her that made her uneasy. At best the boys were indifferent to her but unlike her two friends and some other students, they had never been malicious or mean and certainly had never made fun of her slightly bulky figure. For all their sakes, Rosie was going to pray that Sanjay and Kamal would have the grace not to retaliate. Rosie had thought of turning away from Uma and to try to get Shivani to support her in the interest of caution. This did not happen as Shivani for her part was drifting into a world of her own, often arriving late for lectures and on occasion sliding towards sleep with drooping eyelids, during afternoon lectures.

On the third day Kamal had recovered sufficiently enough to attend the afternoon lecture on which he tried to concentrate hard so as to avoid thinking about the three girls a tier behind and above him. He, too, did not talk or look at anyone except his best friend Sanjay and that too only when the need arose. The schism between the two camps had deepened. The three girls on one side and the two boys on the other, with Krish leaning more and more towards the girls as he hovered around Uma and tried getting closer and closer to her like a starving mosquito. He wasn't concerned with Shivani and Rosie, though he was friendly with them. As yet, he wasn't fully aware of the growing rivalry between the two camps and although he was condescending and arrogant towards Kamal and Sanjay, as was his nature, he certainly wanted to keep his banter on a friendly basis with them – more fun and frivolity than edgy and competitive, unlike the girls who appeared to have their talons specially sharpened for the northern boys. Krish wasn't close enough to the girls, as yet, to know that it was the leader of the pack, Uma, whose gall was rising, and that Rosie was beginning to have misgivings, while Shivani was indifferent where the two boys were concerned.

7

The dirty red Maruti flashed by the open window and skidded to its usual shuddering halt, catching the attention of those near the window in the common room, including the two solemn and gloomy friends, Kamal and Sanjay. A moment or two later, Uma sauntered in, followed by Shivani, with Rosie in her usual, self-allotted, last place. At the food counter the trio joked with Gopal, the manager who ran the common room single-handed during weekdays and with hired hands and a couple of student volunteers during weekends. Uma plucked his cheeks just as Shivani noticed Kamal and Sanjay at their table. She nudged Uma and they all looked at their victims. Uma's mind raced ahead, wondering how to make use of the opportunity she had been waiting for: How should she rub salt in their wounds? Instinct told her to avoid verbal exchanges as there was no telling where those would lead. She wanted to let them know that she and her camp knew that they knew that she was responsible for the very effective mischief which had worked much better than was planned. She sauntered towards their table, hips swaying in tight jeans, long legs crossing one in front of the other as if she were a top-notch fashion model strutting the ramp, erotically dignified and totally self-conscious. Shivani followed suit, also clad in tight jeans while Rosie ambled behind them in her customary frumpy calf-length frock of mercifully forgotten pattern and cut. She knew it was better to be in Uma's good books than in the boys' bad ones.

∽

It was Friday evening, and in the past five days Kamal and Sanjay had nearly resumed their normal routines, except Kamal would have to drink cold milk for some days yet to keep his recently stormy stomach pacified. The tsunami had finally ebbed but the after-effects still lingered. Both were in the common room at their usual table. In deference to his friend, Sanjay had forgone beer and substituted it with a bottle of a horribly sugary, fizzy soft drink with a sickly drooping straw in it. The usual Friday evening was very distant from them, like a nearly lost memory. Kamal rested his elbows on the table, head in hands, and by now a familiar glass of milk in front of his face. Sanjay sat on the edge of his chair, leaning forward, cap pulled down as low as it would go. This was far from his usual Friday evening, when he would be sitting in a typical languid sprawl.

As the girls paraded by, the boys exchanged looks and Sanjay tried the impossible – to pull his cap further down – as Uma patted and primed her newly streaked, waist-length hair, prancing and winking at Sanjay at the same time. That's where the idea had come from. The streaking, except it had been magnified manifold. The signal reached Sanjay.

'What are we going to do, Kam?'

Before and after the forlorn plea struck him, Kamal's mind was firmly cobwebbed in the very same tangle but he needed to tame the vagary of time. It could work against him or for him. Timely or not, Krish's flamboyant arrival annoyed them both immensely, especially Sanjay. Despite knowing where the girls were, Krish still strode towards Kamal and Sanjay. Not having the full facts at his fingertips, the blundering Krish used them to prise the cap off Sanjay's head and 'frisbeed' it to where he cared not. Immediately, Sanjay tried to hide his shiny hairless pate. All he could do was to cover it with his large hands and cower downwards, much to Kamal's regret, pity, loss of pride, and much else at the downfall of his friend and by default, his own. Krish, who knew not what territory he was stepping onto, blundered on, swiping the bald head with the back of his hand as if to spirit away a fly. This was to impress one girl out of the watching three. Krish wanted to perform, without knowing how.

'Hey, Sanjay, man, it's a vast improvement. Should've always been like that, yea. Girls are gonna gush all over you, but you know, Samson and all that! Ha! Ha!'

Heroic task accomplished, Krish homed into his second target and planted an unwanted kiss on her powdered cheek. Uma hardly reacted and Shivani seemed to be dozing but Rosie was surprisingly alert to what was happening, as the twinkle in the eyes behind repaired spectacles suggested. She turned her sparkling gaze to Kamal and Sanjay. Without his hair, Sanjay, once a Kublai Khan, Genghis Khan, and Mick Jagger rolled into one, was mightily downgraded to a blissfully innocent baby-faced boy, much like the kind he saw in nappy commercials. Despite that, his anger was contained and controlled as he watched Kamal, who had been kind enough to retrieve his sad cap. Sanjay liked him even more for that as he pulled the ill-fitting cap back over his ears.

'They've done us in, Kam. Are we going to do anything?'

Quietly, Kamal rose and walked out, his milk remaining untouched. Sanjay followed him out of the common room.

Monday was round the corner, which compounded their miseries further. Preparations for the coming week's workload had to be done. Until Friday, which seemed aeons away, nothing would take precedence over studies. Like every other student, both friends knew this and accepted it. It was only the thought that was bitter but it was sweetened by the fact that Friday's eventual arrival was as inevitable as night following day.

8

The caretaker peered over his thick lenses. He did that whenever he was annoyed and full of disapproval.

'Not allowed. Not allowed. You know that well.'

Kamal and Sanjay, unusually loaded with heavy books and a few cardboard boxes for good measure, looked at each other. Kamal took matters in his already full hands.

'Please, Uncle, these things are heavy. Just two minutes. I know you let Uma have it.'

The caretaker, though fond of every student even if he called some of them rascals and asses, was unmoved, and clutching *Principia Mathematica* to his chest, turned around. Sanjay had to try his tactic, which was totally misjudged, even by his own standards. From one of the other boxes he was juggling, he deftly produced a half-finished bottle of whisky and held it out.

'Please, Uncle, some refreshment for you. Helps with concentration.'

The caretaker turned around and immediately his eyebrows shot up.

'Concentrate on what, Mr Sanjay, rascal! Working out where the next bottle is coming from! I'm keeping an eye on you two!'

Kamal tried to repair the damage.

'Very sorry, Uncle. Sometimes Sanjay is very stupid.'

'Sometimes! Look at him! One extreme to another. Long girly hair one day and the next he decides to be bald as a walnut. You're all getting careless, Mr Kamal, and you, Mr stupid Sanjay, ass, better start concentrating on studies, preferably without that bottle for company.'

Both friends were downcast and pondered over their next move under the intense glare of magnified eyes, but both lit up when, unexpectedly, the caretaker turned to the rack of keys. He removed the master key and handed it to Kamal, who easily freed one of his hands to receive it.

'Most grateful, Uncle.'

Kamal and Sanjay hurried to the stairs, loaded with heavy books, empty boxes, the all important key, and their intentions. True to his word, the caretaker kept his magnified 'eye' on the two hurrying backs till they turned a corner up the stairs, disappearing from his view. He shook his weary, white, tousle-haired head but also permitted himself a gentle smile and a pithy little sigh before returning to his inner sanctum where he would try to pick up Russell and Whitehead from where he had left them in the thick book. He was studying the book for the sixth time, understanding it a little more each time.

9

It had become a regular weekend date and it was widely accepted that Krish and Uma were well on their way to being a pair, unless one or the other or both were merely following convention without meaning it. Each Friday evening Krish would arrive on his powerful motorbike at block 'A' and spend as much time as he could in Uma's room before they both drove away in her Maruti. Uma hardly saw Shivani or Rosie except on weekdays when they went to lectures together. While Shivani was indifferent to what Uma and Krish did or didn't do, Rosie took a keen interest and noted all the developments around her.

This Friday evening, Krish's arrival was watched with much interest by Kamal and Sanjay, who were perched at the window in the black room with the hanging skeleton. Kamal turned around and sat at his desk on which a radio receiver was set up. He rubbed his hands and switched it on.

'Today's the day, I bet you.'

Sanjay sprawled on the bed and ran his hand over his bald head, missing his hair.

'Na. Few more weeks or maybe never. Uma is a big tease, the bitch.'

Kamal adjusted the radio receiver and increased the volume.

'Doesn't matter when they get to it but we better get it right. The whole thing depends on the timing.'

On the radio receiver, a knock on the door was heard followed by the muffled but audible voices of Krish and Uma. Kamal turned up the volume to its maximum and a rustling of clothes was heard.

'They're kissing, Sanj.'

Sanjay sat up.

In the room below, that was precisely what was happening, till Uma pulled back after a long and passionate kiss, red lipstick smudged and some of it on Krish's heavy-breathing mouth. Both tidied themselves and Uma applied more red lipstick while Krish put his arm around her waist, looking at her in the mirror.

'Let's stay in, Umi. We'll catch the movie, later.'

'In case you haven't noticed, I'm all dressed to go out.'

'Just for a bit. Just a cuddle.'

Uma picked up her handbag. She was dressed to impress, not just Krish but anyone lucky enough to catch a sight of her in faded designer jeans, a low-cut satin blouse and high heels which made her almost as tall as the hapless Krish.

'You're so cruel, Uma. Just a cuddle.'

'Let's go, honey.'

In the room above, Kamal and Sanjay heard the door open and close and made disappointed faces at each other. Kamal switched off the radio receiver and leaned back.

'One got away for the moment. Wait for the other two.'

Sanjay arose from the bed and stretched.

'Waiting's boring. Let's go get a beer.'

'No, we wait Sanjay, boy. Patience. Patience. Good pranks need patience. It takes time to plan and to execute them with timing being crucial. The best ones are the simple ones. Okay? Besides, it's too early for a beer, even if it's Friday.'

Before Sanjay could plead further, a scream pierced the calm from the room below his. It was Shivani. Kamal gave Sanjay a thumbs up sign.

'One down, two to go.'

In her room, Shivani was on her side, curled in a foetal position on the floor, her chair on its side as if both were stuck to each other, which they were. No matter how hard she tried to prise the chair away, it would not budge as her jean-clad bottom was glued hard to the seat of the chair. That she was a little drunk did not help. Earlier in the afternoon, she had decided to study for an hour, sleep for another hour, then freshen up and wait for Rosie to turn up and then walk with her to the common room. She made the mistake of opening the brandy bottle which she hid in her room, planning to have a small drink while she studied, after which she would sleep well. The small drink became a large one, followed by two more, before she arose reluctantly from her easy chair and sank into her hard desk chair and opened the book to the chapter on the olfactory function section that she wanted to revise. Perhaps it was the reek of brandy that created the slight petrol like smell around her. It was certainly the combination of brandy and tiredness that made her fall sleep at her desk, forehead resting on the open book, cradled in the nook of one elbow. Twenty minutes or so later, she awoke with a start and attempted to move to her bed but screamed instead as she tumbled sideways to the floor with the chair. The industrial strength super glue, normally used to stick leather, had set, and her bottom and the chair had become inseparable.

'Bastards,' she muttered over and over as she continued to struggle to free herself but to no avail. She thought of shouting for Rosie but realized that she had not arrived yet. In any case she had locked the door from the inside. What was she to do? Eventually, she unzipped her jeans and tried to wriggle out of them but the super glue had seeped through to her red knickers and to her skin, sticking all three to the seat of the upturned seat. Within minutes she sobered up and by pulling at one of the drawer handles on her desk and pushing at the floor with her feet, she managed to pull herself upright along with the chair. She looked around and realized quickly that she would not be able to reach the scissors in the cupboard. Instead she could use the small penknife in the top desk drawer but first she would have more brandy which was, mercifully, within reach on the desk. After twenty minutes of slashing away with the small blade in between slugs of neat brandy, she was both free and slightly drunk, again. She stood up and tugged at the untidy oval of denim, and the remnants of her red knickers firmly attached to her behind. The pain was unbearable but the materials refused to part from her posterior. Shivani tried to calm down with the solace of the brandy but only got angrier as she tried to think of what to do. She struggled into a skirt as she heard Rosie arrive next door. She thought of seeking Rosie's assistance but felt too embarrassed and ashamed. As she sat on the edge of her bed, bent over, elbows on knees, head in hands, trying not to cry, she tried not to return to the stomach-turning worry as to why she had chosen to be a doctor, a healer, in the first place. When the tears started, fuelled by a mixture of self-pity, anger, and the brandy, there was no stopping them. Shivani tried to cry silently but a sob escaped her every now and then. What had she done to deserve this? She did not hate Sanjay or Kamal as much as Uma did. So why had they done this to her and not to Uma who had planned and carried out the dirty pranks on them? Why? Why? The questions faded eventually but the crying did not and Shivani stopped worrying about anybody hearing her. If anything, she hoped Rosie might hear her and come to her rescue.

In the next room, Rosie had kicked off her manly shoes and rested in her easy chair, having done her two hours of study in the deserted library. Every student claimed not to touch a book or study in any shape or form after the last lecture on Fridays but almost all of them did for an hour or more. Not only was this to keep up-to-date but it also soothed the conscience, and come seven o'clock, the common room would be all the more rewarding. Rosie was thinking ahead, looking forward to the weekend, particularly to her regular Sunday visit to the church near the campus. She decided to relax by working on the very nearly complete matchstick model of the church. It needed only a couple of hours of work and trimming and it would be ready to present to the Mother Superior in Panjim. Rosie hated the thought of completing the model as it would mean parting with it, and it would create a vacuum within her before she started another model. She was yet to think of a subject but was already mulling over something circular and made of halved matchsticks, as that would require more skill, patience, and an even more steady hand, all prerequisites if she was to be the best neurosurgeon of her generation. Rosie studied her right palm and flexed the fingers, clenching and unclenching. At the same time she got up and sat at her desk, gently pulling the model and the box containing the required paraphernalia. She decided to spend only ten minutes on it as she selected one headless match, applied glue to it, and carefully guided it to its allotted place on a top corner of the model, only to see the whole model collapse in front of her very eyes as if a spell had been cast on it. Rosie gasped and gulped in a deep breath of air as a reflex action, staring at the crumbled model in disbelief. She cupped her face with both hands and shook her head. As she stared, she saw that the model had been neatly sliced as if with a surgical scalpel, into many different sections which had been stacked back into place. Rosie picked up one section of the expertly butchered model and brought it close to her eyes for a better look. A teardrop rolled gently down her cheek as she put down the section and crossed herself. She turned to look at the picture of the crucified Jesus Christ on a side wall and her right hand trembled with grief. It was as if her real church in Panjim had crumbled and her childhood lay trampled in its ruins, while her God had forsaken her. Rosie wasn't sure what to do next. The idea of meeting Shivani was ruled out and the call of the common room dimmed to gloomy silence as her anguish increased in the small study room.

That was not so for Kamal and Sanjay in the crowded, large common room. The beer was going down quickly as they looked around but none of the three girls had presented themselves as yet. It was Uma they were waiting for. They were sure the other two had got their just desserts, having heard a primordial scream from one and deafening silence from the other, both of which left them unconcerned, even smug, as they justified their actions to themselves. The girls had tampered with their bodies, destroying Sanjay's hair and imploding Kamal's insides but at least they themselves had not stooped as low. Kamal had recovered and in time Sanjay's hair would attain its former glory even if the mental scars would remain. In return Rosie would get over her ruined matchstick model and Uma would get over the trauma awaiting her. As for Shivani? Her pain was physical, yes, but it served her right as she never missed an opportunity to flaunt her posterior. With time, she would get over it as well. The job was nearly done but patience was running out as the prime victim was yet to show up. Satisfaction would not be complete without her comeuppance. Kamal and Sanjay decided to take a bottle of whisky to share in the black room where everything was set up, ready and waiting. As luck would have it, Sanjay caught a glimpse of the red Maruti flashing by the window. It did not stop by the common room but sped on towards block 'A.' Sanjay grabbed Kamal by the elbow and both sprinted out, knocking fellow students aside, the bottle having been forgotten.

Breathless and back in the black room, both made for the radio receiver. It was switched on zealously. The kiss that had been stopped three hours earlier had resumed with a vengeance, as the moans and groans of pleasure testified. Kamal rubbed his hands in anticipation.

In the room below, Uma broke away to shed her high heels while Krish flung his jacket somewhere. They were back in a wrestling clinch, edging towards the bed. Multitasking was the call of the moment. Clothes rustled as each undid the buttons of the other. Both were already breathless and flushed with good food, alcohol, and aching desire. Uma tore off her blouse, mascara smudged eyes blinking.

'You got the condoms, Krishy?'

In the black room above, upon hearing the muffled question on the radio receiver, Kamal was orgasmic and the slower Sanjay was near it. They started the countdown. 'Five, four, three...'

In the room below, Krish pulled down one of Uma's bra straps. She reached for the other one when suddenly a strange loud buzzer went off. It was as if a few thousand hornets had been set into action. The multitasking came to an abrupt and total stop as Uma pushed Krish away and leapt up from the bed. Breathless, she looked around to see if she could locate the source of the buzzing sound by sight. Her ears were more helpful as they led her to the top unused storage space in her room. She pulled her bra straps back to their assigned places and on her tiptoes reached for the handle of the topmost door and pulled it open. In a blurry cascade, glass jars of different sizes raced past her as if fired from a canon, some thudding on her shoulders and others crashing to smithereens at her feet. It was a full second before a strangled scream from deep within her reverberated around her room. Krish jumped up, looking at her and then at the floor. The screams were in full flight, rocket fuelled by hysteria. The familiar smell of formaldehyde wafted about the room. On the floor all around Uma were wet splashes, broken glass, and doll-like, rubbery human embryos of different sizes. They were reposed in their familiar foetal positions with one on her desk and another one on her bed. They had all been dislocated and disturbed in as extreme a way as possible, yet that expression of serene calm remained on each one. In a contrast to the nth degree, Uma's hysteria was boundless and when Krish tried to put an arm around her, he was pushed with such unexpected force that he was almost knocked over. Still screaming, Uma unlocked her door after much fumbling and fled out of the room, not caring that she was barely dressed. Krish did not know what to do, as was usually the case.

10

Shivani had a sleepless night apart from snatches of brandy-induced naps as she lay on her side in the dark, feeling sorry for herself. The searing stabs of pain on her posterior reached down her thighs to the back of her knees. She also realized that she needed medical attention urgently, before the gaping wounds formed rusty scabs or worse, but the faculty infirmary, despite its excellence, was hardly the place to be treated in. Questions would be asked and explanations sought. Immediately the decision was made to get to a hospital far enough from the academy. All the same, an explanation would still be required wherever she went. Shivani was tempted to tell the truth without revealing that it was a prank by fellow students but felt shamed by the admission. She would call it an accident in a carpentry workshop where she designed furniture. She permitted herself a rueful half-smile at her ingenuity, which was brave given the circumstances. That left the question of how to get to the hospital. Now that Rosie knew, having spent long hours the previous evening comforting and commiserating with both herself and Uma, she would go along for some moral and physical support. For Uma to drive the two of them was out of the question as she was still fast asleep under heavy sedation, which Rosie had cajoled out of a fellow

Christian nurse at the infirmary. Involving Krish would be too complicated and also embarrassing. As yet, he wasn't aware of what had befallen Rosie and her by way of Kamal and Sanjay's pranks, as he and Uma were out at the time of Shivani's screams; but both would find out soon enough. The old caretaker knew everything as usual, having heard Shivani's screams and later those of Uma, following a series of loud thuds and clatters on his ceiling, which was under Uma's floor. He was kind enough to have Uma's room cleared and cleaned immediately but he wasn't aware of the extent of Shivani's injuries as she had finally changed into a long loose skirt after having cut herself free. She did wonder though, if the friendly caretaker would report the events to Prof V, desperately hoping he wouldn't. Finally, she summoned enough will to get up from the bed albeit very slowly, and made the supreme effort of swathing her posterior in bandages that were cut out of a towel, after which she slipped on the long skirt. She would get the ever reliable Rosie to get an autorickshaw to the accommodation block and get to the hospital by nine in the morning.

11

In the three weeks that passed since the incident of cascading embryo jars in Uma's room, Krish had tried almost every weekday to plead with Uma but to no avail. She would not even look at him let alone talk to him. In the lecture theatres and labs it was difficult to plead and outside of them, she would simply walk away from him as if he wasn't even there. She refused to answer his phone calls and ignored the notes he slipped under her door. All he wanted was to resume their friendship and in time, get to where they had stopped. What frustrated him most, apart from missing her desperately was the 'why' of it. Why was Uma bent upon punishing him when he had no part whatsoever in the dreadful and ugly events of three weeks ago? He could not even begin to comprehend an explanation as he was clueless about young female psyches, emotions, or thought processes. He was aware that Uma was shocked, angry, and upset, but it failed to strike him that she was also ashamed, regretfully guilty, and even shy that in a slightly drunken moment of misguided passion she had come very close to having sex without being anywhere near married. Despite belonging to a 'hip' new generation which every one of its members seemed to flaunt about, somehow some core values of their parents' generation still remained, and this was also the case with her. These were what made Uma avoid eye contact and close proximity with Krish, who would never realize that in a hundred years. In the cold clinical sobriety of the aftermath of the embryo incident, these thoughts had hit Uma forcefully. For her, she admitted to herself with bitter relief, the only good of the ugly incident was that it made her stop where she did. This, too, evaded Krish, who was determined to win Uma back. For him what was to blame were the pranks, which were no longer childish or harmless but were escalating towards unacceptable levels. This was an opportunity for him to prove his leadership and skills of diplomacy by putting a stop to them and thereby impress Uma so he could start talking to her, at least. Furthermore, he was part of the study group, whether he liked it or not, though he neither sided with the girls nor the boys. Being in the study group also meant better chances of being near Uma. Another reason he had to lead the group was that apart from Uma, he had considered the others to be of lesser stock than himself. Consciously or not this compelled him towards leadership, so that he could knock some sense into these lesser beings. More so after he had learnt from Rosie what had befallen her and poor Shivani at the hands of Kamal and Sanjay. Then he understood why they had hardly been seen around the campus. If for nothing else, an end had to be put to such pranks simply because they were wrong, Krish had further reasoned to himself. There was no doubt in his mind that he had to do something. With Rosie's assistance, a meeting was arranged on the worst day of the week.

∽

Monday was the best day for the common room as it rested and recuperated while being thoroughly rinsed of the weekend's excesses, mainly cigarette butts, chewing gum, bits of food, and empty bottles. The floor was being swept and small clouds of dust swirled up before curling down to death. The study group had taken a corner table that had already been cleansed. The three girls sat on one side and the two boys on the other. Krish headed the table where the ice of three weeks had been broken, but only just. Krish sensed that more needed to be done and he needed to be direct.

'What I'm saying is for the good of us all, all of us. Just stop the pranks, childish or not. That's all.'

Rosie watched her fellow study group members intently, one after the other in the pervading silence. Pretending to be reluctant, she absorbed it all, eyes flitting from one face to another. To break the ice further, she sallied forth.

'They started it first, throwing water on Uma, spoiling her clothes. We didn't do anything.'

All eyes shifted to Kamal and Sanjay. Kamal cleared his throat, collecting his thoughts and remembering.

'Months ago, right from the start, Sanjay and I introduced ourselves to the girls because we were all in the same study group and our rooms were also in the same block. Nothing wrong with that except we were treated like aliens, like we had two heads, like we were untouchable or something. All we were trying to do was to be friendly, to be sociable.'

Eyes turned to Krish, adding to his self-importance. He felt the leader in him stir as he glared at Kamal.

'Slashing Rosie's model that she had spent months on, putting super glue on Shivani's chair. She had to have treatment for her...er...backside. Giving Uma a nasty fright, making her almost catatonic. Call that being sociable, do you!'

Sanjay swiped off his cap and hammered his bald head.

'What do you call this? And putting stuff in Kamal's coffee! It could have made him seriously ill.'

Kamal jabbed his finger at the girls.

'They overreacted. Totally! Totally, Krish, man! It's their fault not ours. We only chucked some water on Uma and look what they did. Well, after that we had to hit back. You would have as well. It was only water, for God's sake, man. We didn't want things to go this far! They did!'

The ensuing silence seemed to confirm this and seconds later Uma gave in.

'I don't want any of these stupid pranks. If they stop, we will stop.'

Krish's diplomacy and leadership had triumphed, welcoming a much needed smile. He stole a quick glance at Uma who had her head bowed all the time. Still, the meeting was going well for him.

'Excellent! Excellent! Don't get me wrong. I am no spoilsport. By all means let's have fun, but only harmless fun. Let's all be friends and help each other to get through. We all know medicine's tough and we all have to let off steam sometime but let's be sensible about it.'

Rosie was concentrating as hard as she did during lectures, looking at all of them and nodding every now and then. She wanted to contribute to the possible state of peace.

'Rules, Krish. We have to have rules. Everything has rules.'

'Right on, Rosie. Let's see. Rule number one, no messing around with food and drinks, putting chemicals and things in it. Number two, no messing about with...um...bodies, top, bottom or in between. No messing about with personal property and most importantly, no messing about with studies. We're halfway through the year and before you know it the first-year final exams will be upon us. If we don't make it or if we barely pass, Prof V will have us for breakfast. You can be sure of that.'

A deathly hush followed the mention of the 'e' word till Kamal got up and asked Rosie for a quiet word. Away from the others he apologized for destroying the church model and offered any recompense Rosie would care for. Rosie smiled broadly.

'It was only a model, Kamal. Don't worry about it. The real thing is here.'

She touched her heart, eyes twinkling. Both smiled, and watching from the corner, Krish sensed he had yet to close the deal, although he was close to it. He shouted across.

'Come on you two, join us and let's all shake on it.'

Rosie, instinctively, offered her hand to Kamal, who shook her hand happily. She went to Sanjay and did the same and the others had no choice but to do likewise, though Kamal made it clear this was done only for Rosie's sake, which was confirmed by Sanjay, word for word. A beaming Krish rubbed his hands together and summoned Gopal, the common room manager, who was caught in the middle of a great leonine yawn, it being a Monday afternoon. He jumped up and rushed to Krish, where orders were whispered into his ear and five hundred rupee notes were thrust into his hand. Gopal left smiling and Krish turned to his five friends.

'Right, you lovely people, drinks are on the way. Party's on me. Couple of hours of harmless fun isn't going to kill anyone! Right, Uma?'

12

The dirty red Maruti, still striving to be cleaned, swerved dangerously through the main gate and skidded to a late halt as usual. Uma and Shivani scrambled out of the front seats and Rosie from the back one. They collected their spotless white lab coats, books, folders, and files, slammed the car doors and led by Uma, with her long strides, marched towards the entrance to block 'A.' Shivani was still struggling as the pain in her posterior was still raw, despite the extensive treatment that lasted nearly four weeks at the hospital, initially under local anaesthetic. Shivani was preoccupied with herself, muttering at times while Rosie trailed at the back as they crossed the small car park.

As they entered the block, Shivani vented her annoyance.

'I mean, I really can't see why you have to drive like a maniac all the time! I really don't, Uma!'

The shaking, rocking, and rolling of the car on potholed roads had given her jolts of pain on her posterior. In spite of that, Uma put Shivani in her place without turning or breaking her stride.

'Gives me a buzz, darling, gets the adrenaline going. Got to live a little, Shivani! Yea, I'm a speed freak. What of it!'

They hurried past the caretaker's window but he was waiting.

'Ms Uma and you two, I'm keeping an eye on you all. Tests are due and the exams are sooner than you think. Don't leave it too late.'

The three had reached the stairs but before they turned in, he shouted after them that one of them wasn't going to make it and shook his head.

All three were exhausted with the day's studies and the evening's revision. Uma was sprawled on her bed, not even having kicked her designer sandals off while leaning back in the easy chair, Shivani winced with pain every time she moved. Rosie sat on the hard study chair facing away from Uma's cluttered desk, head bowed, her chin rested on her chest. For each of the last four days all three had been exhausted and fatigued and they would be so for the next seven days before the pre-exam tests began. Though all were hungry, food was all but forgotten. Uma stirred and blinked at the other two as Shivani winced and groaned with pain as she tried to get up. Uma worried about her.

'Stay for a bit, Shivo. Keep sitting. Rosie, please pour us all a brandy. Small one for me. I can't be bothered with any food.'

Rosie did so and Shivani did not mind the small measure, as from some time ago she had started to keep a permanent supply stashed away in her wardrobe, which her two friends were not aware of. In a few minutes she would get to her room and take recourse to it. Comforted by the thought she drained her brandy and stood up, groaning and pretending it wasn't that serious by attempting some humour.

'Whole thing's a pain in the butt, if you ask me.'

As she stepped towards the door, Uma raised herself and drained her brandy.

'Let's have a look, Shivo.'

Surprised, Shivani turned around.

'What! Are you serious?'

'Trust me, I'm going to be a doctor...unless a bus runs over me. Nothing kinky, Shivo. Purely professional. Show us your butt.'

Uma was serious, Rosie realized, looking from one to the other with blazing eyes, fatigue forgotten. Shivani took a step towards the door. Her brandy was awaiting her and she had no intention of baring anything.

'I don't think so, Uma. It's my butt.'

Rosie always wanted to be in Uma's good books so she joined the campaign.

'We are both trying to help, Shivani, because we are concerned. It is more than obvious you are in pain as you walk, which you're just about managing. Believe you me, we both share your pain and want it to end soon. We want to see if we can do anything, suggest anything. That and nothing else.'

Shivani was touched but had her dignity to protect.

'Rosie, dear, it's just discolouration and some loss of tissue. The bloody glue got through my jeans.'

Uma sat up on the edge of the bed and glared at Shivani.

'Some stupid men say all women are sitting on a gold mine, except some know it and others don't. Yours may be damaged and you may not know it. Understand?'

Rosie understood immediately but Shivani wasn't so sure and the need for more brandy was becoming urgent. Her hands shot upwards and then back down. She started to unbuckle her belt.

'For God's sake, you two! Let me warn you, it's not a pretty sight even for medicos!'

Groaning with pain, Shivani unzipped hurriedly before she could change her mind and pushed her jeans down to her feet. She raised her shirt to waist level and turned her back to Uma and Rosie. Immediately, Uma's face contorted as if with agony, and with a deep intake of breath and a spasm of shock, Rosie held her head in her hands. They stared at Shivani's posterior in silence. Underneath and around the thin gauze were botched maps of pink, red, yellow, blue, purple, and black merging into each other. Mouths agape, Uma and Rosie looked at each other. It was still early days in their training but both had already seen enough injuries and disfigurements on human bodies, dead or alive, that they had become immune to the shocks and horrors of it. But this was different. Shivani was not a stranger they wouldn't see for long. She was more than a fellow study group member. She was a friend.

Shivani bent down, groaning, to pull her jeans up. Uma sprang to her and gently helped her pull up her jeans and buckle her belt, and led her back to the chair, slowly easing her into it. It was then that she saw the silent but huge tears flowing down Shivani's face as she looked up at her, helpless and hurt. Uma patted Shivani's shoulder gently and hurried to the brandy, filled three glasses to the brim, and handed them out, draining hers before refilling it to the brim again and gulping half of it. She sat on the edge of the bed, close to Shivani, who was sobbing, eyes covered with one hand. Uma stared at the floor and saw glass jars shattering all over it with waxen embryos tossing about. A huge sigh was heaved and for a moment she shivered. Rosie came and sat next to her and when she noticed Uma's eyes had welled up, she put her arm around her and tried not to cry, seeing the matchstick model of her beloved church collapse over and over again. She was tougher than the two and managed not to cry. Soon, the two of them had recovered and Uma's protective instincts surfaced. Snivels had subsided and noses were blown. More brandy was drunk in silence and quiet solidarity and a strange calm settled in the room. Uma looked upwards at her ceiling.

'Somebody remind me of the rules.'

Rosie was lost for a moment.

'What rules, Uma?'

Uma made a face at her and mimicked her.

'What rules, Uma! You're the one who suggested them, Rosie!'

'Oh, that. I thought we'd agreed to be out of it, pranks and all that. Like Krish said, grow up and all.'

Uma had a fixed, stern look, determination increasing by the second.

'Krish has his place in the scheme of things. Besides, I'm not charitable enough to let them get away with it. Not my style. Those scars will remain on Shivo's butt for the rest of her life. I still have nightmares about those blasted jars of embryos which cooled things between Krish and me, maybe for good, I don't know. And your church model, Rosie? Hours and hours of hard, solid concentration gone in a second. No, harmless fun is what they'll get. All we have to do is to stay within the rules. Now, what was it? No messing with food and drinks and...and...'

Shivani perked up immediately.

'Yea, keep away from food, drinks, possessions, physical attacks and don't disturb studies. That's it, but what do we do? I wouldn't mind hitting back with or without rules. The bastards!'

Rosie stood up and paced the room while Uma thought as hard as she could, analysing and musing.

'It can't be physical so let's make it mental. Let's go for the minds if not bodies or possessions. Simple, logical. Shock, fear, terror, anxiety, tension... shock. Extreme shock.'

Shivani was impressed.

'My God, that's a textbook of a whole lot of neurosis.'

Rosie's eyes sparkled behind her spectacles.

'I know. Start with Kamal. He's the weaker of the two. Talk him into a mission that'll give him the creeps. Something simple that'll give him a jolt...I think I've got it. The morgue...darkness at midnight... It's a simple idea but you can develop it further. But keep it simple. You'll have to talk Kam into it, Uma. You'll have to use all your charm. I'm sure you'll manage. Girls, all we need are some sweets.'

Uma exchanged a wide-eyed incredulous look with Shivani.

'Sweets!'

Whatever Rosie's simple idea with sweets was, the first step on the road to trouble and to the morgue was taken. The mischief that was to unfold was going to reach beyond itself and was to have strange, unexpected, and long term domino effect repercussions for the group of six, in particular for one of them. Except that Uma delayed the execution of the idea for three reasons, two of which were sound. First, the execution of the idea would not happen till it was fully developed and the planning worked on till it could not be improved further. Second, and crucial above all, was the timing. For the execution to be flawless and to do justice to the idea and its planning, it was of paramount importance to select the right month, week, day, and exact time. The less sound third reason was that being the undisputed leader of the faction, Uma wanted everything to be done her own way and all the factors – the idea, it's planning, execution, and timing had to have her authority and hallmark on it. The other two would just have to wait and see for as long it took. Wait and see. Wait and see.

13

Time flies even when no one is having much fun, apart from Fridays and Saturdays, but that too had become a 'wait and see' game for the two factions within the study group, which had to stay intact whether its members liked it or not. So, the four on the one hand, so to speak, and the two on the other were to be stuck with each other for nearly another four years. Prof V's reasoning – and no one argued with him – was that this was the best way to forge lifelong friendships and professional networks for the benefits of all concerned. As such, he selected groups of people with compatible personalities who had similar academic, reasoning, and intellectual abilities. Accordingly, accommodation was arranged so that members of a study group were roomed next to each other to promote near and regular contact even out of study hours. The professor hardly ever misjudged, though a tweak of adjustment was sometimes needed here and there. As yet, he wasn't aware that the dynamic of his ablest study group – from which he expected much – was heading in a peculiar direction of its own and not the one he intended for it, which was for its members to seek and attain excellence both in their personal and professional lives. So much so that other students would want to emulate them.

As days rolled into weeks and quietly slipped into months, Kamal and Sanjay stopped feeling concerned about when Uma and her gang would strike back at them. Months ago, soon after their own pranks with the super glue, the matchstick model, and the jars of human embryos, they were expecting imminent revenge but nothing happened. The girls actually became incrementally more sociable as the exams approached, as if there was some unknown correlation between the exams and their behaviour. Edging from hostility to indifference to normal social decorum was laudable and sensible on the part of all concerned, but only if it lasted. Whether it lasted or not, the exams were not going to stop creeping up on them, like demands which never stopped till they were met. To get to the second year, one could not avoid the first-year final exams. If anybody was foolish enough to attempt the impossible, all of a sudden they had only six weeks left in which to do so and these would flash by faster than any student imagined.

There was less of a buzz in the common room even during weekends as the final exams crept inexorably closer. No one pretended they were not studying any more. Everyone knew everyone else was staying up late and squeezing out every minute of every hour to study and revise.

This Friday evening, Uma had summoned a meeting of the study group, all except Krish as the matter did not involve him. Besides, considering what Uma had in mind, it was better if Krish weren't there. Seated with Sanjay and facing the three girls at the same table, Kamal weighed an incongruous packet of red sweets in his hand and looked up, mystified.

'It can't be that simple, surely. I work with the damn things almost every day, in case you haven't noticed.'

Although the tension amongst the study group had diminished, Uma was still determined to be her most charming, coquettish self. Six weeks before the first-year final exams were to begin had been judged as the right time to execute the idea which had been planned for Kamal, and she wanted him to oblige. The time for the idea had arrived.

'Kamal, dear, it really is simple. The three of us leave to camp in the hills on Saturday afternoon and exactly at midnight you will go to the morgue and place one sweet in the mouth of each cadaver. You have to go on your own and you have only one attempt. It's as simple as that and it's definitely within the rules. We come down from the hills on Sunday and check if you've done it. Nothing more to it.'

Sanjay felt uninvolved and remained silent, which was unusual for him. Kamal remained mystified.

'What's the point of all this? Doesn't interest me one bit because it's pathetic! Anyway, we all agreed months ago to stop this sort of childish rubbish especially if the exams are only weeks away. Thanks but no thanks. I can't be bothered.'

Uma dazzled a smile at him like never before.

'It'll take some of the exam tension away. Something to relax with. A tiny little diversion from studying and revising. See Kam, we've already made a bet that you will fail in which case that's the end of it. If you're successful, I, for one, will be your slave, at your beck and call for the rest of the time we're here. Be a sport, Kam. Deal?'

This was the first time Uma had addressed him by his nickname. Some interest flickered across Sanjay's face and tempting possibilities flashed across Kamal's mind.

'What exactly will you be at my beck and call for?'

'You name it, Kam. The only exception is a personal relationship between you and me but you don't seem that bad a guy, now that I know you more. We'll see how we get on. It might click between us, you never know. Deal?'

Sanjay could not believe what he heard. Uma was more or less offering herself, almost falling into Kamal's lap. Kamal narrowed his eyes, smiling and suspicious. What is usually too good to be true is usually exactly that – not true.

'That's an obvious "come on" considering you can't stand me, so no deal. I'm no fool. Your motive is more than suspect, unless it's a pathetic attempt at some sort of retaliation.'

Sensing a refusal and being ever on the spot, Uma changed tack quickly from siren to vixen, from fairy to witch.

'Not really. It's just to deal with exam tension. Just a bit of harmless fun, that's all. Anyway, it won't ever come to a relationship because I am totally convinced, we all are, that you won't have the guts. The morgue is a different prospect for a solitary person at the dead of night, especially for a wet wimp who is without much of a backbone, all gas and no guts, which is what you are, Kam, despite your blustering ways.'

The barb hit Kamal exactly where it was intended, with such accuracy that Uma herself was staggered, but it had a strange effect. Kamal burst into fits of uncontrollable laughter, surprising even Sanjay. Unexpectedly, the frenzied laughter came to an abrupt halt and the stony face reappeared. The blazing look was as spiteful as the silence was deafening, and even the normally unflappable Uma worried for an instant that she might have overdone it. Rosie was certain of it. Kamal shot to his feet and smiled, baffling everyone by his instantly changed personae, as if he was a master of magical masks, replacing one with another in the blink of an eye. Even Sanjay, who knew him best, was taken aback.

'Being insulted by you, Uma, is like being licked by a little pussycat. Nice but can be annoying.'

The face of stone returned as he glared at the packet of sweets resting on his palm, and Uma and the other two were convinced that she had blown it. He pocketed the sweets, slowly and calmly, glaring at Uma all the while.

'You're on, but you're going to regret it big time. The first thing you'll do is clean my shoes and fetch my coffee, every day. The rest we will see about. Believe you me, I'll hold you to it and you'll never talk to me about backbone, ever again. You understand? Believe me, you don't know what you've taken on because you don't know the real Kam! Nowhere near! Once you're my slave, I'll change your name to...I don't know... How about "Pussy"? Better get used to it, Pussy!'

With that the totally incensed Kamal clicked his heels and marched out, closely followed by the ever faithful Sanjay. They left a shattered silence behind them. Rosie was nervous and Shivani was worried.

'Uma, what if he does it? He might just do it.'

Uma was the only one smiling.

'Don't underestimate me, dears. Come, I'll treat you to dinner tonight and I'll fill you in with some details.'

As Rosie followed them out, she wasn't sure if Uma was as relaxed and confident as she appeared to be, but the prospect of eating out had cheered her up as Uma only went for the best. It used to be Krish and Uma who went out for dinner but they had only just started to talk to each other after the embryo prank, although, for some reason, they were still uneasy with each other. Rosie had pondered over that and tried to guess where the two were headed.

14

On Saturday night, Sanjay refused to accompany Kamal to the morgue but promised to remain awake and await his return. Kamal wasn't too offended as the mission was as straightforward as it was stupid and silly. What else was expected of second-rate minds, even if there were three of them!

At the morgue entrance he showed his identity card to the bulky Purshotam, the security guard who was more interested in his bodybuilding magazine full of rippling, polished, and hairless male and female bodies, than to attend to Kamal. The excuse for this late entry was to retrieve a briefcase left behind. With a cursory look, a key was unhooked and handed over with only a slight admonishment.

'Make sure you switch the lights off when you leave. I don't like going up there. How all you half-mad people work there I don't know.'

The entry book wasn't bothered with. Purshotam buried his nose in the magazine and Kamal bounded up the stairs, wanting it done with and out of the way. He had better things to do. Inside the morgue which was only too familiar during daylight, the mischief was about to get beyond itself. Kamal got the strip lights on and with only the slightest trepidation, opened the first metal drawer but could not prise open the jaws of the cadaver. Quickly, he realized the jawbones would have to be unlocked at the earlobes. Once he became familiar with the technique, he became proficient at feeding the sweets to the cadavers. The only moment he felt a slight jolt came when he nudged the chin of the open-mouthed first cadaver to close the jaws and it happened with a loud snapping 'clack'. By the time Kamal had fed the fifth cadaver, his slight initial uncertainty and doubt had turned to glee. There was nothing to it. How could a medical student used to cutting up and rummaging inside cadavers be afraid of the stupid dead things! How stupid could Uma get? He started to hum and the prospect of the well heeled, bolshie and classy Uma being his slave brought a smile to his face. He would leave all the menial tasks to 'Pussy'. Cleaning his room and taking care of his laundry, a chore he hated, would be just two tasks for his glamorous slave. What's more, over time and with close proximity, a personal relationship wasn't that unrealistic, if he played his cards right. Four years was a long time. Anything could happen. Uma would drift away from that wet shirt, Krish, and edge towards him instead and nobody in their right mind would refuse her, her with the body of Venus. He opened the sixth drawer. Six more after this one and the job would be done. He'd get back to Sanjay and cajole some whisky out of him. His hands were about to reach down to unlock the jaws of a clean, fairly young, waxy-yellow cadaver when its mouth yawned wide open and the packet of sweets flew upwards. Untouched, the jaws of the cadaver had split open. Then, as suddenly, the jaws snapped shut. For a fraction of the briefest second, Kamal was frozen, then his heart pounded almost out of him and blood raced around his body like a driverless express, and at the same time a warm patch grew between his shaking legs, spreading quickly downwards. He had suddenly lost control of his bladder and himself. A strangled cry followed a sharp intake of breath as he turned and ran to the door, crunching scattered sweets. Taking four steps at a time he ran down to the main exit, past Purshotam who needed two looks away from his magazine before he realized what was happening, by which time Kamal had bolted out like a wild horse with its tail afire, his unbuttoned white lab coat flailing behind him.

∽

Sanjay's head was sagging and his eyes were drooping, and he took in nothing of the diagrams of the human brain spread in front of him. Heavy and hurrying footsteps in the corridor failed to rouse him till the next door banged shut violently, making him jump. Everything came back to him in a flash and he flew out of his room.

In his black room, Kamal was hunched over, sitting on the edge of his bed and staring intently at the floor by his feet. He was oblivious to the warm patch between his legs. He was still wearing his lab coat and his signature black necktie. Rapid shallow breathing made his back rise up and down in quick small heaving motions. Rivers of sweat flowed into his eyes and down his face. His hands were shaking and his knees were knocking together. Sanjay stood at the door, watching and assessing, which didn't take long.

'Kam, what happened, man?'

He came and sat by Kamal, putting his arm around him, and took a closer look and immediately got worried. He caught hold of Kamal's wrist and took a pulse reading, with the back of two fingers he touched the dripping forehead, which was red hot. He tilted Kamal's head gently upwards and had a very close look at the pupils shading them now and then. Everything confirmed what he had already surmised. He also noticed the wet patch on his friend's trousers but was going to pretend that he hadn't.

'Kam, your pupils are wide open and non-reactive. You've got palpitations. Pulse and heart rate twice the normal rate. Temperature, sky high. You're in deep shock. Trauma. You've run away from something dangerous or frightening or both. The old fight or flight syndrome and you're pumped up with adrenalin. What happened, Kam?'

Finally, maniacal, deformed, almost aborted wheezes of strangled laughter hiccupped out of Kamal as if expelled by evil. These intensified to a feral savagery and Sanjay was confounded but he knew of a remedy for all seasons, smart, silly, or serious. Accordingly, he reached for the trusty bottle of whisky from behind some books and filled a glass to the brim and handed it to Kamal.

'This will check your adrenalin flow, Kam. Get it down.'

The invitation superfluous, the proffered glass was grabbed by both hands and drained immediately. Kamal held the glass up for more and more and as the amber coursed down his gullet and eventually the pit of his stomach, its warmth rejuvenated splattered speech into a stutter.

'They got me, Sanjay. The bitches, they got me. They got me. The bitches! One of them...one of them...'

Drinking the fourth glass at a much more sensible pace, Kamal painfully relived the nightmare for Sanjay, concluding needlessly that one of the 'bitches' or one of their cronies was made up as a cadaver. He wasn't expecting anything like that. Kamal tottered to his feet, swaying and reaching out to hold something. Before Kamal collapsed in a heap on the floor, Sanjay got hold of him and pushed him on to the bed, straightening his long legs out. Kamal tried to get up, mumbling.

'Got to finish the job... Can't...won't let them...got to finish the job...one of them...one of them...'

'You're in no shape, Kam. Forget the whole thing. Get some sleep. Smart move on their part, I must say. I can imagine what it must have been like. Come on, Kam, you can't help it. Your body and its systems reacted as they should. Somebody else might have dropped dead from shock. That's the way we're designed. There's no shame in getting frightened. You'll get over it. Just relax. Take a deep breath.'

'I'm Kam. I'm Kamal... Nobody beats me...nobody. I've got to finish the bloody job even if it kills me...'

Sanjay removed Kamal's shoes and the black necktie but struggled with the lab coat as the latter was already snoring, softly at first and then like an enraged bull, blowing and snorting at the same time. Sanjay covered his friend with a blanket and watched him for a bit, taking a swig of the remedy of all seasons before switching off the light and closing the door, leaving the gently swaying Mr Bones in pitch black darkness, not that it mattered to him or to his comatose master.

15

Kamal woke up, startled, thirsty, and with the taste of sawdust in his mouth. His head throbbed behind bloodshot eyes. The events of the previous night played in the screen of his brain, like an indulgent avant-garde film, projected by a banshee with a mind disorder of its own, slow motion here and there, backwards and forwards there and here. Slowly, the film became sensible but that only made the viewer, Kamal, angrier still. He had failed himself and he would have to accept the humiliation of defeat. It was his own fault and as atonement he decided to find and add another two hours to his studies and ignore everything else. That made him leap out of his bed. It was the Sunday morning of Prof V's monthly lecture and nobody missed it, not the teaching staff, juniors or seniors, not even final-year students or even lab technicians, if they could squeeze in. Kamal had only enough time to shower, gulp down three cups of lukewarm coffee and three tablets of aspirin; but before brushing his teeth he would gargle with the whisky and even swallow a little bit of it, and while sitting on the toilet he would have some minutes to contemplate upon Prof V's lecture which he remembered was "The role of Medical Ethics in Contemporary Society".

In the packed lecture theatre of the academy, Kamal managed to get a seat next to Sanjay but apart from a nod, not a word was spoken as Prof V's entrance was imminent, and he was never a single second late for his monthly lectures. Everyone stood up nearly at the same time, shaking the old building with a clamour of bustling which was repeated as the Professor strode to the lectern and commanded them to sit with a slight wave. The bustle of a hundred or so adults ebbing to total silence gave Kamal a few seconds to rapidly scan the rows around him. While he spotted Krish, and Sanjay was next to him, there was no sign of the remaining three members of his study group. A moment later, despite the alcohol-induced depressive inertia combating the caffeine stimulant in his brain, Kamal had to concentrate on the lecture. He was soon engaged with Professor Verma's highly informed and charged oratory, amusing here, anecdotal there, but with deadly serious intent the whole time.

∽

The effect of a mild sedative and possibly Prof V's lecture or very likely both, meant that Kamal slept soundly all afternoon instead of mapping the human neuron network in the lab as he had planned to, despite it being a Sunday. His own nerves had settled considerably, and on waking he immediately reaffirmed and strengthened, again and again, his resolve to acquiesce humbly to Uma and her gang. It was a clever prank and Sanjay was right. Any human body would have reacted to fear and fright with exactly the same reflex even if the extent and effect varied according to the condition and the frame of mind the person was in. The sooner he got the capitulation done, the better it would be as he wanted a clutter-free mind to study hard and gain top marks, but that would remain an undeclared but firm intention. Having showered and dressed, and already feeling better, he went down to the girls' floor and knocked on three adjacent doors, one after the other, only to find them all locked as he had even the previous day. The girls were to have returned the previous day towards early evening but no one had seen them. As it was a Monday and furthermore the exams were looming large, the common room would be deserted but he would start a new search there and rope Sanjay in as well.

The common room, in keeping with its Monday moroseness, indeed was bereft of all and everything apart from Kamal and Sanjay and a yawning Gopal behind the counter. Kamal had already planned his capitulation. The girls, especially Uma, were bound to be full of gloating and triumphant glee. They would savour their victory to the maximum and extend it as much as possible but for his part, Kamal would remain calm and dignified and leave quietly after conceding defeat. He wanted to get back to his books as soon as possible. To ensure this he turned to Sanjay and let him in on one of his resolves too, as if this would commit him further to it.

'Sanjay, I'm out of "pranking" for good but you leave the talking to me. I want to handle this my way whenever they turn up for their pound of flesh.'

'Yea, sure, Kam but where the hell are they? No one's seen them. They weren't at Prof V's lecture. That's unheard of and they aren't in their rooms. I checked. The caretaker hasn't seen them today but he's not there on Sundays.'

'Knowing Uma, they probably decided to stay overnight just to let me stew a bit more. They'll be around, you can be sure of it. I just want to get it over with.'

Kamal sat facing the entrance at which he glanced from time to time, slightly apprehensive but also relieved that there was only Gopal to witness his humiliation, and he hardly mattered anyway. He was irked when he saw Krish walk in, dragging his feet, hair tousled, shoulders slouched and head bowed – not at all his debonair self. Sanjay followed Kamal's steady gaze and both saw Krish slump on to a stool at the counter, holding his head in both hands, elbows on the counter. Gopal, the common room manager, waiter, illicit barman, and cook at times, patted Krish on the shoulder and looked both ways before producing a green brandy bottle and pouring a large measure in a teacup which he pushed towards Krish. At their table, Sanjay was the more observant of the two.

'Brandy, eh? He's starting early for a Monday.'

Kamal was more dismissive, weighed down by other matters.

'That toad! Probably the effect of Prof V's lecture on the son of a bitch!'

'Now, now, Kam, he can't be a toad if he's a son of a bitch, can he. Different species, no?'

Kamal was unimpressed by this shoddy attempt at wit. He was itching to get back to his studies, especially his notes on Prof V's monthly lecture.

'Sanj, after the lecture I saw many groups huddled together, whispering and all. Prof V is out of this world – a one off genius. Didn't use any notes. What did you think of his lecture?'

Sanjay was more intent on watching Krish knock back another large brandy than answering any of Kamal's questions.

'Let's go ask him. He's bound to know since he's never a sniff away from Uma.'

Both strolled to the counter and Sanjay tapped Krish's slumped shoulder. Krish turned around slowly and with some effort raised his head. His eyes were red and seemed swollen, possibly the result of long hours of studying.

'What's up, Krish, man? You look like you've seen a ghost.'

Krish's head sank in the cradle of his elbow on the counter and his back heaved as he sobbed quietly. Kamal and Sanjay exchanged baffled looks and turned to Gopal, who was shaking his head at being the conveyor of bad news and at the news itself. Looking down, he whispered it.

'It's his girlfriend, Uma, and her two friends. They were coming down Nandi Hill very fast, and rammed straight into a bus going uphill. The two people in front passed away on the spot. The person in the back of the car is in hospital, very serious. The whole thing is very bad. Very bad, sir.'

Gopal continued to shake his head as he wiped teacups which were already clean and dry. Sanjay's mouth dropped open and remained so while Kamal's tired eyes blinked rapidly in disbelief. He wanted to be sure he had heard correctly.

'Sorry, say that again.'

Sanjay had heard Gopal clearly but still wanted to make sure.

'Are you sure about this, Gopal? Are you sure it was them? The girls?'

Gopal sighed heavily.

'Sanjay, sir, the car is at the police station. Red Maruti, all smashed up. Their parents are on their way. Professor Vermajee is very upset, identifying bodies.'

Kamal's brain had a synaptic storm while Sanjay still had his wits about him.

'Where are the bodies, Gopal? The police morgue?'

'First they were in the police morgue. Now they're here.'

'Here? In the faculty morgue?'

'Yes, Sanjay, sir. Professor Vermajee arranged it. The police morgue is very upsetting for parents. It's not private. They have to confirm identification, also. Very, very sad, sir.'

A sob escaped Krish. Kamal shook his head wildly, as if to clear cobwebs walked into unseen. Surprising himself and others, he almost shouted.

'Rubbish! Rubbish! I saw one of them...one of them, late Saturday night, midnight, Saturday...in the morgue...'

Kamal trailed away not wanting to relate or relive the trauma of cadaver feeding. He was lost for several moments till Sanjay tugged at his elbow.

'One way to find out, Kam. Go to the faculty morgue and check it out yourself. I know you had a nasty fright there but it's the only way to find out for sure. I'll come with you. I'll come with you, Kam.'

Kamal was downcast, which hardly ever happened. Furthermore, the flashes of a cadaver's jaws yawning open and snapping shut still sent shivers down his spine.

'No, no, I'm not going there. You go, Sanjay.'

'Kam, you can't avoid going into the morgue because of what happened to you in there. You're going to have to go there and work on the cadavers hundreds of times, yet. You've got to get over your fear sooner or later. Going to be a doctor and you don't want to go into the morgue!'

Kamal continued to stare at the floor. Sanjay shrugged his shoulders at Gopal and a tense silence took over in the common room apart from Krish's heavy breathing. Suddenly, Krish's head and hoarse voice shot up.

'You bastards! You bastards! It's all your bloody fault! You and your bloody pranks! I was...I was going to propose to Uma. Just waiting for the right moment... Uma, Uma, she always drove like she owned the bloody road.'

Krish folded like a shirt, head back into the solace of the cradle of his elbow, and the sobbing and heaving recommenced. Kamal looked around the deserted common room for someone, anyone, to tell him it did not happen. He rushed to the two second-year students who had just strolled in, joking and smiling. They did not know anything about the doubly fatal car accident. Sanjay rushed to Kamal, held him by both shoulders and looked straight into his eyes. He lowered his voice to a loud whisper so the others could not hear him.

'Listen carefully, Kamal. The morgue is locked up on Mondays for maintenance. Nobody is going to be there. Now is the time to get your nerve back. I'll come with you and look after you. We've known each other since we were kids. I can't let you go on like this. You've got to go in there and get back to your normal self. At the same time, we'll find out the truth about the girls. We owe that to them and ourselves. Whatever we thought of them, we were all study group mates. Don't worry about getting into the morgue. Leave that to me. I'll get the key off the security guy, Purshotam. I know him well. Come on, Kam.'

Sanjay almost manhandled Kamal out of the common room and to the morgue. The morgue had enough daylight peering in through the skylights. Even so, Sanjay switched on all the overhead strip lights, which came to life one after the other. He pushed Kamal towards the metal drawers after closing the door.

'Go on, Kam. Go, have a look.'

Kamal stayed rooted near the entrance.

'Come with me, Sanjay.'

'I see enough of the damn things day in day out. Go on Kam, you have to do this on your own. I'm right here for you, if needed. We'll get a stiff drink after you've checked the stiffs. Ha!'

Sanjay chuckled at his own remark as he tried to ease the tension. He pushed Kamal again. As stiffly as a zombie, Kamal staggered to the first row of the metal drawers and quickly opened the first one, looked in and closed it. Within minutes he had looked into all of them. One was empty and none of the others contained Uma or Shivani. Kamal looked around and noticed a solitary red sweet against a wall. The others must have been cleared away by the cleaner. It sent a shiver down his spine and he hurried back to Sanjay, who was waiting by the closed door, watching intently.

'One of them is empty, Sanjay. See, I told you one of them was here, made up like a cadaver. That one. There. Look for yourself.'

Kamal pointed but Sanjay snapped at him, which was most unlike him.

'Forget the fucking prank! Are Uma or Shivani in one of them?'

'No, no, they are not. They're not there.'

'Are you sure?'

This time Kamal snapped back, which was also unlike him.

'I know what they look like, damn you!'

Sanjay looked at the 'prep' slabs lying in a dark corner and flicked on a light switch. Immediately, four spotlights shot down, suspended on extendable cords, revealing two glaringly white, crumpled sheets covering what seemed like bags of potatoes. Sanjay pushed Kamal, almost unbalancing him.

'Check the slabs. Go.'

Kamal edged to the slabs and slowly lifted a corner of one sheet. A pair of female feet with red nail polish pointed upwards, accusingly at him. A sharp intake of breath knocked him back. He knew Uma always painted her toenails red, which he noted whenever she wore open sandals or slippers. From the doorway, Sanjay shouted at him to go to the other end but Kamal could not move. He strode to Kamal purposefully and led him to the other end of the slabs and pointed. Kamal lifted the sheet and let out a strangled scream. Uma's bare shoulders and head were swathed in soaking red cotton wool and lifeless wide open eyes stared up at the ceiling. A blood-soaked towel was draped across her forehead. Her face was a nasty blotch of black, blue, purple, and red. Kamal dropped the sheet and blinked rapidly at Sanjay, who lifted the other sheet and Shivani's equally smashed and bloody face looked up, lifeless as stone. Sanjay dropped the sheet quickly, grabbed Kamal by the elbow and rushed him out of the morgue, not bothering to switch the lights off or close the door.

∽

Back in the Monday desolation of the common room, a bottle of brandy stood boldly on the counter, even if half-empty.

As soon as Krish, Kamal, and Sanjay emptied their teacups, Gopal would replenish them. The bottle had appeared on the counter on Kamal's instructions and would be added to his tab. The three sat on adjacent stools at the counter, heads bowed, the conversation sparse and sporadic. Every minute or so, Krish would bang his fists on the counter, making the teacups rattle while questioning no one in particular with a 'Why? Why? Why?' Finally, Kamal felt compelled by the growing weight of guilt.

'I am to blame. If I hadn't accepted the stupid challenge they wouldn't have gone into the hills and this…this wouldn't have happened. You're right, Krish. I am to blame.'

Sanjay did not want his friend to feel such dejection all alone.

'We're all to blame, Kam. Not Krish, but the rest of us have been silly, stupid, and idiotic. I feel so helpless. Two brilliant lives snuffed out. Talk about saving and prolonging lives! Huh!'

Krish blew his nose, finished his brandy, and nodded at Gopal, who obliged with more brandy and excused himself to make a call on his phone. Kamal helped himself and Sanjay to more brandy.

'I cut up Rosie's church model. I hope to God she pulls through.'

Krish blew his nose again and looked into his teacup.

'Rosie does not have a chance. She's in a deep coma, on life support with a fractured spine. She's brain dead.'

Gopal came back and took his place behind the counter and noticed the empty bottle. Kamal asked for another one which was duly produced, opened, and placed in front of the three gloomiest first-year medical students on campus, who were getting drunk as fast as they could. There was nothing else to do except be miserable. Death was difficult to handle and here were two, possibly three to cope with. Honed over millennia of evolution to perfection, it came to this – deathly stillness, bone and tissue, corpses, cadavers. Death was a great leveller. King, queen, pauper, peasant, great beauties, ugly ogres, unequal in life had the same equal finality imposed by death. This was a Monday like never before. Gopal knocked on the counter in front of Krish as if to awaken him and when their eyes met, discreet nods were exchanged. Krish whirled around, took a quick look at the entrance and turned back, a beaming smile across his face.

'It's show time, folks!'

On cue, Gopal switched on the sound system and a hip bhangra track assaulted the common room. Kamal and Sanjay exchanged bewildered looks and swivelled around to see what had transformed Krish and the common room so dramatically. Standing at the entrance were Uma and Shivani, unmistakably so, but bedraggled with wisps of red cotton wool tangled in their hair and hurriedly washed faces streaked with blue, red, and black rivulets of watery paint. Barefoot and dressed in untidy tops and old jeans, the two sashayed towards the counter, hands on swaying hips like unhurried alley cats out to have a good night, walking the tiles. Behind them, a normally sloppy Rosie appeared, prim and tidy. Krish could barely control himself, clapping and whistling. Kamal and Sanjay rose from their stools at the same time in slow motion as the girls broke into a dance matching the music, in perfect unison and with eclectic choreography that combined grace with daring – a hybrid bhangra with bits of jive, breakdancing, flamenco, and tango for good measure. Kamal was singled out as the girls whirled and twirled around him, fixing him with the widest of smiles. A smiling Gopal laid out three teacups and a beaming Krish poured brandy into them.

'Good thing we have a bottle chaps. We have company. Well done, girls.'

Abruptly, Kamal stepped forward to Uma and offered his right hand which she shook with a snarl worthy of a sated tigress. Kamal turned to the counter and drained the brandy, gritted his teeth and instead of placing the empty teacup on the counter, squeezed it in his fist till it shattered to pieces, which clattered to the floor followed by drops of real, brightly crimson blood. The others stopped their dance and watched as Kamal strode away holding out the slashed palm of his cut right hand. He left behind a bloody trail of amazingly equidistant droplets of blood on the floor. Sanjay hurried after him but Kamal was already out of the common room.

Outside, Sanjay caught up with him on the footpath but Kamal kept his soldierly pace. Sanjay got in front of him and faced him, walking backwards, pleading.

'Kam, Kam. That looks bad.'

'Get out of my way, you bastard!'

Kamal brushed Sanjay aside with his intact left hand and marched on towards the accommodation block. Abruptly, he stopped and turned around. When Sanjay reached him, he grabbed the front of the former's shirt with his left hand.

'You're in with them, Sanjay. You all ganged up on me. I know it. I know it.'

'Your hand, Kam. You need urgent...'

'You pushed me on. You made sure I fell for it. You...you bastard!'

'How can you say that! We've been friends since we were kids. You're like a brother to me. Kam, your hand...'

Kamal jabbed Sanjay in the chest with his left forefinger.

'I didn't want to go to the morgue but you made sure I did and then you got me out of there fast enough, before I could think straight and have a good look. They couldn't have done it without you. You made sure it worked for them.'

The blood had formed a jagged, uneven circle on the cinder path. Sanjay got his handkerchief out, reached for Kamal's bleeding hand and tied it.

'Got to get this patched quickly, Kam, and don't get paranoid. Don't you see, if you give in they will have won. These are mind games, Kam. Don't give in to them. Come on, let's get this wound seen to.'

Just as Sanjay had quickly pushed and pulled Kamal into and out of the morgue, he led Kamal to the infirmary, much in the same fashion.

In the common room, the dance had reached a crescendo with Krish and Gopal trying to keep up. It was a dance to end all dances – exuberant with exaltation. Finally, a breathless Rosie flopped into the nearest easy chair, followed one by one by the rest of them, Shivani being the reluctant last one. Krish was beyond elation.

'Amazing, you guys pulled it off! I had my doubts but, hey, well done all.'

Uma was still panting as her paint stained top rose and fell.

'You did your bit, guys, and thanks mainly to Rosie for the arrangements, we did our bit. I was worried the anaesthetic might wear off but you judged it perfectly, Rosie, darling.'

Shivani rubbed her eyes.

'The only things we overlooked were the spotlights. Wish we'd kept our eyes closed, despite the gas and sedation.'

Uma was totally upbeat and gushing.

'Done is done. For the second time, we've taught him a bloody lesson he'll never ever forget and this time we stayed within the rules. Mental, mental. It was all mental. Excellent planning and execution. See, you take your time and you get rewarded.'

Rosie's eyes twinkled and sparkled as never before. She looked from one to the other, finally settling on Uma.

'All credit goes to you, Umi. Mine was a simple idea with the sweets but you turned it into a masterpiece with your live cadaver idea and the final touch of genius – the accident, the car crash that never happened.'

'A grand finale was called for. Go out in winning style, eh. This is where "pranking" ends and exams take over. Play time is over.'

The mention of the dreaded exams dulled everyone to silence. Exactly five weeks were left for the first-year final exams.

16

The nameplate on the heavy door had gold letters on a background of blue – PROF VERMA. It was the last and largest office in the long corridor, with smaller offices for assistant professors and senior lecturers. If students were to be found in this corridor it was either for pats on backs for exceptionally exemplary work or for slaps on wrists for gross misdemeanour, mischief, or prolonged absences, or finally for poor work or results which was hardly ever the case. The extent of such meetings with individual students or their full study groups depended on the magnitude of excellence achieved or the severity of misbehaviour or misdemeanour.

Inside Professor Verma's ample office, prints and paintings of landscapes were bathed in bright sunlight, allowed in by a large window overlooking ornate gardens. One wall of the office was totally bedecked with framed certificates, empowered with blue and red wax seals heralding solid achievement. This was his world, a workplace laden with thick hidebound books and dominated by a large, antique mahogany desk with a soft leather working surface behind which he paced from one side to the other, stirring his coffee with a letter opener.

'Medicine requires discipline and dedication of the highest order if you're to get anywhere worthwhile. There is pressure. Oh, yes, there's pressure for sure. Not least from the likes of me but I am a reasonable person, especially to my students. So I can turn a blind eye to your antics in the faculty morgue. I can turn a blind eye to your shenanigans in the accommodation block and the common room. Yes, I get to know about everything happening around here but take heed, I have only two eyes to turn blind!'

All five stood as stiff as steel rods, eyes fixed on Prof V; Uma, Shivani, and Rosie on one side of the antique desk and Kamal and Sanjay on the other, all of them in their starched and spotless white lab coats. Prof V stopped behind his desk and glared at one after the other. They were about to witness his other side as he raised his voice, seething with anger.

'Misuse of my faculty, your faculty, is out of order! Completely and utterly! From now onwards, you're all denied access to the faculty outside of normal hours and until further notice you are totally banned from all social and recreational facilities. That includes the common room and don't think I don't know what goes on there!'

Like the others, Uma and Kamal had lowered their eyes to the floor but what Prof V said next shocked them both into staring at him in total disbelief.

'In the meantime, be aware that sending all of you down for a year remains under consideration, but that will be denying your future patients and you'll all be a year late in qualifying. The pity of it all is that you're all highly capable. That is why you're here. I want your potentials to be fulfilled and realized, not wasted. Final word, don't get sidetracked. Don't let the mischief get out of hand. Don't let it get the better of you, especially as your final exams are days away. Now, go off to your lecture. You're already seven minutes late.

Next time you're summoned, it had better be for different reasons. Be sure of that! Off with you!'

Heads bowed, each of the five filed out of the office, one after the other. As Kamal walked by, Prof V looked at him and his heavily bandaged hand very disapprovingly, shaking his head with much disdain.

That night, a Friday night as it happened, the girls were closeted in Uma's room in the accommodation block. The snacks bought from the neighbourhood shop had been eaten in silence and the faces were as glum as a dark day, which Uma was fed up with.

'It's like someone died in here, like being in mourning. So what if Prof V told us off? It's not the end of the world. It's Friday evening and we can't go to the common room, right. So we can always go into the city, can't we?'

Rosie stirred and got to her feet.

'It's so expensive in the city and it's not the same. I hate to mention exams but I better go and do some work. There's not much time left.'

As Rosie left, Shivani followed her out, having given up on any offers of brandy. She would have to reach for her own hidden supply in her room. Uma was left alone and frustrated.

'Hey, hey, what's this? A mass exodus! Something I said or what?'

She stretched on her bed, sighed heavily, then reluctantly went to her desk, opened *Gray's Anatomy* at a bookmarked page and was soon immersed in it.

In his black room, seated at his desk, Kamal poured a third cup of black coffee and turned to his bed and sprawled on it. Sanjay was beginning to annoy him.

'You know what it'll do to you, Kam, this sleep deprivation? You'll go catatonic. Crazy. Nuts. Gaga. Loopy. You're halfway there anyway. From paranoia to schizophrenia, it's a short road. Hey, Kam, have you ever wondered where the mind is? We know where the brain is, alright. But where's the mind, the spirit, the soul? Big question, man.'

Kamal got up and shot back to his desk and was soon immersed in studies, his ever-present coffee cup by his books, but Sanjay called to him again and was met by a glare..

'Sanjay you're beginning to annoy me. Just a little. I'm going for top marks and nothing's going to stop me. Not you, not even this.'

Kamal raised his heavily bandaged hand while Sanjay yawned.

'Who cares for top marks? A pass will do just fine.'

'Yes, but you're not me.'

'Thank goodness for that.'

'What? What did you say? Go and do some work if you want to get anywhere and let me get on with mine, okay. I am very serious about being the topper. Did you get that?'

Sanjay got up to leave but couldn't resist a parting shot.

'Okay, okay, got the message. Friendly advice though. Don't overdo it with the coffee. You'll end up like your friend here, Mr Bones.'

Sanjay nudged the suspended skeleton in the ribs on his way out, as if he were tickling it. There was no laughter or protest in return and the skeleton's owner was getting edgy.

'I know what I'm doing. Trust me, I'm going to be a doctor. All is well and under control with the coffee. Good night, Sanjay.'

Sanjay was already out of the door, banging it shut, making the swaying ivory skeleton that was Mr Bones shudder for a moment, as if jolted out of lazy complacency by a minor seismic tremor.

'All right, Mr Bones. Settle down. Going to be a long night for us both.'

Kamal sipped his black coffee and turned a page.

17

Sanjay's hair had sprouted to inch-long black spikes but he still wore his ill-fitting cap while Kamal's stitched hand had healed a little. Every time they and the other four members of the study group passed by the common room, they would without fail, cast rueful glances inside it. Kamal did contemplate breaking the ban but Sanjay had pulled him away from the entrance one Friday. Meanwhile, Krish had voluntarily given up the common room most of the time, not only in solidarity with Uma but also because he was spending more and more time with her, always sitting next to her in lectures and labs and ever so slowly taking their soured relationship back to where it was before. Where others bent over microscopes looking at wriggling sperms and such like, Krish would look at Uma dreamily and wistfully soak in her misty perfume. Work, revision and the long early morning and late night hours spread like an endless pain for all students.

As if to compound the misery of preparing for the fast approaching exams, the very last lecture of the term was on the subject of pain and the lecturer revelled in it, pacing in front of slides, passing by and making the lecture as complicated as possible so that it became its own subject.

'Pain may seem like a pain in the butt but it's easy to grasp. It may be due to inflammation or ischemia. What is that? Ischemia. Anybody? Don't all shout at once!'

The lecturer paused for a moment but no one came up with the answer although Uma, Kamal, and one or two of the others knew the definition. Unconcerned, the lecturer continued.

'Ischemia is the lack of blood supply to any batch of any tissue. Remember that. These two, inflammation and its friend ischemia, cause injury to the tissue which then releases or forms several pain producing agents – histamine from mast cells, 5-hydroxytryptamine from disintegrating platelets and the active plasma polypeptides.'

The lecturer paused for a moment's breath and at the same time, out of habit, surveyed the students to check on concentration levels. Shivani's eyelids were drooping with the weight of sleep while others struggled to understand the topic of discussion. The lecturer returned to the subject.

'Now, if these substances occur in high enough concentrations they stimulate nerve endings causing...'

The lecturer stopped abruptly, eyes clamped on Shivani, who had fallen asleep, head having dropped to one side. Everyone tried to see the cause of the lecturer's consternation but before Rosie could nudge Shivani awake he was upon her, shouting.

'...causing what, Ms Shivani?'

Shivani's eyes popped open and she jerked upright. The stern lecturer was unforgiving. He was going to make it painful for Shivani as was his want and privilege.

'Yes, Ms Shivani, causing what?'

Shivani was totally blank, taking a moment to realize where she was as the other students tittered. The lecturer seized his moment.

'Pain, Ms Shivani! That's what! Pain! And the pain you'll go through when you fail your exams will be a different sort, I can assure you!'

Again, it was Shivani who was laughed at as the cause wasn't the lecturer's remark. The last person who needed to be reminded of pain was Shivani as she had suffered it for nearly a month and had the remaining scabs and the permanent scars on her posterior, which mercifully she could not see without a mirror. Pain she knew, and how, but the science of it she didn't and didn't want to either, even if a question on it turned up in tests or, God forbid, in the first-year final exams.

Later that night Shivani was determined to make amends and never be a laughing stock ever again. Accordingly, sitting on a chair with a new soft seat, she pummelled her temples as if to cram the information from the textbook and notes in front of her into her brain. She had been studying for the last three hours having resisted all temptation to reach for her friendly brandy bottle. Suddenly fatigued and weary, she rose as if in a trance, and summoned by the hidden brandy bottle, reached for it only to find the last remnants settled at the bottom of it, teasing her. Immediately, she felt disappointment, but a moment's reflection replaced it with relief as she decided that this would be the last bottle she would buy. From now onwards she would get up fresh and early without the heavy hangovers which only became bearable after being fuelled with yet more brandy. Shivani swigged the bottle empty and consigned it to the bin, covering it with waste paper and was suddenly overcome by a spate of elephantine yawns she could not predict or stop. She resumed her losing battle with information cramming.

In the next room, Uma rubbed her eyes and checked the time on her diamond studded watch, pushed her laptop aside and began to pace her room, having stiffened up with hours of sitting at her desk. She examined the tips of her long fingernails and proceeded to remove them one by one. Being false, the fingernails obliged freely. Next, in the dead of the night, Uma placed her hands on the shapely cello like curves of her hips, that Krish and many others drooled over. She looked around her room, lost for what to do as a short break from the books and the laptop.

In the room on the other side, Rosie was scrawling fast and furiously in a notebook with many pages of compacted writing and many doodles in the margins. The crumpled and slashed matchstick model rested nearby, as if in its death throes, on a corner of the desk. Without warning, the door by the side of the desk flew open and Uma barged in. Rosie snapped the notebook shut and hid it on her lap, very quickly. Uma stamped her feet on the bare floor.

'I'm fed up! Tired! Bored! What am I doing here? Fuck medicine! Fuck everything! Fuck everyone!'

Despite the tirade, Uma had noticed the resting notebook on Rosie's lap and snatched at it and read the first page.

'The six friends. A short story by Rosie Braganza. What's this? Change of career? There's still time. Might do you good, fatso.'

Rosie snatched the notebook back. Uma was bent upon venting her frustrations on something or someone. When she wanted to, she could be more than condescending.

'You should be studying, Rosie fat bum, if you want to be the neuro-butcher you want to be and not concocting fancy little stories.'

It was unlike Rosie to hit back but this time she resented the intrusion, the intruder, and its manner.

'Need a break sometimes. At least I have a hobby unlike the rest of you moronic jerks around here!'

'Grown out of matchstick models, have we, fatso. Hand's steady enough to dissect a pubic hair, end to end, yea. Sum total of your talents, eh, fatty.'

'Cut it out, Uma! What's up with you? Time of the month, or what?'

'I've just decided I'm going for top marks, fatso. Best way to beat the bastards, specially that big bastard Kamal. Nothing will give me a better thrill.'

'Not even Krish?'

'That I'm working on. But I'm deadly serious, fat bum. I want to outscore Kamal, Prof V's blue-eyed pet boy. I'll show him who's boss. I'll show them both. I'll show the lot of you.'

'You two are not going to grow up, are you! You and Kamal. When is it going to stop, eh, and stop calling me fat whatever. I can easily think of calling you something, Pussy!'

Rosie put aside the notebook and pulled *Gray's Anatomy* towards herself, signalling that it was high time Uma shut up and hightailed out of her room. Instead, Uma reached into her waist pocket, pulled out a sleek handgun with an ivory butt and pointed it at Rosie's forehead at close range, making her jump first and then smile up at the gun.

'Cigarette lighter. Too bad I don't smoke, unlike you.'

'This baby is real, fatso. As real as they come. Isn't it beautiful? Italian job. I love playing with it, especially when I'm bored and fed up, like now.'

Uma waved the gun around and stroked its shiny ellipsoid silver barrel between a slender forefinger and an elegant thumb, tongue sticking out. Rosie's disdain increased and she wasn't impressed with the gun, real or not.

'Why don't you use something else? Does your father know about your little toy?'

'I should think he does. An Italian General presented a pair of these beauties to him and he gave them to me on my eighteenth birthday because they are lady guns but expensive, he said.'

Uma swooned. Rosie's patience was wearing thin and she was prepared to risk annoying Uma whom she otherwise looked up to and even admired.

'Uma, take yourself and that thing out of here. I've got a lot to catch up on.'

Uma made a face.

'Oh, the tension, the tension! Some can handle it and some can't. Sort the men from the boys. I could have a lot of fun with this baby.'

Uma put the gun to her own temple. Rosie stared at her. Uma pulled the trigger and clicked a blank, laughing hysterically before recovering.

'Only papa's hidden this baby's real spunk – shiny little phallic bullets. He wouldn't let me near them but I know his hiding places.'

18

It happened every year without fail. Imperceptibly, with each passing day, the tension in and around the faculty increased till, with just five days remaining to the exams, it became a palpable burden weighing every student down. The common room became a ghost of a place even on Fridays and Saturdays, the very air stilled and hardly a leaf stirred outside, as if in complicity. With no lectures to attend and the labs and the two libraries open for revision only, there was hardly any movement let alone the bustle of a few months ago, which was not even a distant memory. Smiles were not to be seen and laughter was forgotten, which also seemed to affect the teaching staff and lab technicians as they prepared to turn into chief examiners and their assistants. Attendance at the infirmary increased for treatment of stress and study related ailments such as headaches, anxiety attacks and posture related problems due to prolonged sitting. Only the five accommodation blocks saw more activity as most students chose to study in their rooms in between frequent trips to the kitchens and the bathrooms. Every window in every block was alight with heavy gloom even as darkness came, and most of them remained gloomy till the early hours of the morning when some students started their long day with a run around the blocks.

Block 'A' for the first-year students was no different though the tension seemed heightened compared to other blocks, as this was a new experience for its lodgers. Its kind caretaker ensured that all facilities were in clean and perfect working order and put up notices on each floor urging students to contact him for any immediate or urgent needs. This was the quietest time of the year for him but he made sure he was always available in his small office and as students passed by, he would have a word or two of encouragement for all of them.

Uma, Shivani, and Rosie kept to themselves like other students, and if they did meet it was just for minutes and the talk would invariably be about which questions and topics were the most likely ones for the exams. Some students had the risky strategy of selecting topics to revise while others revised everything despite the sheer volume. Uma had chosen to do this and the other two followed suit. Matchstick model making, story writing, brandy drinking, fashion and film magazines were abandoned in favour of medical texts, diagrams and charts. After six more days of cramming, the first of seven written exams would start at nine in the morning followed by practicals in the afternoon. There would be a five day respite during which the written work was marked and practical work assessed. Extensive notes were compiled on each and every student's exam performance. In particular, mistakes, errors, and weaknesses were noted in detail and for a reason. Then, after five days which flew as one, it would be viva voce time, a form of torture where a panel of three professors would fire question after question to a hapless student, all of which were based precisely and exactly on the weak areas exposed in the written and practical exams. The thinking behind this strategy was that an opportunity was offered to the student to extricate him or herself out of blunders already made; a second chance was given. This did not work out for nine out of ten students, who flustered nervously and sank deeper in the mire, and yet the torture didn't end there. After the merciless inquisition, the dreaded box with its instruments of torture was wheeled in by an assistant. At the behest of the three professors, numbered intact human bones, small, large, and in-between, would need to be identified by name, location, and function in the body. This was when many a student wished for human bodies to be transparent or for the more likely possibility of the earth opening up to swallow them and put them out of their misery then and there.

Outside of the torture chamber the suffering student would be pestered by those awaiting their turns with the dreaded box to find out which bones it held. The realization that a human body had enough bones to arm the box with myriads of permutations and combinations seemed irrelevant. Despite this, one student had better chances than the others, in theory, at least. Where others had to be content with periodic acquainting sessions with bones and bodies in labs and the morgue, Kamal had a skeleton slung in his black room which he saw many times every day and studied it thoroughly whenever it took his fancy.

Kamal had allowed his friend Sanjay the privilege of getting to know Mr Bones better as well but Sanjay had soon lost interest, a bone being a bone being a bone. In fact, Kamal had to prod and prompt Sanjay several times to spend more time on studying and less on pumping iron in the gym but old habits die hard, besides, muscles had to be kept primed and toned at all times lest they turned into flab. There was no doubt Sanjay would pass easily and since he was happy with just a passing grade, Kamal had stopped pestering him to study harder. His own study schedule was completely on track to get the highest marks; his right hand required no further treatment and best of all, his handwriting was back to normal, the speed as it was before and no discomfort anymore either. Even so, Prof V had agreed to allow him ten more minutes in each exam but only if required. The six stitches had been removed and apart from a slight itch, all he had left were the six small butterfly scars on the palm of his hand to remind him of how his arch-rival, together with the other two, had gotten the better of him in the 'pranking' world, which mercifully was no more. Getting the highest marks was his urgent priority and his dearest and most passionate wish. He knew perfectly well that Uma was studying as hard and for as many hours but he had started serious study long before her. As such, his confidence was sky high and he was perfectly convinced, and confirmed it over and over again that scoring the highest marks was the best possible way to hurt Uma where it mattered most, as she was also hell-bent on achieving the same. All he had to do was to keep to his thoroughly planned study schedule, add to it if possible, continue during the exams and most importantly, prepare for viva voce, which didn't terrify him like it did the others, including Uma.

Kamal had kept himself motivated with such thinking and constantly looked forward to the pride and pleasure he would have when the marks were announced. The sight of Uma's blighted face would be worth the intense effort he was extending in studying and he had no doubts or second thoughts or any struggle with it. However, with three days left to the start of the exams, in the early hours of one morning when he had finally decided to sleep for a short while, out of nowhere, a tiny niggling thought set itself in the base of his mind and kept him awake as if a mosquito with a drill was at work. Not being able to sleep he went back to his desk but could not concentrate as the thought started to buzz and grow. He had been extremely lucky that his writing hand had healed in good time. He dared not think what he could have done otherwise. There was only one way he would not get the top marks and that was if he had to miss, or somebody made him miss or arranged for him to miss one or more of the exams. He had to ensure that he stayed safe, sane, and healthy by being on guard all the time. How could he do that? The snide thought became an avalanche of all-consuming questions. Two hours wasted by it was going to cost him dearly. He had to deal with the untimely thought immediately and also to his satisfaction if he was to concentrate fully and only on studies. He looked at his healed hand and saw the cadaver open and snap its jaws shut. Sanjay was right. These were mind games. Mind games! He shot to his feet and flew out of his room, propelled by rage.

In the corridor, most doors had narrow slits of light underneath except Sanjay's. Kamal hammered on it loudly, shouting for it to be opened up immediately. After a minute or two, other doors began to open and heads popped out to see what was going on at four in the morning. A half asleep, unkempt Sanjay opened the door and was pushed back into his room. Kamal rushed in and banged the door shut. One by one, heads popped back into their rooms and the doors shut.

Inside his room, a shocked Sanjay, who was wide awake by now, was pushed again, ending up sprawled on his crumpled bed. The time had come for Kamal to dislodge the thought that had overpowered him and to spit it out for good so that his mind was cleansed of it. After that he would concentrate on his studies and nothing, but nothing else. Kamal glared at Sanjay so intently that holes could have been bored in the latter with his vision.

'I know you're stronger than me but I can deal with you and those lunatic girls at the same time. Admit it! You're in with them. All of you planned and pulled off that morgue stunt together. You made it possible for them, all that time ago. You made me go there, you pulled me out of there before I found out they were not dead! You...'

Sanjay stood to his full height and straightened his T-shirt. Suddenly, he grabbed Kamal by the shirt front and clenched his teeth.

'You're right, I'm stronger, much stronger than you. I should knock you out and throw you in your room so I can have some peace and quiet. You're the lunatic, nobody else. How many times do I have to ram it into your block head, I had nothing to do with the morgue rubbish! Nothing, whatsoever! Now get the hell out of here before I pulp you. Out!'

Kamal was freed but stood his ground.

'You'll have to prove it to me, Sanjay. I have to know. I need to know. The sooner the better. You'll need to prove it to me by this afternoon or forget it. I'll come for you at two o'clock. You better be ready.'

'Go and get some sleep. You'll either feel better or you've become loony sooner than I thought. And never ever push me like that again or I'll make mincemeat out of you. Friendship or not! Go! Bloody lunatic!'

'Two o'clock. I will need proof. I will need evidence.'

Kamal got out and Sanjay flopped to his bed, clutching his head, too tired to work out what had triggered the outburst after so much time.

Back in his room, Kamal sat on the edge of his bed, staring at the floor as he had done on the night he had got a fright in the morgue. His mind was in similar but lesser turmoil and after days of abstinence he reached for his whisky bottle despite the early hour. As he drank straight from the bottle, the words 'mind games' kept swirling in his overused and overheated brain. He was more than determined to resolve everything at two o'clock. The first part of dislodging the thought had started with Sanjay, and the rest of it would follow after that. A meeting was called for but first, sleep was to be attempted as it would make him feel better, and having rested he would be able to handle the meeting better, Kamal thought, as he laid back.

Rested and showered by two o'clock, Kamal did indeed feel better but also a little sheepish wondering why and what had prompted his outburst, harking to the past. It could not be exam tension as he was convinced that he was not prone to it. He was relieved to find that Sanjay was in a better frame of mind and not as angry as a few hours before, but all the same, the persistent thought needed to be dislodged and removed for good.

In his room, Sanjay pleaded for more time to provide evidence that he had no part in the morgue prank or the car accident that never happened or the supposedly dead bodies lying on the prep slabs in the same morgue. For the sake of an old and lasting friendship he was granted it. Especially after he pledged loyalty and recounted their past history of growing up together in the same street in Chandigarh. He would do anything for Kamal, who was, now, ready to deal with the rest of his troublesome thought. Before he did that he wanted Sanjay's loyalty confirmed and cemented.

'Sanjay, you said the girls were playing mind games after those morgue pranks of theirs. I just wanted to say you were absolutely right. They did play mind games but will they stop, have they stopped? I don't trust that Uma one bit. Knowing her, I'm sure she's going for top marks and I have a feeling she knows I am as well. I think she will try to stop me by any means she can.'

'No, no, Kam get that out of your head straight away. This is no time for pranks or mind games. Already things have gone too far. You might be right about Uma going for top marks but how could she possibly sabotage your exam preparations or performance?'

'Think about it Sanjay. She's done it once, she can do it again. That morgue prank of theirs must have taken some planning and preparation. And why do it weeks before the exams? Can't you put two and two together? If they can go that far, they can do anything and blame it on a supposedly harmless prank. If they can lace my coffee with laxatives, and your hair manure with acids, what's to stop them from using more lethal stuff? You said things have already gone too far. When that happens, going that much further is not a big deal. That is the underlying principle of escalation. That's what makes it what it is. It happens without people knowing it. Don't you see? Once you go down the path of pursuit, there's no stopping it, unless you're a weak, wet wimp and Uma is anything but!'

'Neither are you, Kam, except you're getting paranoid. You've already accused me of something I would never dream of doing even if my life depended on it. The girls are as terrified of the exams and preoccupied with them as we are. Do yourself a favour. Relax. Nobody is going to do anything.'

'I can look after myself, Sanjay, but I suggest very strongly that you keep your eyes and ears open as well and be on hyper alert. When people like Uma get obsessed, they will do anything and everything. Don't tell me I didn't warn you.'

'Kam, I need to convince you of this for your own sake and as your best friend. You're in a highly disturbed state, verging on paranoia. I know that because I've been reading up on it. If you don't ease up, the increased stress and anxiety during the exam period will break you up. You will destroy yourself, nobody else will. I wasn't joking about sleep deprivation and caffeine overload. Look at it this way and I hope it will convince you enough to ease up. It's our turn to hit back, not the girls', but we've all agreed that childish pranking nonsense is a thing of the past. It has been stopped by all of us. You said so yourself, okay!'

'Yes, we've all put a stop to it but I can tell you what it did to me. I've been humiliated not once, not twice, but three times, each one worse than the one before, while all they did to you was to mess up your hair. That's why, Sanjay, your thinking is different from mine. There are times, even now, when I want to, not only hit back, but outdo their two morgue pranks, totally and utterly. Then I'll regain some of my dignity but I can't be bothered with all the planning and the rest of it which will take some doing. It still bothers me they got away with it but I have let better sense prevail,

Sanjay. The best way for me to hit back, especially at Uma, is to be the topper and that I will be, take it from me.'

Kamal took a deep breath and leaned back. Dislodging the thought that had burst out from being a cold niggling thought to a raging inferno was turning out to be a major, draining effort and it wasn't complete, yet. It had tired Sanjay as well, who was loath to offer any more comfort. He checked the time on his watch.

'What time is this meeting with the girls, Kam?'

'Few minutes. Before we go, Sanjay...'

Kamal got up.

'Yes, Kam?'

'I want an assurance from you we will forever remain the friends we've always been, support each other and do for each other whatever is called for. Can I count on you?'

'Sure, Kam. Sure. What a question to ask! Kam, anything, anything for you.'

'Come here, give me a hug.'

Sanjay got up from the bed where he had been sprawled and the two friends hugged each other. Sanjay was surprised how hard Kamal's hug was. Kamal checked the time on his watch.

'One last thing, Sanj, good buddy, before we go and meet the girls, let's promise each other there will be no more time wasted with hitting back or the like from either of us. There are four more blasted years left for us in this blasted place. We'll put all our energy and effort into qualifying and then we'll head back home to Chandigarh and set up big. I mean set up really big. What do you say?'

There was relief written large on Sanjay's face.

'You said it, Kam. Four years are going to fly by. Let's not keep the girls waiting.'

~

The common room was closed until the evening of the day of the last exam when it would reopen with a literal bang, so the meeting was held outside it on a large log table and benches, lying idle on the lawn. Kamal and Sanjay, friendship renewed and strengthened, sat facing Uma, Shivani, and Rosie, their friendship and solidarity also equally empowered. Perhaps it was the shared terror of the exams that were upon them or simply a maturing process, as all had amicably agreed to meet for what Kamal had suggested was a mutually beneficial arrangement that would enable all of them to concentrate on the exams without fear, tension, or worries of any sort. Lest he appeared cowardly and timid, Kamal asserted himself five minutes into the short but tense meeting after requesting and demanding to be left alone and untroubled.

'I'm deadly serious about this. I'm not frightened of anything or anyone, but you lot I cannot and will not trust. I can handle anything and everything thrown at me. So, either I plead with you or I threaten you. If any of you disturb or interfere with me in any way, shape, or form before or during the exams, I will tear you to bits. I don't care who it is! Like I said, I don't trust any of you, anymore. You've done it before and you might do it again. In return, Sanjay and I will guarantee that we're out of pranking for good and will not do anything to distract anyone from their studies for the rest of the time we're here. Agreed?'

Uma had tried her best to remain patient but she had a limit, and it had been reached much earlier as she felt that the onslaught was aimed at her specifically, and she had her corner to defend.

'Get to the real point, Kamal. Exams are making you shit bricks, aren't they! It's no secret you're going for top marks. Every stray dog for miles knows that. But, fear not, none of us three are going to do anything to you or your precious cramming. But one thing I can assure you. You won't get the top marks, try as you might. You will be beaten fairly and squarely and I'll tell you something for nothing. I might be the bitchiest bitch you'll ever come across but you'll be beaten fairly and squarely. So there!'

Uma got up to leave. Kamal smiled graciously at her.

'I take it I'm being challenged. Is that so?'

Uma stopped in her tracks, hands on hips, and turned around. The ensuing silence seemed to be longer than the few seconds it lasted, and while the others seemed indifferent and lost, Rosie looked from face to face, eyes sparkling behind the tape-repaired owl spectacles. Her look settled on Uma as if on cue because the latter burst forth.

'I'll take any bet from anyone it won't be you, Kam. Never in a hundred years!'

Eyes shifted back and forth from Uma to Kamal, who was smiling graciously one moment and was stone-faced the next.

'Don't play silly mind games with me, Uma. You don't know me that well, okay!'

'Just watch me!'

'No, you watch me, darling! And the rest of you. Just watch me!'

With that, Kamal was up and away, followed by Sanjay while Uma shouted after them.

'Going to your books, are you, little mummy's boys?'

Shivani and Rosie had not said a word, like Sanjay. Uma got up and paced around. She pointed at Rosie and with a twitching forefinger, beckoned her to approach. Rosie obliged, wondering what was on Uma's mind and soon found out.

'Rose, dear, I was rotten to you yesterday, with the gun and everything, so I wanted to say sorry. I do love you so and I care for you. Sometimes I just get carried away. I love you. Take care. I'm going now...to make passionate love to my books. I just love medicine. Oh, and I'm sorry about this little spat, both of you. It was waiting to happen. At least it's out in the open, now. Got to fly!'

Uma kissed a surprised Rosie on the lips, turned and walked away briskly, full of intent. Rosie watched the tall and elegant figure all the way, till Uma turned a corner while Shivani yawned and yawned.

19

The day of the first exam seemed like any other for everyone except for those being examined. For them, an iota of relief that the day had finally arrived was far outweighed by high anxiety – a reflex condition not yet fully medically explored and thus without total cure. All thirty-six students waited, some wringing their hands, others talking in whispers, starched and spotless white lab coats buttoned up in the hot sunshine. A siren disturbed everyone and the double doors of the hall opened and let the students into the gallows. A sign on the door, which was quickly closed and locked proclaimed: 'STRICTLY NO ADMISSION. EXAMS IN PROGRESS.'

The progress of the exams was as relentless as their unforgiving severity. Sweat and tears were shed with or without friends, sleep was forgotten, food neglected and the world ignored as the exams rolled from one to the next until the last one was done and gone with as much certainty as the arrival of the very first one. The vivas were hostile as they magnified exposed weaknesses not unlike malign tumours. Kamal was the only first-year student who wasn't worried as, sensibly, he had used the five day period to swot on what he had found difficult in the written and practical exams, this being a tip from a fourth-year student he had played against in the final of a squash tournament a month ago. He was totally confident about getting the highest marks as he had seen a very tired, red-eyed and downcast Uma a few times in the corridor, and each time she refused eye contact and seemed to be growing smaller whereas he felt taller and taller.

Finally, the exam season was over and the faculty began the rejuvenation process from ailing geriatric back to bubbling youth. As soon as the double doors of the hall were unlocked and thrown open, thirty-six young adults, all with the exception of one, became children as part of the process, firecrackers exploded, some lab coats were tossed up and came down as monstrous, unbidden snowflakes. The shouts and whistling were incessant. The group of four, Krish being a firm part of it by now, held each other by the waist, lab coats unbuttoned and askew while the group of two, Sanjay and Kamal, were not too far behind. While Sanjay jabbered away, as excited as a puppy in a park for the first time, Kamal refused to be a child and marched ahead, looking straight, smug with a slight, self-satisfied smile. He was more than convinced that he had achieved his cherished aim of being the first-year topper by some margin.

The common room was bursting at the seams and the six of the study group joined the throng, totally oblivious to the ban imposed on them by their hero, Prof V, which they had held to until now. Since all six were Gopal's favourite students, not least because of the hefty tips and regularly settled tabs, they got their beers served ahead of earlier arrivals at the serving counter. The only pity was that none of the six were able to finish their drinks as Prof V's personal assistant came hunting for each one of them. They had been summoned barely an hour after the last exam and they had no choice but to comply. Each was surprised and each one had to switch from a mindset of relief and joviality to some sombre guess work. What could Prof V possibly have in his considerable cranium for the lot of them? Smiles wiped off, each one donned their discarded lab coats, buttoning them up as they made their way to the office of their respected and feared faculty head.

All six marched down the corridor that was becoming familiar whether they liked it or not. They waited silently outside the door with the nameplate of gold letters on blue. Each one stared at the floor, apprehensive and concerned. Finally the waiting was over as a red-faced student came out, head lowered and shoulders slouched. Clearly he had been soundly disciplined for one reason or the other.

As usual, the four stood together on one side of the antique desk and the other two on the other side. Smiling, Prof V got up from behind his desk and poured himself a very small malt whisky as he turned to the six students he considered the brightest of their year.

'Last exam done with, we all deserve a drink but I seem to recall you're all banned from the common room. Apart, that is, from Mr Krishnamurthy here.'

Prof V placed his whisky tumbler on the desk and chose to single out Krish while ignoring the others, all of who thought they were in for another wrist-slapping session for daring to go into the common room while being banned from it. While the common room was, indeed, one reason for the summons, it was to come later.

'You see, Mr Krishnamurthy, the six of you have the sharpest and fastest brains I've come across in a very long time, with one exception that is reflected in your average mark across all the final exams. Perhaps I shouldn't be lauding you thus but you all deserve to know. The student who has achieved the highest in the first-year finals is in this study group and so is the second and third best achiever. Some study group, eh.'

Prof V took the smallest of sips from the tumbler and reached for a single sheet of paper resting on his desk. Outside, fireworks and crackers were still exploding while inside the office, six minds had whirlwinds swirling around in them. All eyes were on Prof V and the tension never more consummate as he raised the paper.

'The average mark across all the exams for this study group including today's last one, is as follows, in ascending order, Ms Shivani, forty-nine per cent. Mr Sanjay, seventy-two per cent. Mr Krishnamurthy, also seventy-two. Ms Rosie, seventy-six. Mr Kamal, eighty-eight. And the topper, Ms Uma, eighty-nine percent.'

An agonized spasm shot across Kamal's face while Uma radiated with the brightest smile of the year. Prof V looked proudly at the topper.

'Very well done Ms Uma, Mr Kamal and Ms Rosie. As for you, Ms Shivani...'

Abruptly, Kamal stepped back and was out of the office before anyone could blink. Prof V allowed silence for a few seconds before continuing.

'Kamal's disappointment is understandable, though a certain amount of rivalry and competition is healthy, I dare say. It'll make him work harder, one hopes. Ms Uma, topper by just one per cent. Don't let it go to your head and slacken your work rate. Last of all, as of now all restrictions are lifted and that includes the common room with all its debauchery. Ms Shivani will remain behind for a word or two. Off with the rest of you!'

By seven in the evening the common room resounded with much merrymaking, of which the six had missed only twenty minutes or so, Shivani being detained by Prof V for a further ten minutes for a mild rebuke about her low exam results, which had already been forgotten. Trays laden with glasses of beer, raised at head height by Gopal's hired hands were criss-crossing with those with empty glasses through the throng of carefree student revellers. There was only one exception. Kamal was perched on a stool at the end of the serving counter, the only one still cosseted in his buttoned lab coat and his ubiquitous black necktie. His gaze was fixed on a glass full of neat whisky by his elbow and he was totally oblivious to the carnival around him. He had been dragged away from Mr Bones and the black solitude of his room, where he had already taken recourse to his whisky bottle to dull the pain of humiliation and what amounted to failure for him, even if he had the second highest marks and missed being an outright topper by just two per cent. When Sanjay had come to drag him to the common room, he had only complied after a long raving and ranting outburst, followed by pledges of mutual support, trust, and loyalty between the two good friends. Sanjay was itching to hit the common room but had to endure and listen to yet more of his friend's regretful laments, the lambasting of Uma and her two cohorts Shivani and Rosie. More rambling followed, plans were hatched and discarded and new ones drawn up and details explored until Kamal had almost exhausted himself. Finally, only when he was satisfied with what had transpired between the two, and yet more affirmations of their friendship and solidarity were expressed, Sanjay was able to cajole him out to the common room to join in the annual revelries, which weren't so for everyone, not least Kamal, who seemed lost and distracted, which was totally unlike him.

In the common room only a small handful of students were sober while two or three had already vomited because of inexperience and hasty overindulgence through peer pressure. Sprawled around their usual table, the four were pretty drunk. Uma and Krish were engaged in light petting and hasty kissing while Shivani and Rosie grunted over a drunken arm-wrestling tussle which Shivani was losing, till she cheated and used both hands to floor Rosie's right hand, hurting the latter's wrist and making her swear in a most unchristian manner.

Sanjay was drunkenly busy playing an imaginary guitar with much gusto to the heavy metal bursting from the speakers, thanks to Gopal. He was so intensely happy that the misery of his friend, Kamal, was a forgotten consideration till his attention drifted and he saw him sitting as morose and still as a forgotten and desolate, ignominiously toppled statue. Through a haze of smoke-ridden ribaldry he staggered to the stool next to Kamal and with some effort planted himself on to it and tugged the elbow next to him.

'Come on, Kam! Who the fuck cares about one per cent! Only one per cent and it looks like your whole blasted world is crumbling around you. What's the matter with you, man! Hey, let's get totally sloshed. What do you say?'

Kamal lifted an eyebrow without looking at Gopal, who was very happily busy behind the counter. Despite the fact that two glasses of whisky appeared before the two friends faster than a flash, Kamal remained as he was, comatose and clammed up enough to concern Sanjay, who was drunk enough to be anything.

'Kam, Kam, if you go on like that, rigor mortis is going to set in. Hey, hey, ease up, man. Not the end of the world, you know. Bloody hell, man, only one miserable per cent!'

The only time Kamal shifted was to look at Uma entwined around Krish and each time the one per cent deficit stabbed him in the middle of his forehead. Sanjay shouted for more drinks and then found he did not have enough money and Gopal had no time to go looking for his tab and add to it. Without much ado, Kamal reached for his wallet and extracted all the notes in it, amounting to several hundreds and slapped them on the counter in front of Gopal, who received clear and concise instructions.

'Don't ever refuse Sanjay a drink, understand, Gopal? Give him whatever he wants. That lot over there, Uma and her friends, get them whatever they're having. Clear my tab and the rest you keep. Understand?'

Gopal looked at the scattering of five and one hundred rupee notes together with lesser ones and hesitated before picking up the money, by which time all of this registered in Sanjay's addled mind.

'Wait a minute. Wait a minute. Those bitches aren't going to get a drink from you, Kam! You crazy, man! After what they did to us, to you, I mean. Heck! Look after my drink. I'll show 'em!'

Sanjay got off his stool, stumbled and fell. He scrambled to his feet, laughing, and started playing his imaginary guitar while he waltzed like a deranged penguin towards Uma and her group. Kamal turned back to his whisky, took out all the coins he had in his pocket and placed them on the counter before asking Gopal for a cigarette, which surprised him.

'I didn't know you smoked, Kamal, sir.'

'Neither did I.'

'Anything the matter, Kamal, sir? You look worried.'

Kamal's face split into the widest possible grin but the next instant was back to his stoniest, making Gopal step back with as much surprise as concern. Both missed seeing Shivani and Rosie trying to bait Sanjay and pull his jeans down. A very drunk Sanjay flapped back to Kamal, pulling up his jeans and nearly fell over him, laughing like an overfed hyena.

'Hey, Kam, Kam, don't look so worried. I'm with you and everything is under control. You know something. I've known you, boy and man or is it man and boy and I've seen you drink like a fish, even if you're a man or a boy, but you never seem to get drunk. Me? I get rat pissed but soon everything gets under control and I'm ready for the takeoff anytime, buddy boy. Sorry, got to take a leak. Got to point Percy at the porcelain. Bladder's bursting. After that I gotta get lost. I gotta get to work. Ready for takeoff, capitano! Anytime!'

Sanjay staggered towards the toilets but fell flat on his face very close to Uma and her friends, all of whom enjoyed the spectacle, laughing and clapping. They cheered up even more when a tray heavy with all kinds of drinks was deposited on their table and the benefactor pointed at. Kamal had been distracted by the cheering and laughter caused by Sanjay's drunken fall and he was looking towards Uma's table when she raised her brandy glass and waved it at him. She shouted above the din.

'Hey, Kamal. Why the drinks? Have you gone mad or what? Listen, one per cent this time. Twenty per cent next year and every year and that's a challenge, boy.'

Kamal turned to his whisky, finished it and smashed the empty glass at the wall behind the counter where it shattered to smithereens, disturbing no one except Gopal, who missed it by a few inches.

∽

The next morning almost everyone in every accommodation block awoke near or after midday, a lot with hangovers and many a headache, and chief among them was Shivani, who found herself awake in Uma's room, wearing dark glasses. She could not recall how or why she was there, which hardly mattered as a strongly tempting coffee aroma drifted around her, nudging her senses awake. Uma was towering above her, holding out a promising, steaming mug and kicking her awake. Shivani struggled to sit up in the easy chair and gratefully accepted the coffee while her mind was beginning to reassemble itself and speech came back, though still heavy-tongued.

'Never again! Never ever again. Man I'm never touching a drop again.'

Uma, coping with a lesser headache, was terse and unfeeling.

'Go and sleep it off, Shivani. No one told you to drink the whole damn bottle. Serves you right.'

'Please, don't mention any bottles. Tell me, did you manage to hook Krish? You were all over him.'

Before Uma could spit out an unsavoury response, her door was kicked open and a bedraggled Rosie burst in, holding out her right hand.

'My hand! My hand, Uma. It's all swollen. Shivani, you bitch, look what you did. You and your stupid arm wrestling. Look, Uma.'

Uma reached for the hand and felt the wrist at several places, making Rosie wince with pain.

'Nothing serious, Rosie. Stretched tendons. Lucky you didn't snap them.'

'Me! You mean this Shivani bitch didn't snap them!'

Shivani put her hands to her ears.

'Rosie, do you have to shout? I'm aching all over. Earache, headache...heartache... Oh, Uma, did you give yourself to Krish? Body and soul? Or body, only? Or anything?'

'I dumped the idiot. He was stone drunk, thinking I was his to do as he pleased. Then he threw up on my new jeans.'

Shivani perked up a little bit.

'I don't know. Lovey-dovey one moment, and war the next.'

Rosie's interest was aroused and she forgot her injured wrist for a second and stopped flapping it about as if she were shaking drops of water off her hand.

'So, not husband material then. What a shame. I thought you'd make a nice couple. Oh well, such is life.'

As often, Uma was totally dismissive.

'Sorry, darlings. Not for me. Not in my league. You're welcome to Mr Style and so is the world and its mother.'

Shivani and Rosie lapsed into a lazy silence which was pierced by a terrifying overhead scream, making all three of them jump and look at each other. The scream became shouted words. It sounded like Sanjay.

'Noooooo...oh, God, nooooooo...noooooooo...help... somebody help...'

Rosie was the first one to leap to her feet, followed by Uma and Shivani, who tore off her dark glasses. All three rushed upstairs.

It was clear that the screams emanated from Kamal's room even though they became softer and less hysterical. The door was flung open and the three saw Sanjay kneeling on the floor, his tear-stained face looking up at the black ceiling. The three looked up and saw Kamal suspended by the neck from the ceiling at the end of a short rope. He had changed places with Mr Bones, who was laid out on the bed with an unused cigarette clenched in its jaws. Underneath Kamal was an upturned chair near which Sanjay was on his knees, wringing his hands and crying.

'What's he done? My God, what's he done?'

Rosie was the first one to wake up from the nightmare and uprighted the chair and got up on it, reaching up to the black ceiling, inches away from Kamal's popping eyes and his slightly protruding purple tongue, the mouth agape. She tried to ease the rope from the hook in the ceiling, using all her might, but neither the hook nor the knotted rope budged. She yelled at Sanjay.

'Lift him up, Sanjay. Lift him up. Sanjay!'

Sanjay was lost in a daze, still kneeling by the chair and crying. Uma and Shivani stepped up, clasped Kamal's legs and tried to lift him up as Rosie tried her hardest. Suddenly there was a sickening crack and a cry from Rosie. She jumped off the chair, face twisted in agony, her shaking right hand held by the left one. It was the wrist that was hurt in the common room arm wrestling with Shivani that had snapped. Sanjay shot up to his feet and wailed.

'Please go, all of you. Just go. It's much too late. Just leave us alone. Go, please go. I beg you.'

Uma tried to comfort Sanjay by putting her arm around his hefty shoulders but was harshly pushed away as were Rosie and Shivani. Sanjay herded and pushed the three shocked girls towards the door and out of it.

'Please, just go and leave us alone. It's too late. Too late. He's been like that for hours. It's much too late. Just go, will you!'

Uma and Shivani left quickly while Rosie, still in agonizing pain, took a long, lingering look at the scene in the black room before the door closed on her.

Back in Uma's room, the three stared at each other until Uma turned away to face her window, which was being slashed by unseasonal rain. The other two continued to stare at her back, which started to heave. Rosie stepped up to her and gently turned her around and saw large silent tears flow down. Shivani started to cry and left immediately as she needed a drink. Rosie stayed on and managed not to cry while comforting Uma, even though her wrist was pulsating with unbearable stabs of pain. Outside, the rain intensified with a vengeance.

Rosie's mind was racing, new, overflowing thoughts crashed into each other, some remaining incomplete, others spawning many more. She needed to get to her notebook. She needed to scribble. She needed to exorcise away what she had seen.

20

Despite Professor Verma's great regret, sorrow and untold anguish, he completely understood Sanjay's plight and grief and helped him to arrange a flight to Chandigarh within hours of discovering Kamal's suicide, so that Sanjay had flown out of Bangalore with the body of his truest friend before much of the faculty knew. This was done to spare Kamal's elderly and frail mother, his only parent, as much of the trauma as possible of her only child's suicide. For the frail lady, suffering from various ailments, to come down to alien Bangalore was out of the question. Instead, he would take the body to Chandigarh and whatever needed to be done would be done there. Arrangements were made accordingly once he had managed to control his own grief, which he knew would never leave him. For the moment, there was much to do. He would also make all the arrangements for the cremation in Chandigarh and share as much of Kamal's mother's grief as possible, having known her since childhood and having stayed in her house and eaten food cooked by her many a time, just as Kamal had at his house.

Sanjay was so heartbroken, disillusioned, and disgusted with the academy and the faculty that he vowed never to return. He was sick of medicine as well but after a few days of consideration and much petitioning by his family he decided to continue with it in the institute in his hometown, even if it was less prestigious than the Rajiv Gandhi Academy of Medicinal Sciences in Bangalore where he had spent a whole eventful academic year with its woes and wows, ups and downs, tragedies and joys. Despite that or because of it, he was not going to miss it, except, maybe Prof V and perhaps the old caretaker uncle with his thick lenses, which seemed organic to him. He would certainly not miss his study group members, for sure, though he had developed a soft spot for Shivani and at times regretted his part in harming her with a silly prank. He felt like a total idiot for it.

Three of the – by now infamous – study group decided they could no longer bear to live in their accommodation block even though the academic year was at an end and the three week holiday period had already begun. Upon Uma's insistence the three decided to shift to a rented flat, found with her father's help, three days after Kamal's suicide. Two porters brought down their boxed possessions, which were mainly books, clothes, laptops, some sports equipment, a lot of shoes, and some other personal effects. While Rosie had the least to pack, she still needed Shivani's help as her right hand was encased in plaster and rested in a sling. In contrast, Uma had the most to pack and both Shivani and Rosie helped her. As the porters piled their cases and boxes into a hired van, the girls took their places in the perpetually dusty red Maruti, watched by a forlorn Krish to whom Uma would still not talk to, the vomiting incident being still fresh in her mind and nostrils. This was the second time Uma had stopped talking to Krish, who feared that their relationship, which he had striven hard to repair, was at an end. Krish walked to his motorbike unnoticed by anyone. He had never felt so alone in his life but consoled himself that he knew where Uma's family home was and that her parents had taken a liking to him, particularly her mother, who was much taken by him and the fact that he was a local boy of excellent stock, to boot. There were still four more years to come at RAMS during which he and Uma would have to attend the same lectures, do the same lab work, and prepare and sit for the same dreaded exams. There would be ample time to get back into Uma's favours. Failing that, where one door closed, others opened. The only problem was that hardly any of them would have polish and veneer like Uma. Krish knew he was going to miss Uma badly for the next three weeks of the much needed annual year-end holidays.

Before the red Maruti sped away in the customary haste to which it had resigned, the old caretaker came out waving at it as if to reprimand it for its dirt. For once he was without his indispensible *Russell and Whitehead* tome.

'Ladies. Young ladies, one moment.'

His magnified eyes looked benignly at all three of the girls one by one before he approached Uma's side.

'Very sad. Very sad. He was one of the brightest, young Kamal, but regretfully tragedy too is part and parcel of life. His friend, Sanjay, has decided not to return, also. Must be very hard for him. For your part, you're doing the right thing. Settle down quickly in your new place, try to put the past behind you and get on with your studies. Understand?'

Shivani and Rosie had lumps in their throats and Uma was touched, which didn't happen often.

'Thank you for everything, uncle.'

She shifted a gear but the caretaker was still leaning on the car.

'Listen, I will get my thanks when all of you become big expert doctors but I know one of you is not going to make it.'

He was about to turn away but Shivani felt slightly irked, shaken out of her slumber.

'Thanks for the warning, Uncle.'

The caretaker ambled away and the car sped off towards the gate and out of it, followed by the waiting hired van. Inside the car, Uma was puzzled but unconcerned as she dismissed the prophecy of one of them not making it as the ramblings of an old man whilst Rosie wondered if she would ever see Caretaker Uncle again. He was nearing retirement and Rosie was unlikely to come to accommodation block 'A', which she had thought would be her home for five years, but that was not to be. During the one year she had spent there, he had always been kind and considerate to her, much more so than anyone else. Rosie decided that near each Christmas she would come and see him with a card and some small present. After all, there were four more years to spend at RAMS and apart from studying, life had to go on.

Rosie's thoughts shot in a different direction, pricked by a red motorbike flashing past the Maruti, which was creeping along in the heavy traffic like a sluggish snail saddled with the load of carrying its home with it, the same as Uma had to ensure that the van behind her with their belongings in it kept pace with her. The flashy red motorbike with the hapless Krish atop it had already zigzagged out of view, blazing a trail of possibilities in Rosie's mind. Was this the end of the road for Uma and Krish or would they, should they, get back together? Rosie's curiosity got the better of her, making her put on her soft dolly-doll voice as she leaned forward.

'Umi, sweetie, would you mind if I asked what's up with you and Krish? Has it ended if you're still sore with him or are you going to wait and see or is it that you can't wait to pair up with him again? Sorry, not prying, only wondering.'

Uma had seen Krish and his motorbike flash by, and waves of moments spent with him, happy ones, annoying ones, and sad ones had similarly flashed across her mind but she wanted to erase those and avoid her impinging feelings, wherever they originated from and whatever happened to them, wherever they died or lived, buried or grew, and whether they got hammered or pampered on the way. The heart or mind or brain, each one was welcome to feelings, happy or sad, like hell they all were! Now, here was Rosie with her innocent enquiry that was asking her to unfold and make order out of the rampant rainforests that human emotions were, growing and spreading where water and light commanded. Rosie's enquiry was best avoided until the will to do it full justice was restored or came unbidden or best of all, never visited. Uma slowed her car as if that would help her concentrate more on her interior world than the exterior one.

'Rosetta, sweetheart, right now I have many, many more concerns on my mind apart from Krish, considering all that happened and the rest of it and more worrying, what is going to happen. What is our future? In the scheme of things, Krish has his place but I don't know where. It's very likely he doesn't know either. If we could place ourselves in the right place in the scheme of things all the time, we would all sail through life, laughing all the way, catching all the fish we needed. What I know is that we have two weeks to regroup and get our heads sorted out before we get back to the madness at RAMS. I strongly suggest we concentrate on what we came to RAMS for and forget the rest which is peripheral, transitory, unimportant, and a total waste of time. Let's get to this new flat of ours and settle down, shall we? We're nearly there.'

Uma sped the Maruti and Rosie was perplexed as she had expected a simple 'yes', 'no', 'don't know' kind of lazy response instead of the sanely educated analysis and prescription which landed in her lap. She did not know what to do with it. Uma had surprised her with gravitas of the highest quality and substance, or had she simply evaded her innocent enquiry?

'Uma, all that means is that you don't know whether you want Krish or not. Leave it to chance, no? Can't make things happen. Let them happen as they want, when they want. Right?'

Uma braked suddenly for no other reasons than to jolt Shivani awake and avoid further probes from Rosie. Shivani shook her head, trying to dislodge the brandy-induced sleep out of it and rewound the tape running in her mind to where she thought it had stopped.

'He's always been saying that, Caretaker Uncle. "One of you is not going to make it." Like who? What does he mean? I know, I know. Simple. He means me since I always get the lowest marks. He's trying to goad me to do better. He means well, old uncle. Where are we? Where we going?'

Much needed laughter escaped Uma and Rosie joined in. The van behind them flashed its lights, not in laughter but for some other reason that Uma could not decide, not that it worried her. Rosie enjoyed the moment and wanted to prolong it. From the back seat, she got hold of Shivani's tousled head by the ears and shook it as if it were a coconut whose water content was dubious and needed to be determined.

'Welcome back to the real world, Shivo. What makes you think you're the one who is not going to make it? It could be any of us. Maybe all of us. Who knows? I mean Kamal didn't make it for one, did he. Maybe Caretaker Uncle was right and it was poor Kâm.'

Deathly silence settled inside the car while outside the traffic wailed, whined, laughed, and guffawed with incessant hoots, all to no avail, leaving Uma to recede back into herself, which was better and more preferable to what was going on outside of the car.

'Time will tell, girls. Time will tell but it will take its own sweet time.'

Rosie sat up in the back seat, perked up.

'Time? Time? No, Umi, darling, time tells nothing to no one. Nothing. That's its big secret, don't you see. That's its power, its stranglehold on us. Without that it's nothing but passing by, like the shit that it is. No, it is change that needs watching. Change. Long term evolutionary change having made us what we are, perfection personified, give or take a minor slip here and there, like in my case. That we can't control, can we? What we can control, that which is in our hands is the instant 'snap', 'snap', 'cut to', 'cut to' change like in the movies. Cut a long story short. Cut to the chase. Change is what needs watching. Yea, what else is there? Only change changing to change, only short-changing us and others on the way, sometimes giving out bad coins.'

Rosie could not help laughing as the other two, she knew, had no idea what she had rambled on about. She wasn't too sure herself. Uma was miles away and Shivani was drifting back to sleep. Rosie got back to the real world as the stabs of pain in her wrist flared up. Change was what they all wanted.

PART TWO

21

Change over a long period of time isn't often discernable as it creeps in incrementally and unannounced. Over a period of five years, like everything else, noticed or not, RAMS had changed in several ways. Students were allowed shorter lab coats and ties were no longer compulsory. The dress code had generally been relaxed and more foreign students were taken in, particularly from China and African countries. The five accommodation blocks were refurbished and the common room enlarged and two more pool tables added. Of course, with every year, a batch of new students arrived while those who qualified left for employment. Some students chose to stay on in Bangalore and work in one of its many internationally renowned hospitals, while others returned to work in their hometowns and cities to be with their families and relatives. Yet others applied to work abroad.

Being Bangaloreans, neither Uma nor Krish had to move far. Both returned to their family folds and found themselves working in the same hospital in general medicine. Much more than that they even found themselves married to each other, given what life was with its winners and losers and those who didn't care, and the rest of its undisputed and unchallenged, sometime vulgar and at other times happy vagaries. With their first baby, they were well-settled in a select suburb in south Bangalore, and Shivani, the other Bangalorean of the defunct study group at RAMS was only a few streets away. Of the remaining two, Rosie and Sanjay, little was known.

The only blot on the otherwise comfortable horizon that was life were Uma's occasional nightmares, which she could cope with, but lately these had become recurrent and more frequent to the extent that she couldn't cope with them anymore and neither could Krish. Almost every other night, it was the same face whose eyes would pop open, the jaws would part wide, then snap shut, and the torso would rise in slow motion to a sitting position and extend its arms outwards, inviting a hug. It was always Kamal. Without fail, Uma would scream and sit up. Krish would wake up startled and switch the bedside light on and the baby would start to cry. Uma would be glistening with perspiration. This time, when it happened three nights in succession, Krish did not conceal his annoyance or impatience despite being utterly considerate and tolerant as always. Switching on the main light in their bedroom, which had an unmistakably sumptuous red decor, he picked up his tiny baby boy from his cot and rocked him gently back to sleep before turning to Uma.

'This is not fair on Krishnan or me. You have to get this sorted. It's more than a nightmare and it's recurrent and deep-seated. You know very well where this will lead to. I'm going to ring Khanna right now.'

Krish returned the baby to the cot.

'Don't disturb him now. I'll see him in the morning.'

'Doctors are used to being disturbed. That's what we're there for. Besides, you keep putting it off. I hate self-perpetuated neglect! That's where health problems start and get worse. I'll use the lounge phone.'

Krish stormed out. Uma sighed deeply and reached for the water glass on her bedside table and debated whether to let another sleeping tablet do its work or remain awake for the two hours remaining for dawn, which always arrived whether it was wanted or not. The unasked for but often welcome bird cacophony of a mad feathered orchestra and the barking mad endless territorial disputes without any top dog being in charge of the dog world, she was used to. The occasional nightmare, she was used to. Perpetual, unneeded, and recurring nightmares, she was not used to.

~

A few streets away, Shivani had fared even worse and had already fixed an appointment with a specialist. She made the decision with the greatest of reluctance and had cancelled several previous appointments at the last moment. Now, she faced Dr Shah across his consulting desk as he finished going through her file. Shivani was wearing crumpled clothes and her hair was a tousled mess. Dr Shah looked at her disapprovingly.

'At least we know the source of your anxiety which is half the battle. The bigger problem is your alcohol dependency. That, as you well know, is not the way to deal with anxiety attacks, no matter how serious. You do know what excessive alcohol does to the body and mind. All doctors do.'

'That's not what...'

'You qualified from one of the best academies a year ago but you've been fired three times already and divorced...'

'Let's go to the source of my...'

'Let's just do that but we have to give a context to your problem, Dr Shivani. Didn't they teach you that at RAMS? You blame yourself for the suicide, at least your part in it. That leads to guilt-ridden anxiety to cope with, for which you rely on alcohol. Now, you know it and I know it, you can't remain intoxicated and numb for every second of every day, try as you might...'

'The reason...'

'I know very well the reason you came to see me. I want you to try something out. Have you met the others lately?'

The question surprised her. How would that help her?

'No. We all went our separate ways after qualifying. Rosie used to phone from time to time but hasn't for a long time. She had to leave after the first year as she hurt her hand very badly. Also, partly my fault. Uma and Krish I met some time ago, they are here in Bangalore but Krish was not directly involved in the...in the...'

'You're fortunate in one sense in that it was a shared experience, no matter how tragic. Find your friends. Meet as a group and talk about the suicide as much as possible. Share experiences. Share the guilt. Then talk about the guilt itself. Keep talking. Meet as often as you can. Talk the guilt to death, so to speak. Talk it to extinction, to use a better word. Do you understand me, Dr Shivani?'

Shivani nodded her head, relieved as Dr Shah had finally delivered the goods, though he still had a parting shot for her.

'Cut down on the alcohol and you'll live longer.'

Shivani was determined to do exactly that and on the way back to her small flat her mind drifted to the past, while the crowded bus she was in ploughed through dense traffic. The very first time she took a sip of brandy in Uma's room in the old accommodation block at RAMS, she had choked on it, vowing never to touch it again. Yet it had snuck up on her like a snake does on a rat before striking. She had become a closet drinker and vodka became her master as the chances of it being detected on her breath were lesser than with brandy or whisky. Even this morning she had knocked back a quarter to enable her to venture out of her flat and mercifully Dr Shah, despite all his experience had failed to smell it, thanks to an after drink cardamom, and also because after a drink, Shivani came close to functioning normally. Without it, the shakes and tremors made it difficult for her to walk and mundane tasks like writing or extracting change for the bus fare became humiliating impossibilities. On this bus journey, after almost a year of confusing uncertainty, Shivani was in a positive frame of mind thanks to Dr Shah, despite his brusque manner. She would take up both his suggestions. Cut down on alcohol stage by stage until she wasn't dependent on it and contact Uma and Rosie. She was hoping their phone numbers hadn't changed during the intervening six years.

~

Fourteen hours away by land and two hours by air from Bangalore, in a poor part of Panjim where she had grown up and subsequently lost both her parents, her father to alcohol and mother to cancer, Sister Rosie was conferring deeply with the mother superior at their church. As usual, Sister Rosie was reflective and sombre as she looked at her right hand, lifting it from her lap. It had a slight but uncontrollable and so far permanent tremor, and she had given up seeking anymore cures after years of trying every possibility.

'It's deserved retribution, Mother Superior. It has to be. I wanted to be the greatest neurosurgeon of my generation and I ended up with this ever so useless shame of a hand.'

Rosie was in the mother superior's living quarters in the church, sharing an old sofa with her. As always, the mother superior listened intently. Coffee and biscuits were in front of them but went untouched as Rosie continued.

'The silly prank in the morgue was my idea but it was meant to be simple and harmless. Just to go into the morgue at midnight and feed sweets to the cadavers we used for dissection. I thought that would be frightening enough on its own, but then Uma added her own two twists at the end which I told you about – a cadaver that would open its mouth, that was a friend of ours, made up – and a terrible car accident that never happened. Unfortunately, these only worked far too well, way beyond intention, certainly my intention, anyway. Then, there was the pressure to do well and Kamal's arch-rival Uma was the first-year topper which he so desperately wanted to be and, what was worse, it was only by one per cent. Maybe that was the trigger that unhinged poor Kamal, I don't know but I had my part in it, too.'

Rosie lapsed into silence and looked at her feet, suddenly burdened by all the weight in the world. Mother Superior had nodded encouragement all the time and wished her to continue, which she had to.

'We never really talked about Kamal's suicide. We just moved out of the accommodation block and got stuck in our studies in a rented flat. Somehow, Sanjay managed to take Kamal's body home the same day and never returned. My hand had little spasms from time to time but within weeks it came to this and I returned home to you and my church where my peace will surely return. That is the full story, Mother Superior.'

Rosie despaired. She had returned to her church with a yearning to be a nun after what had befallen her at RAMS. The mother superior, knowing much better, had advised caution and patience, as the arduous path to becoming a nun required total conviction which Rosie had yet to understand. Not wishing to discourage her, the mother superior had counselled Rosie towards being a sister at first and to wait to become a nun till the call became unmistakable and impossible to ignore. Now, easily sensing Rosie's unease, the mother superior felt moved to be more than a listener to her protégé.

'I will pray each and every day for you and for your hand to heal. Your peace will return but you are still disturbed, which is why you are here. Is that not so?'

'Yes, Mother Superior. Shivani phoned with many tears after many years. She and Uma want us to meet and talk about what happened. They are in turmoil as well. I can't decide whether to meet them or not. It will all come back but then again it will be nice to see them. I spent all of eighteen months with them and we became such good friends, but for this hand I had to return here to my sanctuary and to you. A lot happened.'

The rosary beads in the mother superior's right hand deftly followed one after the other, confined but orderly.

'Thanks to Almighty God, you will be healed, your heart, body and soul, Sister Rosie. Trust in the Almighty and don't you panic. You must assist Almighty to do the same for your two friends and pray for their healing.'

The mother superior crossed herself and taking note, Rosie, impressed and overcome, did the same. She stood up, partly delighted and partly upset.

'It's so obvious, Mother Superior. Why didn't I ever think of this? Of course I will pray for my dear friends, Umi and Shivo, with all my heart and soul and I will go and meet them.'

'Of course you will, Sister Rosie. Now, sit down and have your coffee. Don't get too excited.'

For the first time in many a gone year, Rosie smiled as she sat down and picked up a biscuit.

22

Uma and Krish had a very large, free-standing, fenced and security-guarded house with extensive gardens and an impressively long drive in a select part of Koramangala in Bangalore. Both were earning handsome salaries now aside from having ample financial security from their families. Employing a maid, a babysitter, a cook, and an occasional gardener hardly stretched them financially. Uma's recurring nightmares aside, all was well with them.

On this bright and crisp morning, Krish reversed his red Mercedes out of the drive as he did most mornings at around eight o'clock, unless he and Uma were late getting up because of her nightmares. Thankfully for them, with Dr Khanna's prescription of high-dose sleeping pills, the young family had undisturbed sleep, except it made Uma dull and woozy in the mornings, almost as if she were mildly inebriated. Her pillow always had soggy patches of saliva which had leaked from the corners of her mouth during the heavy, drug-induced sleep, which went unnoticed when she woke up. As doctors, both husband and wife knew this had to be a short and temporary stopgap.

The red Mercedes pulled out of the drive, revealing the old red Maruti at the end, rusting and dusty as always. Krish wanted the old car junked but Uma, seated next to him, couldn't bear to part with the very first car that was her own. It reminded her of her early carefree days at RAMS as well as the later unhappy ones. Both were on their way to work in the same hospital. Krish pulled into the main road traffic, which was always heavy, work on a flyover and digging up for the Metro underground network in Bangalore did not help at all. It wasn't a long way to Green Acres Medical Centre where both worked, but the twenty minutes of crawling in their car gave them the opportunity to exchange notes about this and that. Uma was busy digging into her Blackberry.

'Krishy, can you make it back by six today?'

'Depends on what turns up at five. Why, what's up at six, sweetheart?'

'I'm meeting Shivani and Rosie. I told you about that.'

'Ah, yes. I remember. Good. Good. Shivani's idea. Hope it works.'

The red Mercedes drove past a well-known shopping mall which had a row of trees with benches underneath, where people, mostly IT workers, came out for a smoke or to have some snacks. It was more than a familiar sight for Krish and Uma as they passed by it twice every day, six days a week, sometimes more. Uma looked up from her Blackberry for a moment of relief from her appointments for the day. Just as the car swept along a curve, her breath stopped.

'My God! It's him. Oh, my God!'

Uma craned backwards to look, somewhat panic stricken, while Krish was still jovial.

'What, you've just seen God, or what?'

'I swear it's Kamal. There, at the back. Stop. Stop.'

Krish turned his head backwards and rammed into the rear of the car in front. Uma opened her door and ran back towards the mall as if possessed. Krish had no choice but to run after the wife he loved more than anything else, even more than his little child and his expensive Mercedes, not to mention the huge house with its endless drive and gardens and his recently whiplashed neck. He stopped by her at a bench a few yards away where she was staring at a man, partly behind a newspaper. The fat man who was driving the car Krish had rear-ended stopped by them, furious and breathless.

'You think you can run away from me?'

The man with the newspaper turned it aside. His turban was remarkably like Kamal's but he wasn't Kamal. Krish dragged Uma back to the scene of the accident followed by the muttering fat man.

'Have you got eyes in your head or buttons?'

Krish pushed Uma back into her seat and slammed the door shut. He was angry. Both drivers examined the damage to their cars, which was superficial, Krish having lost both front lights. He apologized to the muttering man and offered him generous compensation, but despite that he had to add more to it. Back in the car, he paused for a long moment. He was going to vent his anger but seeing Uma's face with her mouth still open with fear and shock, he relented and drove on. Both had a busy working day ahead and Uma's fright would have to wait. For the moment she had forgotten her evening appointment with Shivani and Rosie.

~

The conference room in one of the three best hotels in Bangalore was large and could accommodate up to thirty people. It was bright with light from numerous overhead chandeliers. The ornate wood-panelled walls supported several heavily framed prints of well-known paintings with their own individual spotlights reigning upon them. Photos were being passed around – Krish, Uma and Shivani in their graduation gowns and mortar boards, beaming with broad smiles, photos showing the accommodation block and the forever dusty, red Maruti and even earlier ones including Rosie, Kamal, and Sanjay, messing around in the comfort of their beloved common room during their very first year at RAMS. It brought to mind the varying circumstances under which the three had departed – one, Kamal, committing suicide, the other, his friend Sanjay, mentally scarred and the third one, Rosie, physically hurt and retired so much earlier than she would ever wish, her dreams of being the best neurosurgeon of her generation in total ruins. It was not a great surprise to her two friends that Rosie had turned to her faith and become a sister, having stumbled, through no fault of her own, at the very first hurdle of the open race that grown up life was.

Uma, Shivani, and Rosie passed the photos from one to the other when there was a knock on the heavy door and a smartly-clad waiter pushed in a trolley laden with several bottles and an ice bucket. The whisky bottle was opened as Uma lit the first of many cigarettes and inhaled deeply, not caring where she expelled the blue smoke. The waiter tried to be unconcerned and waited as was his duty. He was fascinated by the three young ladies, who were going to drink and eat themselves silly, he speculated. One was as supremely elegant as the other was unruly and unkempt, while the bulky third one kept adjusting her spectacles. He would do his duty and wait. He sensed Uma was in charge as gravitas was oozing out of her just as the cigarette smoke was.

'When may I bring your main orders, madam?'

Uma considered it for a moment and suggested one hour but was quickly overruled by Shivani who demanded two hours and another bottle of whisky, even if the first one still stood unopened. The inquisitive waiter nodded his useless assent and departed, closing the door. Immediately, Shivani crowded three glasses with ice cubes and drowned two of them with expensive whisky. Rosie stopped her filling up the third one.

'Water will do for me, Shivo.'

Shivani wasn't aware that Rosie, who had partaken her fair share of alcohol at RAMS, had forsaken it now.

'What? Water? Whatever for?'

Uma was much wiser in such matters and saved Rosie an unnecessary explanation.

'The vows, isn't it, Rosie? Austerity and the rest of it for nuns and sisters?'

'There are very strict vows if you want to be a nun but not as strict or stringent for a sister. I wanted to be a nun but Mother Superior advised me to become a sister first and wait till I was sure and ready to be a nun. One day I'll be a nun when the call comes. I'll know when that happens; Mother Superior told me. For now, being a sister is fine for me.'

Shivani poured water for Rosie. She had once joked that the likelihood of Rosie becoming the best neurosurgeon of her generation was as likely as her, Shivani, becoming the next Mother Teresa. More seriously now, her curiosity was aroused, not that she had any inclination towards that particular road for herself.

'Does that include celibacy, Rosie? No partners, no marriage?'

'Yes it does for both nuns and sisters. Suits me fine. I never was the marrying kind.'

The silence returned as Uma and Shivani exchanged looks and realized what Rosie had embarked on was not an ordinary journey and that she was serious about it. Uma picked up her glass.

'Well...here's to...here's to... Hell, I don't know...here's to...'

Uma seemed stressed and like the other two, had aged more than she should have. Shivani snatched her glass and raised it, eyeing it as if it was the last desire of a condemned human being.

'Just drink it, will you.'

She drained her glass and reached for more while Uma and Rosie exchanged looks as they sipped from their glasses. Rosie kept her shaking hand on her lap, keeping it out of view.

Four hours later, the table in the corner of the ornate conference room was laden with nearly empty dishes, half-full bottles and scores of soiled napkins. The ashtray in front of Uma was brimming with mangled cigarette butts. Shivani had fallen asleep and Rosie wondered where this drunken meeting was going to lead. Even though sober, her speculation and imagination had started to cross borders.

It was three in the morning and after several calls to Uma, Krish had fallen asleep in his surgical collar, having discarded his spectacles and the book he was reading. He was concerned and tired but woke up as Uma slipped into their bed, having checked on their baby and swallowed her usual sleeping tablet. Despite the food and drink, she was wide awake and as Krish asked about the outcome of her meeting with their former fellow students, she was more than obliging.

'We managed to get through to Prof V. He thought it an excellent idea. The academy pays for one scholarship and the four of us, well mainly you and me, pay for the second one. Rosie and Shivani aren't that well off. Both are struggling. The scholarships will obviously be named after him. The Kamal Virdee Memorial Scholarships for Remedial Medicine. Sounds good, doesn't it?'

'Hope it works. Then the three of you can get on with your lives and forget the past. I mean Uma, enough is enough. How long can you guys carry the past with you and suffer from it? Surely there is a limit to everything.'

Despite the ungodly hour, Uma was suddenly wide awake, reflecting on the drunken meeting she had with her two friends. Being doctors and new parents, both were used to sleepless nights. Uma wasn't even yawning.

'Rosie thinks it'll appease Kamal's spirit. Her words. Then it'll...he'll rest in peace and won't trouble us, she said.'

'Not exactly a scientific premise, is it Uma? Appeasing spirits? I mean, what is this all about?'

'Well, Rosie's gone all spiritual, taken vows to be a sister and all, what with the tremor in her hand. Maybe that's why she seems to be coping better than Shivani and I. Both of us have fallen to bits but not her. Religion helps, I guess. We should invite her over, Krishy. Incidentally, we got through to Sanjay as well. He's pleased to be at the next meeting. I think it's going to work. I feel better already.'

Despite the hour and a busy schedule awaiting him, Krish was also wide awake, concerned more about the present than the past or even the immediate future.

'You know something? I was really worried you started seeing Kamal in broad daylight.'

Uma smiled and reached for Krish, pulling him to her.

'Come here you.'

Krish winced with pain.

'Ouch, my neck!'

'It's not your neck I'm after.'

'Uma! Crude as ever.'

'Some things never change, Dr Krishnamurthy, do they?'

23

It was Sunday service at the church, with a high cross reaching to the skies on its leaky roof. This only confirmed the fact that the church, in some disrepair, was in a poor part of Goa. The palm trees swayed over the few cars and many motorbikes and scooters outside the church. Inside it, forty or so parishioners of all ages sat on both sides of the aisle down which Rosie handed out hymn sheets and smiled, exchanging greetings here and there. She always wore her sister's habit for Sunday service and any other formal function at her church. As she approached the last row she stopped suddenly and the remaining hymn sheets tumbled out of her unsteady hands. She thought she had seen Kamal seated at the end of the row. The nearest parishioner smiled and gathered the sheets and handed them to Rosie, who had turned pale. When she looked up again, Kamal was no longer there.

∽

At the next meeting of the three in the conference room, Uma was the first one to arrive and immediately noticed that only two chandeliers above the corner of the long table they sat at were ablaze with light while the rest were switched off as if resting. Cutlery and various bottles were already laid. Uma was expecting Shivani to be a little late as she had insisted on collecting Sanjay from the new airport. As she waited, Uma decided to have a closer look at the gilt-framed paintings and prints on the wall. At the other end of the long room, darkness loomed except for equidistant circular pools of light on the thick carpet, above which the prints and paintings were illuminated by spotlights. Dressed in a smart black trouser suit, Uma stepped from one to the next, in and out of darkness, taking a good look at the prints and paintings. When Rosie came in she saw no one but got a fright as Uma stepped out of darkness. Both settled down and immediately, Uma sensed Rosie's unease.

'What's up, Rosie?'

'Nothing. Nothing.'

'Rosie, darling, I spent nearly two years with you before you had to leave RAMS. I can read you like an open textbook with huge diagrams. Now, what's up?'

'My nerves are on edge, a bit. That's all. How are you?'

'What's up, Rosie?'

'Uma, you might think I'm cracking up but I think I saw Kamal in my church.'

Uma was unusually speechless as she sat back holding her head in both hands. She decided not to relate her own experience of seeing Kamal but she wanted confirmation of what Rosie had just said.

'Are you sure you saw Kamal and not someone like him?'

Rosie was a little embarrassed and regretted having mentioned Kamal at all. She wanted to get away from the bizarre experience at her church and hoped Uma wouldn't persist with it.

'Forget it, Uma. Probably my mind playing tricks. Anyway, do you remember the old caretaker used to say one of us was not going to make it? Well, he was right and it was me. Shivani thought it was her and I thought it was poor Kamal after the...you know...but no, it was to be me. Shivo and you made it but I didn't because of this useless shame of a hand. How Caretaker Uncle knew, I haven't a clue but he was damn right.'

Rosie held up her right hand to show the slight but persistent tremor. Instantly, Uma's mind was numbed by an unexpected stab from the past and she struggled for a suitable response.

'I made it, Rosie, but for the past five years the guilt has been killing me and Shivani has not fared any better, as you well know from the last meeting. Still, things can only get better from here on. What happened in the...'

The door opened and Shivani entered, ushering in a well-suited and booted Sanjay. The past was forgotten as everyone smiled. Uma and Rosie got up and were transformed at seeing Sanjay. Hugs and greetings were exchanged and Sanjay was settled into a chair next to Shivani, who also wore a black trouser suit, only hers was crumpled and matched her dishevelled state. Uma poured drinks for them as Sanjay looked around at his surroundings. He had specks of grey in his hair, which was back to slightly more than collar length but not as lustrous and long as years before.

'Just like old times, eh guys, but a lot more upmarket. Makes a change from the good old common room.'

He accepted his whisky tumbler from Uma but Shivani didn't.

'Not for me. I'm off it for good.'

Uma was surprised, almost shocked.

'Did I hear that right? Well, well, bless my soul. Or, maybe that's Rosie's department. Heck, Shivo darling, if I was looking for good news, this is it. Keep it up, sweetie.'

Shivani poured herself a glass of water and raised it to the others.

'I will. Three weeks of rehab so far. I'll drink to that.'

Shivani and Rosie raised their glasses of water to the whisky tumblers of the other two. Sanjay added a proper toast.

'And to your scholarship idea. It's more than brilliant. Wish I had thought of it. It'll keep dear Kamal's memory alive at the faculty, at least. Cheers.'

At the mention of Kamal's name, the room froze and the girls took refuge in their drinks while Sanjay looked at the paintings and prints in their circles of light. Shivani was thinking about how to break the silence and bring some relief, even joviality into the room, when she caught a brief glimpse of a tall shadow – flashing out of the darkness to the edge of one of the circles of light and then disappearing immediately back into the darkness. The glass of water jumped out of her hand and landed with a dull thud on the thick carpet. Everyone was looking at her and her hands began to shake.

'Sorry, sorry. Clumsy of me. I think I'll just have a small drink.'

As if her hands had minds of their own, they shot out and grabbed the whisky bottle and splashed a generous amount which Shivani drained all at once, as the others looked on perplexed, none more so than Sanjay. Shivani's eyes were locked on the whisky bottle as an internal battle raged within her. She lunged out of her chair and before anyone could say or do anything, she was out through the door and gone. The silence in the room continued till Sanjay's anxiety prodded him to speak.

'What happened? She was laughing and joking all the way from the airport. Now suddenly Shivani's...what happened to her?'

There was a knock on the open door and the waiter entered with his pad and pen. As before, he addressed Uma.

'I'm sorry some of the lights are faulty, madam. They will be repaired tomorrow. Ready for the first course, madam?'

There was no response. Sanjay looked from Uma to Rosie, more perplexed than ever. As always, it would take him several moments to decide what to do next.

'What's up, girls? Anything the matter? Shall we order?'

24

Dr Shah looked up from his notes and Shivani wilted under his gaze.

'Obviously, I imagined it but at the time it seemed very real and I got very frightened.'

'You got through the difficult part – delirium tremens, the shakes and the sweats and the rest of it. After three weeks of doing well, you relapse because you think or you imagined, as you say, that you saw your friend from RAMS who committed suicide. What is to be made of this?'

'It's not important. Lately I've been thinking about Kamal a lot. We all have been and we've been talking a lot about his suicide as you suggested, and about the guilt, and it has helped, especially after we came up with the idea of the two scholarships in his memory. That is why I managed to stay away from booze for three weeks. I'll just have to stop the booze again, starting today. I did it before, I can do it again. I'm sure of that. I feel better already. I think we've got this thing licked.'

Dr Shah permitted himself a rare smile.

'Good. On that positive note, let's call an end to this session. Keep motivated and keep to your word. The only person who can help you is yourself. That's all.'

Dr Shah leaned back in his chair and flexed his fingers, always a sign that the session had ended. Shivani rose to her feet unsteadily, as there was still a slight tremor in her thighs and legs.

'Thanks, Dr Shah.'

Dr Shah leaned forward in his chair.

'One minute. Do your two friends also think or imagine or feel that they saw or felt the presence of – what's his name – your late friend?'

'Kamal. I don't know. I don't think so. They would have told me, otherwise. I mean, we talk about everything. Everything, even the smallest things.'

'Ask them, will you, and let me know as soon as you can. It could be important, though I doubt that very much.'

'We're meeting in two weeks time, on the day the Kamal scholarships are launched. I'll ask them. Why could it be important?'

'There's an extremely rare condition called "Collective Delusional Mania". You must have come across it in your studies?'

'I don't think so. Doesn't ring a bell.'

'Never mind. It's so rare, it hardly ever happens. Do remember, keep off alcohol and keep on talking till you get very fed up with the subject. Then it'll ask to be forgotten, and in time it will be, and you will feel better.'

25

The day the two Kamal Virdee scholarships were to be launched arrived and was soon gone. In the evening it was time for the three originators of the idea and their friend Sanjay to celebrate. They were ensconced in the usual conference room, more than half of which was dark as the chandeliers at one end were still resting, unrepaired. No one seemed to mind as that part of the room was superfluous to them. Their usual waiter had already wheeled in a trolley laden with the usual bottles and new additions of chilled champagne and two bottles of mixed fruit juice accompanied by platters of dressed lobster. At Rosie's behest, he took a photo of the group of four beaming friends before opening up the champagne. Rosie stopped him from pouring a third as did Shivani. Sanjay was surprised when fruit juice was poured in two glasses.

'I thought you guys liked your drink. You certainly did at RAMS, didn't you?'

Shivani didn't mind admitting what others would hesitate to.

'My doctor's just confirmed what I already knew. My liver's begun to moan and groan. I'd better not let it get too upset. Oh, and Rosie is now Sister Rosie Braganza even if she's in civilian garb just now.'

Sanjay raised his eyebrows.

'I say, things do change, don't they. So its Sister Rosie. I must say it sounds nice, "Sister Rosie".' The waiter left them to their celebration. Led by Uma, everyone raised a glass and toasted The Kamal Virdee Neurosurgery Scholarships. Sanjay added to the toast.

'To Kamal. And to all of us.'

Light humorous conversation flowed as easily as the champagne and the fruit juice. Rosie said less than the other three, looking from one to the other, smiling broadly all the time, taking it all in. Seeing Shivani and Uma cheerful made her happy. Both were far from their usual morose selves as Sanjay teased and flirted with them. He had not changed over the years as he bantered with them.

'You know something, Uma, I really fancied you like mad all that time ago.'

'Not now, you won't. I'm not the silly dolly bird I used to be. We have a one-year-old and another one on the way.'

Rosie chipped in.

'You have time for anything else, Uma? Keeping Krish busy, eh!'

Sanjay smiled.

'That reminds me. I have a bone to pick with you, Uma.'

'What Sanjay? You've got your hair back, haven't you? Miss your silly cap, though.'

'All that's water under the bridge. No, I mean this is my second trip here and I still haven't seen Krish and you didn't tell me you two got married, let alone invite me to the wedding.'

Uma giggled away Sanjay's concerns, which were not serious at all. For the next three hours or so, the four friends ate and drank while the giggles turned to laughter as they regaled each other with hilarious medical mishaps, real and urban myths such as the woman who was so convinced she was giving birth to a reincarnation of Lord Krishna and the medics had to play along, at least until the difficult delivery was over. Rosie did not have much to contribute, as having left medicine behind after only a year and a third of its study, she didn't have much experience with hilarity in medicine as the others, if any at all. Shivani joined in the laughter but didn't have much else to say mainly because she had won a hard-fought battle to refrain totally from alcohol and was as sober as a responsible neurosurgeon in an operating theatre. The waiter was kept busy as more delectable food was brought in and empty dishes wheeled away.

The eating and drinking had to stop sometime and the celebration had to end as well. By the time this happened, apart from Shivani and Rosie, the other two had removed their jackets as the alcohol and rich food warmed their bodies. Finally the table had been cleared. The waiter had excelled as he completed the last of his tasks before leaving. Sanjay yawned and stretched and Uma thought of bidding her friends goodbye and to call for the taxi she had booked. She rose unsteadily and reached for her jacket, which was hanging on the back of her chair. As she slipped it on, from the corner of her eye she saw a tall shadow dart from semi-darkness into total darkness. It happened again for a split second and Uma flopped back on to her chair. Sitting next to her, Rosie was concerned.

'Uma, you okay?'

'Don't know. Tired. Drunk. Both. I had better get going. Maybe I should cut out the booze as well. I'm sure the little bunny in here doesn't take too kindly to it.'

Uma patted her belly which was yet to show any sign of her pregnancy. She tried to stand again but fell into her chair as she had once more glimpsed the same tall shadow dart in and out of the dim light. Rosie looked at Shivani sitting opposite her to confirm it was time to leave. Shivani's mouth was wide open and frozen and she had turned pale. Rosie followed her stare, fixed at a dark corner. She was in time to see a shadowy, tall figure that looked like Kamal appear and disappear in and out of the shadows with the stealth of a cat. She turned to look at Shivani and their eyes locked before turning to Uma. Uma looked at them. Then all eyes turned to Sanjay leaning back in his chair, staring at the ceiling, eyes glazed. He yawned again and was unsettled by the sudden silence surrounding him, which made him look around before he turned to his three friends and found them all standing up and staring at him.

'Yes, you're right I guess. Time to say our goodbyes. What a day!'

Uma had never sobered up so fast. She was no longer tottering on her feet as she bolted right out of her chair. She had seen Kamal again, darting about. She turned to Sanjay, who had finally sensed that all was not well with the three young women, who suddenly seemed older.

'What's up, ladies? Seems like you've seen a ghost.'

It was left to Rosie to summon enough courage to mumble the dreadful.

'He's here. In this room.'

'Sorry, who is?'

It was the right time and the right opportunity for the three to offload their repressed anxieties and they did not want to hold back. Uma pointed to a painting and took the lead followed by Rosie and Shivani.

'I just saw him over there. I saw him before.'

'I saw him in my church and I saw him a minute ago.'

'I saw him here last time in this very room and I thought I was imagining it. Now, I just saw him a moment ago and I haven't had a drop to drink and neither has Rosie. Kamal is here. What the hell is going on, Sanjay?'

The floodgates had opened. Sanjay smiled as he stood up.

'Oh, Kamal? You mean in spirit? He's always there with me. Nice of you to remember him. He would have loved the scholarships in his name. At least his memory will always be there. Ah, well, such is life.'

Sanjay picked up his jacket and got into it but Uma was determined to get a rational explanation now that the subject had been broached. It was only a matter of time before all of it would spring out.

'Sanjay, don't mess around with us. Is he here or not?'

'Hey, guys. It's only natural we're thinking of him. We spent the whole day in his remembrance. As his friends, we're bound to feel his presence. In fact, it's nice that we do. That's the whole point of these dinner parties isn't it? So that we don't forget him? Isn't it?'

'You took his body home. Did you see him cremated?'

'What is this? Some kind of sick joke or some silly prank? Of course I took his body home. I had to. We grew up in the same street. His elderly mother is still there, frail and lonely, and she lost her only son and I lost a dear, dear friend. Cremation? Damn it, I put the torch to his pyre with my own hands.'

Abruptly, Sanjay turned his back to them and strode into the shadows where what was left of the drinks rested on a side table. Shivani and Rosie, standing on either side of Uma, looked at her. Uma was as still as a stone, breathing deeply and staring straight ahead, determination written all over her. Sanjay returned with a half-full whisky bottle and a glass into which he splashed a large measure and then he drank it all. Tears were rolling down his cheeks. He blew his nose and wiped away his tears.

'I'm sorry. I'm sorry. Happens when I drink and then I can't stop. Kamal is in heaven. How can you claim to see him? Please, please don't insult his memory. How can you? How can you see him...'

Sanjay stopped abruptly and suddenly took a deep breath. His mouth remained open for seconds as he looked at the three, one after the other, before recovering and putting both hands to his head as if to hold it in place.

'Wait. Wait a minute. You all saw Kamal moments ago in this room. All three of you. And all three of you have seen him recently. Oh, my God. Oh, my God. Oh, my God. I never thought I'd come across it in my lifetime and yet it's happening right in front of my eyes and to my friends, of all people. Oh, God!'

Sanjay wiped away his tears and gulped more whisky straight from the bottle. He paced the room, swigging from the bottle. Uma could not decide whether to leave immediately or test Sanjay further.

'What is happening right in front of your eyes, Sanjay?'

'I can't believe it. I can't. I just can't. Collective delusional mania. That is what is happening. Collective delusional mania. My, my.'

Shivani's hands shot up in horror but before any words or sounds of other kinds escaped her, Sanjay continued, suddenly serious and sober. He discarded the whisky bottle.

'See, I majored in the subject of mind disorder in Chandigarh after I left you guys in Bangalore. I know it well on paper and a few, very few case studies of collective delusional mania. This is the very first and almost certainly the last real case I will come across. I don't know what to think or feel anymore. I'll write a paper on this and get noticed but...but it's happening to my own friends, my own friends! Collective delusional mania!'

Sanjay shook his head. Shivani raised a hand but no words emerged while all Rosie could do was to look intently from one to the other. Uma lost her patience.

'Get to the point. You haven't answered my question. Is Kamal in this room or not?'

'Guys, listen to me. Listen to me. Uma, Shivani, Rosie, you all need help. Please, as soon as you can, before it gets deep-seated. Then it'll be too late. You'll all end up catatonic. You'll all...'

'Collective – delusional – mania?'

Shivani was still in shock but she had recovered some speech. A loud bell kept sounding in her mind as Dr Shah had alluded to something similar. Sanjay stepped up to her. In contrast to Shivani, words gushed out of him.

'Yes, Shivani, yes. You know what it is? When delusional mania reaches the same level in different individuals who know each other, its transference begins followed by its acceptance. There was a case of a family – father, mother, and two teenage daughters – all of whom became convinced independently and without telling each other that their neighbour was not a human but an alien. It became collective delusional mania.' The few known cases occur in peer groups, particularly close friends with similar abilities, skills, and mindsets. My God! Your individual delusions have reached the same manic levels and have transferred to each other. It's become connected. It's become collective. You're all sharing the same delusion, don't you see? Please, please get help, get treated. I have already lost Kamal. I don't want to lose you all to some hell of a mental institution. Please. Please, you guys.'

Shivani tugged at Uma's sleeve as silent tears started to roll down Sanjay's face, as he started to splutter.

'You are all still here but nothing, nothing will bring dear, dear Kamal back and we are all responsible. We all played our parts. Yes, I did too. Instead of standing up for him I set up your stupid morgue prank for you. Yes, I did. Remember Uma, you sweet-talked me into it. Yes, you sweet-talked me into it and he knew. He knew. It broke him. It broke him... Oh, Kam, Kam, forgive me, forgive me.'

Shivani tugged Uma's elbow again but got no response. Uma snatched her handbag from the table.

'I'm much too tired for this. I'm going home to my husband, to my baby. I'm finished with this. Count me out. I want nothing to do with this anymore.'

Sanjay removed his hands from his face but continued crying.

'That morning – the day after the first-year exams were over, some six years ago – I found him...he'd been hanging there all night...while we were all asleep in drunken stupors. Remember that...remember that...'

Sanjay started to weep. He flopped back into his chair and dropped his head into the nook of his elbow on the table. His shoulders heaved with sobs.

Rosie shuffled on her feet as Shivani got hold of Uma's shoulders and turned her around to face her.

'Uma, Dr Shah, my shrink, I told you about him, he also mentioned the same thing. He told me to ask you and Rosie if you were also seeing or thought you saw Kamal. He said it was unlikely but could be important if you were seeing Kamal. I didn't ask you because I thought you might think I was mad and laugh at me. Think about it. How could Kamal possibly be here? We saw him…we saw him hanging, dead, didn't we? That's when Rosie hurt her wrist, trying to get him down. Remember? Uma, he died. Kamal is dead. Accept it. First thing tomorrow morning, all three of us must see Dr Shah. It's urgent. Uma we need help. Sanjay is right. It is what Shah said. Collective delusional mania.'

Rosie had registered Shivani's every word and became worried, feeling sad for Sanjay. She walked to him and patted his heaving shoulder. Shivani followed suit. Uma joined them.

'Sanjay? I'm very sorry, Sanjay.'

Sanjay's crying became strange and more guttural. Instead of heaving with sobs, his shoulders began to shake violently. Uma wanted to go home but was also concerned about Sanjay.

'We should either take him to his room or leave him to recover and he can make his own way. I think we should leave and meet him tomorrow after seeing Dr Shah.'

Shivani and Rosie nodded and retrieved their handbags. Sanjay's crying turned into an odd mixture of crying and laughing at the same time till he raised himself and looked up, when it became loud, spluttering, and uncontrollable; wild laughter of the hysterically raucous kind, gobs of spit shooting out of his mouth as he struggled to speak.

'We have company. We have company. Just as well we have a bottle!'

Before the three friends could blink, collectively or not, Kamal stepped out of the shadows into a pool of light. Instantly, the room lit up as the remaining chandeliers that had been resting came to dazzling life. Kamal was resplendent in an elegant black tuxedo, his usual black necktie and a majestic black turban with a large diamond brooch at the apex of it. He had specks of grey in his neatly trimmed beard. He took a deep theatrical bow – a prince bowing to his subjects. His verbosity knew no limits.

'Good evening, girls. Or should I say, ladies. How sweet this moment is! I want to make it last and last. Better than the best orgasm. Just this moment makes it worthwhile. Ahhhh! Oh ecstasy, thy name is Kamal.'

Kamal bowed again and shuddered with delight before suddenly breaking into a bhangra dance joined by Sanjay. They were astonishingly good at it as they danced in perfect synchronized abandon around the stunned trio of friends. Victorious shouts of 'shava, shava, balle, balle' rang out, and in front of the closed door stood two waiters as if on guard, one of whom had served the three friends so loyally. Eventually, Kamal and Sanjay stopped. Kamal smacked his lips.

'Aren't you going to offer your long-lost friend a bit of fizzy? The friend you all missed so much.'

Sanjay handed a whisky laden glass to Kamal, who raised it in triumph, the smirk on his face widening.

'To you all. Your grief was so touching, your concern so heart-warming. This moment calls for the shine of polished diamonds but I am no poet. Cheers.'

He savoured his whisky as never before. An equally greedy smirk settled on Sanjay's face as he pulled out a tiny black bottle from his pocket and waved it about.

'Good stuff this. Brings tears to your eyes better than anything, literally. Ha! The planning, the execution, the pay-off. Such perfection, such patience, epic in its making. The prank of a lifetime. I bow to thee, master.'

Sanjay tossed away the tiny black bottle and bowed to Kamal who bowed back in return with equally blunt and shameless exaggeration.

'And I to thee good friend, for thy faith and thy flawless interpretation of the greatest tragic role since Olivier's Othello. Such feelings...such depth. Whilst, all I had to do was to play dead, dead straight. Ha. Ha. Play dead, dead straight! Get it? Never mind!'

Out of nowhere, Shivani lunged at an unsuspecting Sanjay and clawed at his face with the ferocity of a fighting alley cat before the waiters sprang up and pulled her away, struggling and lashing out. One waiter held one arm and the other held the other arm. Shivani was easily subdued but she had managed to draw blood from Sanjay's face where an angry red furrow was scratched from his nose to his chin, to which he was oblivious, anaesthetized by alcohol. At Kamal's gesture, the sentinel waiters released Shivani, who was too shocked and spent for anymore instant, irrational revenge attempts. Kamal smirked.

'Still the same temper, eh, Shivo? Oh, and your posterior looks so, so positively elegant. Let her be, guys. Such sweet and friendly staff they have at this establishment. Thanks guys. Pleasure working with you. Your reward awaits you.'

Sanjay munched a piece of lobster and followed Kamal, who was pacing about the room, repeatedly making a crushing gesture with his right hand and examining the palm of it. It had an ugly Y-shaped, unforgiving scar with six spidery stitch marks. Kamal held up his palm to the girls then tapped his head with the same hand.

'The scar is on the hand but it's etched deeply in here forever and ever. You should know, Uma, I never give up. You outscored me once, just by one per cent, but you will never outdo me. Not even the three of you put together. Let's see what you lot come up with. But can you follow this, I ask myself. Six epic years in the making. How was it done? All will be revealed in good time. In the meantime we shall await your hit back, for surely you will. Try, try with all your might, if you can. Put some excitement in your small lives. Brighten your blood! Come Sanjay, hero of mine, let's hit the town and celebrate but we won't gloat, will we? No, no we shall not gloat.'

Kamal walked to the door and waited as Sanjay picked up an unopened bottle of champagne and grinned at the girls.

'Good job we have a bottle. We'll drink to your good health.'

Sanjay joined his friend at the door, which was opened for them, but Kamal wanted a parting shot at the girls.

'Rosie darling, Shivo-Shivani, and Uma baby, don't take it too hard but be impressed with it. The prank to end all pranks but only harmless fun. Well might you wonder why one would go to such lengths. Wonder on and you'll get to know the measure of the man I am. That's me. I am what

I am – the maha maharaja of attitude and certitude and Sanjay is what Sanjay is – the bad badshah of loyalty and commitment.'

Suddenly Kamal's leering and sneering smirk gave way to genuine solemnity. The magician of the flashing facial masks as at RAMS was back but this time his expression seemed heavy with sincerity.

'We do have one regret though. Only one but a very severe one. Seriously, one that truly hurts me and Sanjay deeply, profoundly, and that's Rosie's hand. Don't give up, Rosie, darling. Miracles do happen. Sanjay told me you've joined the church and become a sister. We will both continue to pray for your recovery, also. The dead might not be dead and the living dead might live again, Rosie. Other than that, goodbye and God bless you all.'

With that, Kamal stepped out followed by Sanjay and the two waiters, one of whom closed the door gently behind him. The silence in the room was overwhelming. Uma poured herself a neat whisky and sat back in her chair. Shivani came and sat next to her, eyes riveted on the whisky bottle so invitingly close by. Her hand started to itch and a small tremor took over it. From a distance, Rosie watched her silent friends for a good two minutes before joining them. Shivani's hand shot out like a bolt of lightning, startling Uma. The whisky bottle was in Shivani's shaking hand. Uma was concerned and pained.

'Don't, Shivani, don't. It will be downhill all the way. Put it down.'

Not a word registered with Shivani as she threw her head back and poured whisky into her mouth. She did so twice more, emptying the bottle and tossing it aside. Suddenly, she sprang up and rushed to the door. This time Uma's mind was elsewhere but Rosie was worried.

'Shivani, don't do anything stupid. Shivani!'

The door banged shut and Shivani had flown. Slowly and deliberately, Uma extracted a cigarette and lit up, taking quick and deep drags. Rosie looked at her before raising her right hand, which always remained awkwardly gnarled and still except for the slight tremor which never left it. She looked at her hand and a silent tear rolled down one cheek. Uma was staring ahead, resolutely and stubbornly, as still as a cracked wall that knows it will crumble sometime. Wisps of smoke escaped Uma as if from widening cracks. She muttered to herself.

'I'm going to kill that bastard.'

26

Uma tossed another pebble into the pond. It rippled the reflection of green trees and blue skies into concentric circles of disorder, and before default order was restored in this inverted world like her own, she tossed another pebble into it, disturbing it again. For a Sunday, the park was almost deserted apart from makeshift games of cricket in the distance. Uma and Krish sat on a bench by the pond with their baby fast asleep in a pram nearby. Uma cast the last of the pebbles and sat back watching the concentric circles ebb away, restoring calm to the inverted world. Krish resumed their quiet conversation.

'I'm so glad you changed your mind, Umi. Silly student pranks are one thing and being grown up with a child is another. All that was years ago. Why drag it back into the present?'

'Doesn't bear thinking, does it? I was an immature brat then, Krishy. We all were. Kamal and Sanjay have dragged it up again but no, I'm out of it, I really am. I do think of revenge quite often but, no, let sleeping dogs lie. I'm out of it. I've got better things to do.'

Krish was more than relieved as he had suffered Uma's regular outbursts of anger at Kamal and Sanjay and her obsession at hitting back at them over the last few weeks.

Each time, he would try to pacify her and try his best to talk her out of any notions of revenge. Now, out of the blue, Uma had made up her own mind and Krish wanted clear and total confirmation, making sure Uma meant what she said.

'You don't sound too sure of yourself, Uma.'

'Sure, I'm sure. I've got you. We've got little Krishnan, bless him, and another one on the way. We've got the house. We've got good jobs. I'm happy with that. I'd be crazy to go chasing after the whims of a semi-deranged idiot who refuses to grow up. What Shivani and Rosie want to do is up to them. I'm out of it for good.'

'Semi-deranged idiot. I like that. I'd say Kamal is a totally deranged idiot. I always had doubts about the nut and his mad ways. Anyone going to such unbelievable lengths has got to be a lunatic. Do you know he had his room painted black, I mean totally black? Everything but everything was black. What kind of mind is that? Totally, utterly deranged. You guys are best rid of the idiot.'

Uma's mind had wandered. The pond seemed a picture of tranquillity and Krish relished the thought of enjoying his dinner and watching TV in peace, again. At last Uma had come to her senses. Life would return to normal. Krish smiled, not knowing that his wishful thinking would remain just that. His household was about to be disrupted as never before.

∽

Rosie was staying over for the weekend, and Shivani, who had instigated and insisted upon the gathering came for the evening with her camcorder, which Krish had plugged into the large screen LCD television. Pizzas had been ordered and drinks were handed around as per preference. The baby was asleep and Uma and Krish and their two guests were well settled in the airy lounge. Shivani had already seen the videotape several times in her small flat but the other three waited eagerly, not knowing what they would be seeing. Without ceremony, Shivani pointed the remote control at her camcorder and switched it on. A shaky and blurred image appeared on the large screen. It cleared into a distant, sleek, luxury-cruiser boat that skimmed over the surface of a beautiful, rippling lake. Unsteadily the boat zoomed in larger and larger until a tall, turbaned male and a female figure were clearly visible, both wearing trendy dark glasses. It was Kamal, but Shivani wanted to make sure the others realized that.

'That's Kamal and his live-in partner in one of his two boats.'

The others watched in silence as Kamal moored the boat. The top end of a plush glass tower of apartments appeared. Uma shifted uneasily in her sofa chair.

'Don't tell me. I can guess. That's his penthouse suite on the lakefront.'

The TV screen showed one shaky sequence after another with Kamal somewhere in all of them. There were luxury cars, motorbikes, farms, orchards, and yet another plush boat, from which Kamal and Sanjay were fishing. Shivani provided a running commentary which wasn't required as the luxury and ostentation exuded was difficult to miss despite the poor camera work. Kamal and Sanjay were both high-end consultants, owning four major medical centres, Shivani had found out, as she informed the other three. Uma became increasingly restless as several smart residential and commercial streets unfolded on the TV screen. These and other prime chunks of Chandigarh, she was informed, belonged to Sanjay who had invested in property in a big way but as a small side business. Uma leaned across and snatched the remote control from Shivani and switched off the camcorder and the TV.

'What is the point of all this, Shivani? I refuse to be jealous or envious. I like the way I live, thank you very much. I don't give a damn how others live!'

In the ensuing silence, a shocked Shivani stared at Uma while Rosie decided not to interject but look from one to the other as if she were studying them. She feared the unpleasantness that had suddenly pervaded the comfortable lounge, almost inverting it. Krish wanted to end the sudden tension but as usual he wasn't sure how to. So, inadvertently, he managed to add to it.

'What made you do this, Shivo? Going all that way and filming all that? I mean...'

'Uma might have forgiven and forgotten but I've been drowning myself in a bottle day in, day out. I was and still am so angry. I wanted to know what they were up to after what they did to us. I can't hold a job because of drink and poor Rosie's dreams of being the best ever neurosurgeon are in tatters. Just compare our lives to theirs. They're big shots in Chandigarh. It didn't take me long to trace them. No, Uma, I will not forgive and forget!'

Silence returned. Rosie looked at her gnarled and tremulous hand. Uma sighed loudly at her ceiling.

'I will make it as clear as I can, darlings. I'm just relieved the bastard didn't hang himself on my account. I thought he did and it turned my life upside down. Just ask Krish what he had to put up with. Now that my sanity has returned, I want to keep it that way.'

The tension thickened, becoming almost solid. Shivani bit her lip, finding it difficult to contain herself.

'Nobody's asking you to do anything, Uma.'

'Good. And nobody's going to either. Now or ever. It's silly spying on them like that, Shivani. It's right out of their book!'

Calmly, Shivani unplugged her camcorder and packed it. Instead of reoccupying her seat she snatched her handbag from the floor and glared at Uma and almost shouted.

'Thanks for nothing, Uma.'

Krish was concerned but could only make a weak appeal.

'Girls. Girls, calm down. Sit down Shivani.'

Shivani stormed out of the lounge and a moment later the front door slammed loudly. Krish looked at Uma and found her staring at the ceiling as Rosie looked at both.

'I didn't say anything, Uma.'

Uma did not shift her distant gaze.

'No Rosie darling, you didn't. I did. Maybe more than I should have. But you know Shivo and her temper. What's new?'

Krish sighed and got up to refresh his drink.

'Am I glad I'm not part of any of this. Girls will be girls, I guess. And it doesn't get any better as women.'

The front door chime trilled out. Krish perked up and hurried to open the door, leaving behind an instruction.

'You better make it up to her, Uma. Am I glad she's back.'

Rosie was also glad their friend was returning. She decided to steer the conversation to more cheerful avenues.

Uma was also secretively relieved and decided to apologize and make amends to Shivani by treating her to a special dinner at one of Bangalore's top eateries later in the week.

In the hallway, a beaming Krish opened the door, not to Shivani but to the pizza delivery boy.

∽

The first thing that Shivani did was to seek refuge in another more reliable friend which she purchased from a wine shop not far from Krish and Uma's house. Not for a second did the thought that she had stopped drinking not so long ago for the sake of her liver cross her mind. Being shunned and insulted by her best friend of years was more than a blow to her, coming so soon after the discovery that her tormenters lived the lives of kings after reducing hers to that of a sewer rat. Like many an alcoholic, Shivani no longer required an excuse, justified or not, to reach for the next bottle. It was as if she was programmed to do this. She had become adept at spotting wine shops without knowing it just like many a bride-to-be becomes adept with jewellery shops. Except that brides having purchased their desires had no need to return again and again whereas Shivani's need was perpetual. Hence the talent of spotting different wine shops, which became necessary as Shivani avoided the wine shop nearest to her small flat unless totally desperate. She did not want anyone else apart from Dr Shah to know she was degenerating towards extreme alcohol dependency, which she fooled herself she would fight and ward off before it became a debilitating habit. She did not know it had already become that. Back at her flat she stared at the whisky bottle on her coffee table for many minutes, daring herself to open it as she muttered the word 'bastards' over and over again. After what seemed like an hour but wasn't, she reached out for the bottle, still muttering, and with shaking hands, opened it. She kept staring at it before lifting it to her parched lips but did not drink from it. Instead she screwed the cap back on the bottle, lurched to her wardrobe, put the bottle in it and locked it, taking the key with her to resume her seat. The muttering continued and the perspiration started as she clenched the key in her fist till her knuckles turned white. It was very likely that the 'bastards' referred to were Kamal and Sanjay and not the three friends she had walked out on only a few hours before. Shivani shot to the wardrobe. Its key rattled and knocked at the lock but had considerable difficulty entering it.

27

The church with a high cross at the very top was not as grandly imposing or ancient as others in and around Panjim. Coconut and palm trees sheltered it along one length and an open patch of hardened red ground doubled as a haphazard parking space and a rough playing field along the other. This was Rosie's church and her matchstick model of it was amazingly accurate when it had been intact. The only detail the model missed and could not contain was the sad disrepair of the church. The roof was leaky as several slates were missing, some windows were broken and a side wall had a threatening crack meandering down it. Nevertheless it was more than a home to Rosie. Not only did it provide physical shelter to her body but it was also succour for her soul, soothing and nourishing it. Several times, she had tried to raise funds for repairs but had given up each time as it was a poor parish and donations were sparse. Rosie had returned to her church from Bangalore a week ago. At both ends, the modest church had living quarters. The mother superior had the larger flat at the front end and Rosie had a smaller one at the back end. Apart from a single bed, a wardrobe, a work table, and a chair, there wasn't much else in the one room she had. The table was cluttered with paperback novels, notebooks and several pages with shaky scribbles and doodles on them. A cheap laptop and printer as well as a small radio competed for space. In the corner was the ruined matchstick model but it was in several pieces, of which only three had been glued together while other pieces rested nearby, like stranded pieces of an incomplete jigsaw puzzle awaiting their fates. At least, despite its disrepair, the real church was still standing even if its matchstick model wasn't.

Without fail, Rosie kept to her routine, day in, day out. After her day of parish and church duties, she would have supper with the mother superior and mull over the day's events and those to unfold the next. At times, Rosie would summon the distant thought of becoming a nun but this was becoming less and less frequent perhaps because the mother superior always thwarted it, saying Rosie was nowhere near ready. After that Rosie would retire to her room to read, write, or dabble on her laptop. Finally, before offering the last prayer of the day, she would spend twenty minutes or so trying to glue one of the disjointed pieces of the destroyed matchstick model to its rightful place. In the four years of trying she had only managed to glue three pieces together because her right hand refused to be still and steady enough for the delicate operation of fixing it. She needed to apply glue to the broken piece with a brush and then place it delicately in its place, then hold it still long enough for it to stick and stay. She had even tried using her mouth to hold a piece steady. While she could glue it with her left hand she could not hold it in place next to the other three pieces as her nose would get in the way. She had given this up after numerous wasted attempts in the early days, when she would scream with frustration and anger. These days, she was less agitated in spite of the pitifully paltry progress, but the determination to repair the matchstick model to completion remained undiminished, if not stronger, as did the silent cursing of Sanjay and Kamal. At the end of each unsuccessful attempt, Rosie would raise her right hand to eye level, look at it hatefully, and try to stretch out the fingers knurled inwards like unruly roots. Only the forefinger was curved minimally, enough to be of use when she tapped at the keyboard of her laptop, which she did almost every evening, before turning to her attempts to resurrect the matchstick model. She tried her best to do this and also to stop cursing Sanjay and Kamal. Invariably, she failed at both just as she had failed to raise funds to repair her real church.

~

Back in much cooler Bangalore, Uma had finally managed to convince a very reluctant Shivani to have a long leisurely dinner with her at an eatery known for its seafood and kebabs. It was only in the middle of the dinner that Uma found out why Shivani had been avoiding meeting her. Being a doctor, a brilliant one at that, she knew immediately why Shivani's eyes were glazed, her movements lazy and speech heavy-tongued. Shivani was either sedated or influenced by narcotics, possibly both. Uma decided not to probe into it as Shivani was managing to be stable and lucid enough to pass for a normal but very tired person. She also noticed Shivani's marked preference for drinks over the food. Aperitifs were strong and several in number and fine French wine flowed with the dinner. Uma had apologized unreservedly but the rest of the conversation soured the evening as it was predominantly about how the pranks of Sanjay and Kamal had blighted their lives in different ways, in particular the last prank. It had been as outrageous as it had been insane, with its audacity and with its scope of lunatic proportions. To add insult to considerably debilitating injury, which had traversed from ghastly mental realms to harsh physical realities, there were very clear indications that the pranks were going to continue in some form or the other. Kamal had made that clear, inviting them to retaliate even now, after so many years. No longer interested in the food, Shivani had finally staggered out of the denial she was sheltering under and had freely admitted to Uma her alcohol dependency, whereby she could not function or face the day unless she had drunk half a bottle of neat vodka upon waking. Already the inside of her mouth was ulcerated, and without enough alcohol, her visceral insides felt as if they would implode, while the shaking made walking impossible, and delirium tremens made sleep impossible. Once a sufficient amount of alcohol completed its alchemy, all was well, at least till the spell wore out. Shivani no longer bothered to hide her chronic addiction, and instead of shunning the local wine shop for fear of discovery she had come to an arrangement whereby vodka and whisky would be delivered to her flat. The few rare occasions she ventured into the outside world she would be tanked up enough to be immune to its sobering realities, appearing and moving about in what she thought was a normal way. At least that is what it felt like and appeared to her. The truth was that within weeks the whole neighbourhood knew. The shopkeepers would deal with her as quickly as they could. The autorickshaw drivers would steal glances at her in their rear-view mirrors and see her swaying and smiling at nothing. Giggling children would point at her. Her hair was uncared for and clothes crumpled. It was only a matter of months before she would succumb to the ultimate and final clutch of alcohol or arrive at it by killing herself when the money ran out. Twice, Shivani had given up the demon drink only to relapse, largely to cope with the aftermath of what the pranks had done to her. Now, she lived with the realization that once a person became an alcoholic, they remained alcoholic. Her lucid moments were far and few, such as this day when she had to be propped up by other chemical mind-altering agents. Uma had guessed as much, and the good doctor that she was, had listened and counselled and cautioned. Other than that she could not do much else. She owed her friend an apology, and that she had delivered.

Uma's own woes were not as self-inflicted but were involuntary reflexes like Shivani's had become. The severe headaches had begun as mild ones and the strange dreams had exploded into chaotic nightmares, except this time she saw herself killing Kamal, sometimes by running him down under her car, sometimes by stabbing him, and other times by decapitating him with a sword. The methods were different but the theme was always the same. The ultimate revenge this time was not a dish to be served cold, but burning, boiling, and molten, so that it destroyed Kamal from the inside. As before, Uma would wake up with a scream and disrupt the small but growing family in her large house. She was back on sedatives and sleeping pills. In desperation she tried to convince herself that she was right in not having anything to do with Sanjay and Kamal. She had accused Shivani of being childish for thirsting for revenge and had upset her mightily, while her own mind was beginning to be overrun by the very same urge, which was slowly but surely creeping into an obstinate, obsession without her knowing it. This obsession couldn't be more different from the calculated, deliberate, and knowing one of many years ago at RAMS, when she wanted to be the topper in her studies. In that she had succeeded.

Shivani refused to meet in public places or at Uma's house as her behaviour became uncertain and unpredictable, so they met in her small flat. Uma was shocked at how much Shivani and her standard of living had plunged down. There were dirty clothes, unwashed dishes, and layers of dust in every corner. Invariably, during every visit Uma would force Shivani to tidy up and end up doing most of it herself, and on the next visit find the place filthy yet again. For her part, Shivani would try to convince Uma to join her in avenging themselves, while Uma would try to convince Shivani to seek professional help to stop drinking. It was her good friend Shivani's abject deterioration, which was as obvious as the agony etched on the latter's sorry face, combined with her own increasing frustration that finally made Uma agree to hit back. Now that she had reason to be alert and energetic, Shivani promised to seek the help she needed to decrease her alcohol abuse and eventually stop it completely. She would need to lead in the planning, timing, and execution of their revenge so that they could exorcise the demons of badly bruised and angry egos and hopefully return to their normal lives. If Shivani needed the motivation to stop her alcoholism and stay alive and enjoy life, hitting back was surely the answer. Pouncing on this, Uma had extracted a promise out of her, not once but twice, that Shivani would seek treatment for alcoholism and be rid of it. It was only a matter of the mind convincing the body that it did not need mind-altering substances but only nutritional ones.

For her part, if Uma was to regain her mental equilibrium and be ready to welcome her new baby and be the responsible wife and mother she once was, hitting back would surely do it. It would clear her mind of the cobwebs clogging it. The two smiled and hugged and decided on the next step. Hitting back was what Kamal wanted, so he would be hit back. Only it had turned to revenge just as their indifference to Kamal and Sanjay had turned to hatred. As to when and how they would hit back, the planning, timing, and execution of the revenge would be decided in due time. At this stage, the intent and agreement to hit back was more important and so was its consolidation.

28

The shafts of bright sunlight through the imposing but broken stained-glass window of the church highlighted motes of dust swirling in unhurried slow motion without rhyme or reason. Silence was a perfect backdrop to this hazily lazy activity. Rosie, Uma, and Shivani were sitting quietly in the very last pew at the end of the church looking at the distant altar with its creamy alabaster statues, tall candlestick holders, and the surrounding murals. The trio seemed deep in meditation or prayer but neither was the case. After the initial excitement of meeting, some tension had invaded the atmosphere as the real purpose of the visit was reluctantly dragged out after a quick tour of the church. Shivani was beginning to fret till Uma returned to the purpose of their visit.

'I can and did change my mind, Rosie. So should you. I can't let Kamal get away with it. I just can't. First, I thought that I should let sleeping dogs lie but it began to gnaw at my insides. Why should I let them get away with it? They had completely disrupted my life and continue to do so and it's becoming worse no matter how hard I try to fight it. I'm worried about what it'll do to me next if we don't do anything. I really am. We have to hit back, Rosie.'

Instead of becoming concerned at her friend's disquiet, Rosie simply smiled.

'Still the headstrong, obstinate Uma. The years have done nothing to change you. If I may say so, things got to where they did at RAMS because of you. I'm not saying Kamal and Sanjay were totally blameless. Now you want to continue in the same vein.'

In her lap, Rosie turned up the palm of her right hand and looked at it. The subtle hint was not lost on the downcast Uma, adding to her desperation.

'Are you blaming me…for…for everything?'

Rosie did not want to take the useless apportioning blame game further. Once started, there was no end to it. Besides, it always came after the event and did nothing to change it. Instead it only fuelled the dying embers of the past. Rosie sighed so deeply it was heard throughout the church.

'We are all to blame. No one is totally innocent or totally guilty.'

The ensuing silence was louder than before. Shivani was getting irritable as the effect of the vodka she had consumed before the flight, from Bangalore's plush new airport to the small Dabolim one in Goa, was on the wane. Uma wasn't aware that Shivani had never kept the promise she had made to her. Shivani wanted to get to the hotel as soon as possible and to the bottle awaiting her. She wanted Rosie to understand clearly and quickly.

'Kamal is one dog that's not going to lie still. Till he's made to, the bastard! Oops, sorry, I keep forgetting we're in a church. Come on, Rosie come to your senses.'

Rosie held up her trembling hand and let them have a good look.

'See this? I have more reason to settle my score with Kamal and Sanjay but I will not break my promise to my God, in whom my faith is unshakable. You two are free to do as you wish.'

Shivani was incensed but Uma decided to be more tactful.

'Rosie, that stupid prank damaged your hand. It ruined your dreams, your aspirations. Aren't you angry? Not even a little bit? You've lost everything. What about being the best neurosurgeon and so on?'

Rosie did not avert her eyes from the statue of Christ at the altar. She was as calmly forgiving as a thankful sea is after a raging storm has passed, having done its best.

'I deserve whatever my God has chosen for me. I must accept it. There must be a reason for it because the Almighty does nothing without a reason, and I have thought long and hard. I'm human too, you know, but I've decided not to stoop as low as Kamal and Sanjay. And that's final. Just think of it. You both come running to me and you will do so again, believe me, even Kamal and Sanjay. I will make you all run to me and you will. Why? Because during the year-and-a-half I spent with you all at RAMS, none of you treated me with any decency. At best, I was ignored. I was just a fatso, just a fat Goan Catholic from the sticks with not a paisa to her name, while you all were posh and loaded city-slickers with money to burn. And yet you were my friends. How do you think I felt? Now you come running to me and you will again because I'm going to show you all. I am going to make it and make it big with or without this ever so useless shame of a hand.'

Rosie held up her hand again. Silence returned. Uma and Shivani cast their eyes down, heads bowed. Shivani wanted to leave but Uma felt genuinely touched and remorseful. She sighed heavily. It was time for another apology.

'That was then, Rosie dear. I was a solidly stupid, spoilt brat. We all were except you. It never occurred to me that you might be upset. I am so sorry, Rosie. It's been six years now. I never want to lose your friendship. Never. Let bygones be bygones, please, Rosie darling.'

Shivani was taken aback by the unexpected and candidly unreserved apology and Rosie wondered if she had been too forthright with her accusation. Even so, she was going to maintain her resolve not to be talked into any notions of seeking revenge, and she wanted to discourage her friends too.

'Why don't you two do the same as well and just forget Kamal and Sanjay? Let them lead their lives and we lead ours. As you said, let bygones be bygones. Why not?'

Shivani knew Uma was cornered, but Uma got out of it when something new suddenly struck her, or maybe she pretended it was new.

'Goodness Rosie, your matchstick model! It's this church, isn't it?'

Rosie's eyes twinkled and she smiled broadly, happy to be sidetracked from a very sour subject.

'The very same, Uma dearest. I've still got it but it's still in pieces, I'm afraid. This hand...my useless hand won't let me put it right.'

Silence returned, angry at the constant interruptions to it. Uma pondered over what it would be like for Rosie to live with a right hand that was almost completely useless, which had blighted her life. She wanted to offer comfort but remained silent for a long time, examining her fingernails till Shivani nudged her. Uma held Rosie's hand.

'You know Rosie, this might surprise you but I think you're right. It has to stop somewhere and somebody has to stop it but I can't help it. That person is not me. If somebody somewhere is able to put a stop to it, that'll be fine with me. I'll go along with it. You see, Rosie, all I seek is for calm to return to me, to my mind, so I can lead a normal life. When that happens there will be no need to seek revenge, but...and here's the rub...only revenge will return my calm to me... and nobody will take my revenge on my behalf. So I have to do it myself. The same applies to Shivani. How and when we do it, we don't know yet, but do it we will. You're right about something else, too. See, things may have changed around me but I remain what I've always been. That hasn't, will not, and can't change. Sure, experience teaches lessons, but some lessons are so bitter, they can't be forgotten just like that.'

Rosie felt tempted to debate her friend's misperception about experience. A sensible, sane person rules their experience, taking the good from it and leaving the bad well alone. Only insane idiots let their experience rule and take over totally as Uma was doing. The reminder of her friend's obstinacy a few seconds before deterred Rosie from airing her thoughts.

Shivani fretted even more, biting her lower lip, irritation rising as she would have to ensure Uma's resolve to hit back did not take a dive down but shot up. She would have to convince Uma that the two of them should take up the challenge on their own without Rosie. In total contrast, Rosie, serene and calm, was more than pleased as she got up.

'Come, let's meet Mother Superior for a minute or two so she can see the friends I keep talking about. Then we can settle down in my humble abode, where no one disturbs my peace, and have some coffee. Sorry, no booze in the church. I haven't touched a drop for ages. We could talk about the old times but only the good bits, if you promise.'

There was a spring in Rosie's step as she led them down the aisle towards the altar, where the trio stopped as if commanded to do so. They stood in reverence to the statue of Christ with its raised blessing hand. Even Shivani found momentary solace.

'First time I've been in a church. I can't believe how quiet and peaceful it is in here.'

This cheered Rosie even more, not that she needed it.

'Isn't it just that, Shivo, and aren't I lucky to live and work here? This is where the rest of my life is going to be, even after I've become a nun.'

They walked past the altar and took the creaky narrow stairs by the end of it.

29

The last hour of the flight back to Bangalore was a subdued one for Shivani and Uma and not only because of outside turbulence. As soon as the aircraft had levelled in the pristine blue sky, Shivani had launched into her campaign to convince Uma that their return to normal life, out of their blighted, burning, and bitter present ones, would never happen till they put Kamal and Sanjay in their rightful places. She had already convinced Uma of this but felt frightened that Uma was willing to desist if someone, somewhere, stopped her, or if, somehow, her calm returned without them hitting back. Uma had listened to Shivani repeat herself for a while but was soon consumed by her own thoughts. Was Rosie blaming her for what happened to her hand? Did Rosie really mean it? Worst of all, was Rosie right in doing so? A tinge of guilt flashed through her. There was no denying that hers was the leading part in goading Kamal till he came up with the faked suicide prank, which had resulted in Rosie's hand getting damaged beyond repair. What was a passing flash of guilt settled on her and began to sink in. Riddled with remorse and regret, Uma sought sanctuary elsewhere and crash-landed into the real world after the aircraft bumped and jerked through turbulence. What was the distant drone of Shivani's rambling monologue closed in on Uma. After watching and listening, already agitated by her guilt, Uma put a stop to the worsening gibberish about the "bastards who needed to be put in their place" by threatening to change her seat if Shivani did not stop at once. Uma took a close look at Shivani and sniffed her. She knew Shivani wasn't drinking water as she was pretending to, but drinking vodka. In a haze and with blinks of droopy eyelids that took seconds, Shivani realized that their friendship could get damaged if she persisted, and succumbed to sullen silence, breathing quickly and deeply, almost audibly. Uma was already agitated by the guilt of her part in the damaging of Rosie's hand and now she felt infuriated at Shivani's deception, especially after Shivani had promised, not once, but twice, to stop abusing alcohol. After minutes of tense silence, Uma resisted venting her anger and decided to do some good and be kind and supportive instead. So, as many times before, she attempted calmly, almost pleadingly, to convince Shivani to seek professional help, yet again. Sitting next to her, Shivani would have no choice but to listen.

'Shivani, I know what's in that bottle. This is the last time I will plead with you. You keep promising to reduce your intake but instead you've turned to cheating. The worst part is that being a doctor, you know full well you'll be dead within months if you don't stop. Shivani, it's suicide. Did you hear me? It's suicide. I don't want to lose you, please Shivani. You said so yourself, you promised me, not once but twice. Remember? In your flat when we agreed to hit back. Tell me, how are you going to plan it if you're going to remain tanked up half the time? Hitting back was your motivation to stop drinking, remember? This is your last chance. If you don't stop the booze, you can forget me, forget our friendship.

It'll be like I never met you. I mean it. I'm deadly serious about it!'

Shivani listened and nodded sagely every now and then. After a while her head tilted sideways, bowed down, and her hand slipped down out of her lap. She had fallen asleep. Uma watched her before prising the plastic bottle out of her hand. It had only an inch or so of vodka left in it. She was close to tears, and without thinking about it, drank it all, letting the empty bottle drop to her feet just as the aircraft heaved up and down violently enough to make passengers jump, seatbelts straining around waists. Uma looked at Shivani and again, guilt flooded over her, welling up her eyes. This time it was not the flashing guilt about Rosie's hand nor was it to do with her terse admonishment of Shivani. It was many times worse and was to grip her very core. It was about her own unborn child. She had just lectured her sleeping friend yet again about uncontrolled drinking while her own consumption had risen with each passing day, she realized. What she had preached to Shivani applied even more urgently to her. While Shivani was single and without any responsibility, she herself was a mother and a wife. As if that wasn't enough, she was pregnant as well, and to cap it all she was a doctor and knew full well how she was harming herself and her unborn child, even if she wasn't addicted as Shivani was. Several times, Krish had alerted and warned her of this as if she didn't know it, and they had ended up fighting. Was she slipping down the same spiral of self-destruction as Shivani and would she end up like her? No, it was worse, much worse. If she had driven Kamal to a fake suicide, she was driving her unborn child to death, for sure. Could she blame Kamal and Sanjay for driving her to this? Or did she have only herself to blame? In the end, Uma blamed herself and resolved not only to stop drinking but also to mend her ways so that she could become the good mother and responsible wife that she once was. The resolve satisfied and comforted her, but her mind refused to leave alone the subject of alcohol and even widened to the use of other mind-altering substances used and abused by humans. Invariably, these were fleeting and short-term balms that soothed by cheating perturbed souls into believing that all was well, while doing untold and silent damage to bodies. Uma's thoughts were jolted by a turbulent bump. She wished she had more vodka to drink.

The rest of the flight was spent in deathly silence even when Shivani was roused out of her sleep as the aircraft prepared to land. Uma ushered a tipsy Shivani out of the airport and into a taxi, all without a single word between them. All the while, Shivani had nothing on her mind but the next drink and Uma was quietly strengthening her resolve to return to her former, normal self. It was to be many weeks before the two of them were to speak or see each other again.

30

Krish was happy. The perceptible weight gain was proof enough. Family life was good once again as Uma's temper tantrums had declined considerably. Dinner was cooked and ready on time, and if they did eat out, it was not because Uma had refused to cook. Work was going well and promotions were on the horizon for both of them. Little Krishnan was doing well and Uma's second pregnancy was proceeding smoothly. Uma had taken up playing squash and after professional coaching, she played a decent game. One of her two initial reasons for taking it up was no longer as valid as it was in the beginning. It was to vent her anger and frustration at Sanjay and, in particular, at Kamal, that she had taken up the sport. With every mighty thwack of the small black ball into the walls she was thwacking Kamal, and to a lesser extent, Sanjay. Over the weeks this need became less intense and was eventually forgotten, even though she would often let out a few primeval screams when she initially began playing. Of late, she had managed to cajole Krish to play with her at least twice a week but he could only manage two games with ease, after which he needed to rest and stop before Uma wanted to. Ever the competitor, she never made it easy for him, thrashing him soundly each time, though Krish was beginning to improve. Often, Uma would tease her husband playfully on the way home which often turned into passionate lovemaking sessions later on. The second reason Uma took up squash was to tire herself out, till deep sleep would come easily and her reliance on tablets would end, which it did eventually. Her daily nightcap – a good measure of brandy – returned to being hot chocolate as it used to be. Yes, life was good and there was no reason why it wouldn't continue to be so. Once in a while she would contemplate inviting Shivani and Rosie for dinner, but each weekend seemed to get booked weeks beforehand as their list of friends and colleagues, most of them in high places, grew rapidly. She decided to make a special effort to book the next free weekend for Shivani and Rosie. She was more anxious about Shivani and thought about visiting her soon, and wondered if she had made any efforts to get treatment for her alcohol dependency. Recalling the terrible turbulence-ridden flight back from Goa, she hoped her strong pleas had had an effect on Shivani to keep her promise to give up alcohol.

Uma would have been pleased, even overjoyed, had she known that Shivani had indeed made the supreme effort to get treated and had been on a strict detoxification regime for the past two weeks. It had been an extremely painful journey to get that far. On returning from Goa in an annoyed and insufficiently inebriated state, Shivani was mightily overjoyed to discover a half-full bottle of whisky by her bedside even though she had bought another one on her way in. Before doing anything else she had poured herself a huge measure with very little water in it and finished it while changing her clothes and unpacking. It was when she was pouring a second measure that a stab of pain pierced through her abdomen, making her double over. It passed but an eruption arose from the pit of her stomach. She got to the toilet basin in time to spew out a torrent of black vomit. She knew immediately that it was congealed blood from the scar tissue from her liver. She retched again and again till the spasms ebbed and ended. As she stood staring at the black vomit, she did not need to be told that this was the beginning of the end, and that if she did not take immediate remedial action, the end would arrive within a month. She had staggered to her kitchen table and sat there with her head in her hands, with the two whisky bottles staring her in the face, challenging and threatening her. They had fired a salvo along with Uma's earlier admonishing. Uma's words rang out in Shivani's head.

'...forget me. Forget our friendship. It'll be like I never met you...'

It could cost Shivani her life if she did not put an end to her addiction, and before death arrived she would have lost her best friend. Even worse, the two ex-friends who had brought her to this state would get away and her obsession to hit back at them would go to waste. This was a battle she could not afford to lose. She knew what her body would go through if she waged the battle. The withdrawal symptoms – days of sweating and feeling cold, the shaking, the crawling skin, and the horrors of delirium tremens – would carve her up before withdrawing. Even so, this was an affordable cost, which was transitory, as opposed to the alternative one, which was final and permanent.

From where she was sitting, she hurled the two taunting whisky bottles into the kitchen wall in front of her, one by one, smashing them to smithereens, dissipating their contents. Shivani had commenced battle.

Victory returned to Shivani her mental and physical balance. She was surprised by how clear and bright her surroundings were. It kept striking her how idiotic she had been as she started to plan applications for work at one of the many hospitals and health centres in Bangalore. She thought of contacting both Uma and Rosie to give them her good news but decided to wait for a few more days.

~

When Rosie took the call from Shivani, she was genuinely pleased and congratulated her friend, and made her promise not to ever take to drink again, no matter what. As for herself, she had settled into the routine she wanted and was happy with it. Weekdays were spent working with parishioners. There was the mothers and toddlers group she had formed and looked after and there was the elders group as well. Two evenings a week, she taught some construction workers' children, who were living in plastic-sheeted tents in a nearby slum. There was also the alcoholics group and the domestic violence group, and constant contact with the police and various NGOs to liaise with. In between and more so on weekends, her attention turned to the Almighty and All-pervading when she prayed and studied the Bible with Sunday service being the highlight. She gave up all attempts to glue the matchstick model back together, and on most days she didn't even remember it or the events that led to its destruction. Instead, she was spending more and more time on the keyboard of her laptop, tapping away contentedly as her short story, *The Six Friends,* kept on becoming longer and longer. The forefinger of her right hand was just functional enough for this. She had begun to live with the shaky hand she had thought of as 'ever so useless a shame'. She was happily busy, and even happier having spoken to Shivani after such a long time. She even thought of phoning Uma, and the prospect of meeting the two was a cheerful one. Rosie thought of planning a week-long holiday for the three of them in Goa when she could show them places that tourists knew nothing of. Despite the happy plans of the three, for one reason or the other, the happy meeting and holiday remained distant.

31

Eventually, the meeting came about but not for the happy reasons the three friends had envisaged. The circumstances were a little short of being bizarre. The chain of events began with Uma receiving a couriered package at her workplace, to which she had not given a second thought. As a senior general medical professional with a growing reputation, she received several promotional materials and invitations to attend various conferences and seminars, all of which were discarded the next day when she tended to her administrative matters. This particular package was different. It contained a brief handwritten note on embossed paper and an unlabelled CD, which Uma ignored as she turned to the note and quickly scanned the scrawl.

Hi Uma and Co.,

Greetings from an impatient acquaintance of yore. Mightily disappointed at your lack of response. Sanjay and I were and still are waiting to be hit by you three but no such luck! So, to jog your memories we're sending you a reminder of the prank to end all pranks, that none of you will ever forget. You all should watch it and learn a thing or two from its execution.

Come on girls, it's your turn. Don't let us down. Think, plan and execute. Put some red in your blood. Live! Entertain and get entertained! Surprise us! Hit us or get hit! Enjoy the movie!

Cheerio.
Kamal

Uma read the scrawl twice more, each time slowly enough to ingest each acid word. What was left unsaid was worse. Uma's mind clouded and for moments she did not know where she was or what she was doing. Only a phone call from Krish pulled her back to a semblance of sense. She declined lunch together, hesitatingly citing overwork as an excuse. In any case, her appetite had vanished, all too suddenly. She picked up the innocuous unlabelled CD, examining it, wondering what it had to reveal. She crumpled the embossed paper and flung it into the bin by her desk. Innocuous or not, the CD followed the same route. Uma put on her white coat, convinced she had made the right decision to consign both items to the bin where they belonged, more unwanted than the usual suspects. Very much so.

In the ward, Uma reviewed one case after the other with two final-year students in tow. Case histories and family health backgrounds were described, symptoms and remedial measures discussed. Various readings of temperature, blood pressure, and heart rate were taken and recorded. The accompanying nurse would be left to administer any medication or injections as per instructions and the young doctor and her even younger charges would move on to the next bed. Uma probed the two students, asking questions, correcting them and instructing them on examining techniques. Her concentration and dedication were supreme. The CD and the brief note that had unbalanced her not too long ago, were forgotten. After two hours and six case reviews, Uma led the students to a quiet corner of the ward where biscuits and tea for three were laid. Here, the conversation would be informal and very general, the intention being to relax the students for ten to fifteen minutes so that they could regain their energy and dissipate the accrued tension in readiness for the next two hours. Years ago, Uma had gone through similar rounds of case reviews and quick tea breaks as a student, and she knew full well the need for such breaks. Brains and legs got the chance to recuperate. Medicine certainly was not a walk in the clouds. It was here, during a deliberate lull in the conversation, that the CD and the note crept up on Uma and lodged in the back of her mind.

Minutes into the next two hours of case reviews, the innocuous CD and the poisonous note started to permeate her consciousness. Her concentration started to waver and her dedication began to suffer, until by the end of the first hour she was hardly saying anything. She realized it was not fair to the students, who were puzzled during long moments of silence and inactivity. She asked them to wait at the tea table and hurried out of the ward before she came to a complete stop.

From her small office, Uma arranged for the standby doctor to take her place and then held her head in her hands, elbows propped on the desk. After minutes of uncertainty, she retrieved the two offending items and booted her laptop, sliding the CD into its portal. Within moments, the laptop was ready to oblige but Uma's quandary intensified as the minutes ticked on. After what seemed like an hour but was only a span of ten minutes or so, she had still not clicked the command to show the contents of the CD. The chilling worry as to what seeing the 'movie', as Kamal had referred to it in his note, would do to her would depend on what it showed. There was only one way to find out. Uma's finger reached for the synaptic pad, hesitated, hovered, and withdrew. Eventually, curiosity combined with a touch of fear got the better of her and she watched the CD, and spent the rest of the afternoon watching it over and over again.

Later in the evening, Krish made his own way home after finally managing to contact Uma, who had gone home without him. She seemed to sound unwell, and on reaching their house, he found her so. Uma was prone on the large sofa in the lounge and upon Krish's concerned enquiries, pleaded exhaustion from an overload of work, which was not the case. Krish mumbled words of sympathy and went into the kitchen to make tea for the two of them. He had also had a tiring day but not as bad as Uma, it seemed. As much as he tried to coax, cajole, and joke Uma into unwinding and sharing her day at the hospital, he failed.

Late into that night and for the next two nights, misery returned to the large house, of the small but growing family, with a vengeance, as if to make up for its recent absence. Uma's nightmares became frequent and dug deeper than before, and botched her behaviour with carefree abandon. Krish was puzzled and angry. Which feeling was more dominant he couldn't decide, but he knew he couldn't stand any more of it, whatever it was that had brought Uma's demons back. She had stopped going to work, did not cook at all, and even neglected little Krishnan. There was the occasional smashing of crockery and screams at Krish for hardly any reason, and long hours of sleep at odd hours induced by tablets. The resolution she had made to be a good mother and wife, on the bumpy flight back from Goa, wasn't even a distant memory in her mind. It had vanished without the slightest trace as if it had never happened. Something else seemed to have taken its place. On the morning of the third day, Krish decided not to go to work. He fed Krishnan, dressed him, and drove him to his babysitter. He returned home and waited for Uma to wake up but this did not happen till well after midday, when he heard the upstairs toilet flush. After what seemed like an age, Uma came downstairs, wearing a nightgown, hair dishevelled and eyes puffed. She saw Krish putting down his newspaper but seemed not to register him sitting in his usual chair. As she passed him to go into the kitchen, he arose and put his arm gently around her.

'You sit down, darling. I'll make you breakfast. Tea or coffee? Toast, cereal, eggs. Scrambled or boiled?'

Uma sank into her chair and mumbled.

'Just coffee.'

'Come on, you've got to eat something. Look at you. Look at the state you're in. I know it's more than exhaustion. I'm a doctor, remember. Okay, full breakfast first. Then we'll talk.'

Krish hurried to the kitchen while Uma sat back, yawning and thinking hard about what she had been grappling with during brief and fitful moments of wakefulness. Should she tell Krish about the CD and the note? Let him see the CD and read the note? Alone or together with her? He was her husband and she loved him. Guilt flooded her. She could hear the sizzle of frying eggs, the pop of done toast, and the sprinkle of cereal. She made her decision as Krish brought in a laden tray.

'Put it on the table, Krishy darling. I'll have it there.'

The warmth in the voice and the willingness of its owner to eat cheered Krish and he felt positive that from here on it would be plain sailing. Happily, he did what he was told and returned to his chair and picked up the newspaper.

'Enjoy your breakfast, darling. We'll talk after.'

Uma remained seated.

'Krish, upstairs in my handbag is a crumpled bit of paper and a CD. Get them. Read the note and watch the CD. I've seen it hundreds of times. It makes me sick each time.'

Uma got up and so did a very curious Krish.

'What's this about? What's the CD about?'

'Just read and watch. Suddenly I'm starving.'

Uma made for the dining table and Krish dashed upstairs.

He straightened the crumpled paper and read it on his way down. Back downstairs, he muttered, mainly to himself.

'Damn, it's him! What is going on? What's the CD about, Uma?'

Uma was busy with her breakfast and spoke with her mouth full.

'Don't just look at it. Watch it. I mean put it on.'

Krish slotted the CD into the home theatre system's portal. He wondered what was awaiting him this time, and then watched and listened in stunned, opened-mouthed silence with a gasp here and there. His occasional commentary was peppered with words and choice phrases such as: 'I can't believe this!', 'Lunatics!', 'Incredible!', 'I don't understand this!', 'What the hell!'. Minutes later, the visuals ended and the screen turned blue. Krish switched it off, got up and started pacing, hands on hips. Uma brought her coffee and settled into her chair. Krish stopped and stared at her.

'You let this get to you! This rubbish! Uma, baby, why? Why? You should pity the morons. Laugh at them. This is proof enough. They're lunatics, both of them. Are you listening, Uma? All that was years ago, for God's sake.'

'Did you read the note, Krish?'

'I did. What of it?'

'They want us to hit back.'

Krish flopped into his chair, exasperated.

'You will have nothing to do with those two. Not ever. Not if I can help it. Anything else you get from them goes straight in the bin. I'm going to smash that CD to bits and tear up the stupid note and that will be the end of it.'

Uma studied her fingernails.

'Don't you think Shivani and Rosie should see the thing? It's meant for them as well.'

Krish was adamant. For once he was decisive, surprising himself, and Uma, with his single-mindedness.

'What good is that going to do to anyone? The sooner this lunacy ends, the better it is.'

So the debate began. Uma wanted their two friends to see the CD and read the note, while Krish wanted both destroyed immediately. Uma wanted to share with Shivani and Rosie the pain and misery she had gone through, the humiliation she felt, and the stirrings of revenge which she had tried to dismiss after watching the CD over and over again. Revenge or hitting back was out of the question, she convinced herself after much painful introspection, and assured Krish of the same. Not only that, she further conceded that this was definitely the end of their connection with Kamal and Sanjay, and made a promise of it, too. In return, Krish agreed for Shivani and Rosie to see and read the offending items after which both would be destroyed, and hopefully peace could prevail after that exorcism.

Thus the meeting came about. Even so, it was three weeks before the four friends met on a Sunday evening. During this time, Uma had resumed work and the rage she felt had become controlled, although she watched the CD everyday during her lunch break. Each sequence of it was etched on her mind and the words Kamal and Sanjay uttered resounded over and over. Without her and certainly without Krish knowing it, she had become obsessed with the CD and the note. After each viewing, the humiliation, anger, and frustration became that much more, and the emotional mixture more volatile. Yet, Uma managed to keep it firmly bottled. Mercifully, the nightmares remained at bay with Krish blissfully unaware of the stormy turmoil raging within Uma, though an occasional outburst of temper and crockery-smashing disturbed the peace some evenings. The turbulence had returned.

During the same three weeks, Shivani had secured a post at a hospital in Mysore, and accommodation within it, though she still kept her small flat in Bangalore to which she commuted regularly in a nice car she had bought. She was also dating a consultant at her new hospital. The best part of her new life was that the demon which had nearly blighted it had finally been banished. Shivani was simply far too happily occupied, both in her personal and professional life. The need to drink was no longer there so she didn't touch alcohol apart from an occasional glass of red wine while dining with the consultant, who had become the welcome bedrock of her new calm and stability. Shivani had not thought twice about accepting Uma's telephonic invitation to spend a weekend with her and Krish, especially as Rosie would be there too. Shivani had thought of making a romantic weekend out of it by taking her date along but Uma had requested her to bring him along some other time. Even so, Shivani looked forward to the meeting.

During this time, Rosie had not turned to her ruined matchstick model even once. More than that, she had put away the broken sections in her desk drawer, out of sight, out of mind, after contemplating whether she should throw them away or not. It wasn't just sentiment and religion that saved the destroyed model from oblivion. Somewhere in Rosie's mind was a thought, a wish, and a prayer, that a day might arrive when her hand would heal and stop its shaky, unruly behaviour. As a failed but brilliant scientist of the human body, she knew it would need a miracle to happen. Fish might have better chances to run marathons on deserts and birds to swim across chasms of the ocean floor. The damaged nerves in the tendon of the wrist, normally highly durable and flexible, could not be repaired with a snap of fingers and a weld or two. As for miracles, the less dwelt on them the better, even if at the very core of her faith was the miracle of resurrection. Deep in her heart of her hearts, she did not want to rule out the recovery of her hand via a miracle, while in the depths of her mind she knew such a possibility was more than unlikely. It was impossible. Rosie had become weary and at many a time distressed by finding no way out of this impasse. Many times she had sought the mother superior's counsel on this and invariably was told to remain patient and to believe and continue to believe in her faith. Yet Rosie, only too human, could not help this and the tussle continued in her heart and mind. At the end of such soul-searching, Rosie was always left with the same thought. If she became a nun, the wavering of her faith would be a tiresome niggle of the past. She would have no choice but to be totally and utterly committed. This made the wish to be a nun that much dearer to her. Whether the wish came true or not, she had learnt to live with the injured hand, so she spent more and more time at her laptop, where at least the forefinger of the blighted hand received exercise as her short story blossomed. In her mind, science was turning into art. Her devotion to her God and to the needy in her parish was becoming even more consuming as she continued to reach out. Her congregation increased two-fold and rewarded her devotion with much love and warmth. Discussions with the mother superior centred on matters of faith, ethics, philanthropy, and other philosophical tenets with the wish to become a nun surfacing every now and then. Rosie had found a purpose in life and no longer rued her lot or the cutting short of her career ambitions. When she received Uma's invitation to spend the weekend together, she did not have to think long, especially as Shivani would be there as well. Sundays were busy at the church but she needed to be away.

32

Uma was not herself, but she and Krish managed to look after their friends very well. Dinner was at a favourite seafood eatery with cocktails beforehand, wine during, and brandies after, but only for Krish who was determined to make a night of it even though he dreaded what was to follow the dinner. The three young women restricted themselves to mocktails and carbonated water for their own reasons. Conversation was about the good times, with many a splatter of laughter from all except Uma, who seemed to be elsewhere for most of the time. The CD and the note from Kamal were never mentioned. Their time to be aired was to come. As yet, Shivani and Rosie did not know anything about them. Both had assumed it was just a long overdue social gathering for old times' sake, at least the good ones, most of which had been forgotten.

Back at home, Uma dismissed the beaming babysitter with a huge tip. Coffee was the preferred option for the women while Krish continue drinking brandy. The one comfort Uma had was that she was amongst friends and her returned disenchantment with life, such as it was, was about to be shared, which she had wanted badly. No longer was she going to stew alone. She took control of her lounge as the mistress of the ceremony.

'You're all going to watch TV. I shall not say what, but watch. Maybe I should apologize for inflicting this on you but I won't. Krish, switch it on. Oh before that, the note please.'

Krish picked up the straightened page and passed it to Shivani as she was the nearest to him. Having read it quizzically, she passed it to Rosie, who took several minutes to absorb it, squinting her eyes behind her spectacles. Quietly, she handed the note back to Krish. Shivani and Rosie exchanged quick looks. Rosie was in deep thought as she waited, looking at Uma, who was on tenterhooks. On the large TV screen, an image appeared. It was Kamal. He was dressed in a white shirt and a red necktie instead of his usual black one. He smiled and addressed his audience.

'Greetings from Chandigarh, friends, and welcome to the KP show. That is, the keep playing show. Keep playing!'

Rosie was rapt and so was Shivani, while Uma sat on the edge of her seat, even though she had watched the CD so many times that she knew exactly what was going to happen next. Krish helped himself to more brandy, not caring a jot about what the TV was showing. He had seen the CD once and that was enough for him to be sick of it. On the TV screen, Kamal continued.

'After waiting and waiting we have decided to offer you a special presentation that we have been saving for you. This might inspire and or galvanize you into some much missed and needed action. The time has come, so without further ado, Dr Sanjay Dutt, the announcement if you please.'

A slightly drunk Sanjay replaced Kamal on the screen.

'For the delectation of our select, special audience, we present "Seven easy steps to heaven". Hang in there for a special treat. Hang in there, folks. "Hang" being the operative word. We're proud to take you back a few years and reveal to you how the greatest ever prank was executed. Learn from it and hit back, although you all will never come anywhere near it. Here we go. Flashback, rewind to six years ago. The place is Kamal's black bedroom of black deeds, back in the old accommodation block. It'll all come back to you. Sit back. Enjoy.'

In Uma and Krish's lounge, their guests watched a static TV screen before a very busy Kamal walked into view in his black room, wearing a white lab coat. He carried a surgical tray which he proceeded to lay out on the bed. There was a syringe, a small gas cylinder with a face mask, a length of rope with knots on both ends, and a metal hook on the tray. Kamal switched on the main light and drew the black curtains, although there was early morning light outside. He was preoccupied and looked at the slightly wobbly camera while reaching for a chair.

'Put the camera on the tripod, Sanjay. This is more important. Got to get it exactly right otherwise it might misfire badly.'

The picture of Kamal climbing up and standing on a chair to unhook the skeleton from the ceiling became wobblier before becoming steady. Sanjay, dressed exactly as he was on the day of the suicide, appeared in the frame and took the skeleton from Kamal and laid it on the bed. Kamal got down from the chair and extracted a cigarette but Sanjay wagged a finger at him.

'Not a good idea, Kam. You're going to inhale a fair amount of G.A. in a few minutes. And other stuff.'

Sanjay pointed at the small gas cylinder. Kamal nodded his head, reached across and pulled the skeleton's jaws apart and jammed the cigarette into it, and then checked the time on his wristwatch.

'You're right, Sanj. Won't harm Mr Bones. Time check. Twenty minutes past seven.'

Sanjay concurred.

'Forty minutes to lift off, give or take a minute or two.'

Kamal took off his lab coat, picked up the metal hook and passed it through a small reinforced loop inside the collar of the coat. He slipped one of the knots into the hook and tested it for strength. Tied next to the knot was an adjustable noose.

Back in the lounge, Uma drank her coffee, eyes glued to the TV screen. Shivani and Rosie were also riveted to the TV screen, on which Kamal was slipping on his lab coat and slinging the adjustable noose around his neck. Uma pointed her coffee mug at the TV screen and began her commentary, which wasn't necessary.

'He's going to gas in some general anaesthetic and some sedation so he appears dead to us idiots. The bastard! Way beyond what we did to him...he's going to hang by his bloody lab coat, not by his bloody neck. Wish it was his neck...'

Krish was wondering how the women were going to react at the end of the CD. They were bound to be angry, which was pointless and uncalled for. He hoped they would see it as the work of two lunatics, which it was. On the screen, Sanjay entered the picture, opening a small black bottle which aroused Kamal's interest.

'What's that, Sanjay?'

'Watch.'

Sanjay turned his back and a moment later, turned around to face his audience again. His face was wet with tears and contorted with mock sobbing and wailing before he smiled and winked at Kamal, who had climbed on to the chair.

'The only prop I need, Kam. Glycerine.'

'Brilliant. Lots going to depend on you, Sanj. Don't mess it up.'

'No worries, Kam. I've got it all planned. You do your bit, I'll do mine. I love acting. Didn't you see me last night, in the common room? They all thought I was totally pissed, falling about and all.'

On the TV, Kamal pointed at the watching audience.

'Remember, don't let them near me. Any of them. Under no circumstance. Let them have a good look then get rid of them. The sooner the better. Okay? I don't want this to go wrong. Got that?'

'Calm down, Kam. Man, you were excellent last night, sitting there at the bar, still as a stone, lighting up and chucking away your money like that. Brilliant move. Even I thought you were ready to top yourself. And, hey, listen to this. Gopal told me he was worried about you. He thought you might do something silly!'

Kamal took a bow, still standing on the chair, and addressed his audience directly, looking down on them while rubbing his hands with relish.

'Girls, if we pull this off you're going to wonder for the rest of your miserable lives how I made it home. Simple, simple, simple. Lots of imagination. Lots of money and a gift of the gab. And then, even you Uma, even you could pass your father off as the Queen of England...no offence, darling. Just harmless fun. On with the show.'

In the lounge, Uma's face contorted. Her grip on her coffee mug tightened. No one noticed this.

On the screen, Kamal turned to the task at hand. He tightened the noose around his neck, reached up and slipped the knot at the other end of the rope on to the hook in the ceiling above him. He made final adjustments, rehearsing popping his eyes, showing a blue tongue lolling out of an open mouth, head thrown to one side, arms dangling uselessly. He was ready and gave Sanjay a thumbs up sign. Sanjay held up the small gas cylinder and face mask up to him.

In the lounge, a creamy object flew across and the large plasma TV screen shattered into smithereens with a deafening crash, making everyone except Uma jump in their seats. In the deafening silence that followed, only the popping smithereens of frosted glass could be heard as they fragmented further. The baby started crying upstairs. Shivani and Rosie looked wide-eyed at each other and then at Uma, who was panting heavily. Krish shot to his feet, marched to Uma and glowered down at her, eyes flashing with anger that had finally erupted. It was the brandy that released the anger in him.

'Enough is enough! I can't take this shit anymore! One minute you're all sweet smiles and the next a raving monster. Why the hell did you have to do that? Grow up and clean this mess yourself! You better sort yourself out before it's too late, Uma. First I put up with your bloody nightmares, then I had to stop you drinking like a fish to save harming the baby and now this! I've had enough of this bloody hell!'

Krish stormed out of the lounge and bounded up the stairs. Uma kept staring at the screen-less TV. Finally, the smithereens stopped popping and Uma's panting could be heard. Shivani was shocked. Mouth agape, she looked from the smashed TV to Uma. Rosie surveyed the scene around her, panning slowly across the lounge like a motion camera, taking everything in. She remained silently helpless as if her mind was travelling much too fast for her liking. Upstairs, little Krishnan stopped crying. Uma stood up slowly.

'I need fresh air...and a cigarette.'

Uma walked almost in slow motion to an antique dresser by the wall, totally oblivious to the destruction she had caused. Rosie and Shivani watched every step as Uma walked to the French doors with a packet of cigarettes and a lighter. She opened the door and stepped out into night. Rosie and Shivani exchanged worried looks. Shivani walked up to the ruined home theatre and extracted the CD that had caused so much havoc, not knowing there was more to come. Rosie joined her.

'Shall we clear this up, Shivo?'

'Uma did it. She can sort it. Why did she have to do it?'

'Anger, frustration, and hurt. Umi never liked being made a fool of and this was rubbing it in her face, like it was meant to.'

Shivani put the CD in her handbag.

'I want to see the rest of this.'

'What shall we do?'

'I'm going home. What else is there to do?'

That was easy for Shivani as she lived twenty minutes away, but Rosie's home was many hours away, and she did not want to sleep in a house of discord even though a room had been prepared for her.

'Can I ask for a favour, Shivo? Will you put me up for the night?'

'Sure. Let's go and tell her and get the hell out of here.'

The two walked out of the French doors to take leave from their perturbed hostess.

~

Uma woke to a very quiet house. A shaft of bright sunlight nearly blinded her and the sparkle of what seemed like a million diamonds adorning the floor around her brought reality back. The more she registered it, the more she panicked. She sat up on the long sofa surrounded by destruction both mental and physical. The previous night, she had paced the back garden in the darkness after a very brief and awkward goodbye to Shivani and Rosie, when not a word was said about the eruption in the lounge. After about half an hour, she had returned to the lounge not knowing what to do. Her immediate instinct was to go upstairs and check on Krishnan but she was afraid that Krish might still be awake and she would have to face his wrath again. Furthermore, she didn't have the slightest explanation for her behaviour. That the eruption was the culmination of built-up resentment of the worst kind was not reason enough. So she had paced her lounge until tiredness took over and she had stretched out on the large sofa. After much torment and regret, sleep had followed. On waking, she struggled to her feet, her mouth parched and salty, head throbbing. The first clear thought she had was about Krishnan and Krish. When she checked the ornate wall clock she was shocked as it showed the time to be just before midday. More than a few hours had gone by. Krish must have followed his routine of taking Krishnan to the babysitter before going to work. He could have woken her to get Krishnan ready as she did every morning. That he didn't only added to her guilt and increased her fear. She had a lot of clearing up to do as the cleaner wasn't due till the evening. After a strong cup of coffee she phoned Krish at the hospital, wanting desperately to apologize, but had to leave a message as he was operating. Determined to devote herself to her husband and son from that very instant, she armed herself with a broom and began to gather the shards of frosted glass, unable to look at the destroyed TV. After clearing up, she would have a long shower and cook a special dinner over which she would convince Krish of her determined resolve to get back to normal family life and back to her profession. She would enjoy her second pregnancy and plan for the new baby's arrival. It was then that she noticed a folded note on top of the shattered TV, which she had missed the previous night upon returning from the garden. She thought it to be a note from Shivani or Rosie or both, although she had spoken to them before they left, but it was from Krish. Uma unfolded it and read it. It was brief and terse, which reinforced what it had to say.

I have taken Krishnan with me and we won't be back till you've sorted yourself and grown up, if you can ever manage that. Don't try my mother's. We won't be there.'

A loud wail escaped Uma. She stood rooted to the spot, the note clutched to her eyes with both hands. Tears flowed freely as Uma reached for her phone and sought Krish on his mobile. All she could do was to leave a tearful message imploring him to call her at the earliest. Hands shaking, she fumbled with the phone and attempted both of Shivani's numbers but there was no response. Desperately, she tried Krish again and failed to get through. She thought of calling her mother but decided against it. Instead, she kept trying Shivani's phone till she finally got a response. Shivani was on her lunch break at work, in the hospital in Mysore that she had joined recently. Shivani listened as Uma cried and explained. The two decided to meet the next day in the evening after Shivani returned from work.

~

Rosie had taken the earliest flight available from Bangalore back to Panjim. The neatly sliced matchstick model that had been put away weeks ago was out of its drawer and back on the desk in front of her, but she made no attempt to glue it together. Instead, she stared at the pieces and at the shaking right hand trying to rest on the desk beside the pieces. What had brought out the mangled matchstick model into the open after it had almost been forgotten? The open laptop next to it showed a screen saver with cascades of bubbles, unnoticed by Rosie. The contents of the CD she had seen at Uma and Krish's house flooded her mind at every moment it could. It was not the details of how the fake suicide had been set up but the aftermath of it, which was not on the CD, that was etched on her mind. It was like a mental video of her own which looped over and over in her mind and no one else's. It had started the moment the door to Kamal's room had been flung open and she had caught sight of him hanging from a rope, with Sanjay kneeling and wailing on the floor. It ended abruptly, as Rosie felt an excruciating bolt of pain when the tendon in her wrist snapped, while she tried her hardest to lift the hanged Kamal out of the danger of death to a flickering possibility of life. Every time this video ran in her mind, she felt the same pain. Now, in her small room, Rosie got up and turned around to face the painting of Christ on the crucifix. She knelt in front of it, holding both her hands up in deep prayer. On her desk her mobile phone started to ring but Rosie ignored it even after she had completed her prayers and crossed herself. Instead, she walked out of her room to seek the mother superior, even if it was an ungodly hour.

∽

In Bangalore, Uma spent the afternoon waiting for her repeated calls to Krish to be answered. In between, she cried and decided to drive to Krish's parents as soon as possible. She had delayed doing this for as long as she could, desperately hoping Krish would answer her. She had her phone clutched to her chest, where it rose and fell as her breathing became more and more laboured, until it trilled and shook in her hand. Her thoughts took flight. It was Krish, and she had wanted to hear from him more than ever, but what he said was not what she wanted to hear.

'I needed to get away from Bangalore and from you. Krishnan misses you but he'll get used to his nanny. I have made a major decision. In the next few days you'll hear from my solicitor. Don't keep calling me. I'm out of Bangalore for good. It just wasn't fair to Krishnan or me. Everything has a limit. Bye.'

Uma's heart leapt and the wailing began, uncontrolled and feral, emotions reduced to basics. She beat her chest with her state-of-the-art mobile phone and then flung the phone across the room, where it crashed against a wall, exposing its innards. She felt doomed, her life seemed to be crashing. Where was it going and when was it going to end?

There was no other car in the garage. Krish had driven away with Krishnan in his beloved Mercedes, with the front of it still unrepaired from the accident of months ago. The sentimental, dusty, old Maruti wasn't going to start at any price given its years of inactivity. Uma called for a taxi and got to her mother-in-law's palatial bungalow, which she hardly ever visited. Lunchtime or not, her appetite had disappeared, not that she was going to be offered any food. What she was offered chilled her to the bone. Her mother-in-law informed her of a long overdue divorce petition that was on its way. More than that, it would be fast-tracked through the courts, where the family had many contacts. It would be a good riddance according to her mother-in-law, who had never liked her. It did not surprise Uma that none of her urgent questions about Krish and Krishnan were answered. Of Krish there was no sign.

The taxi sped Uma to her own mother and father's equally palatial house. She was in total turmoil, and breathless, tears coursing down her face. She rushed into her childhood home leaving explanations to the minimum. Her father, being a retired general who had travelled widely, was more understanding than her mother, who stayed at home out of choice and misplaced tradition, and who thought highly of Krish. The retired general hugged his only child, except Uma wasn't a child anymore. He had nothing more to offer and returned to his single malt, quietly convinced that it was no more than a temporary domestic tiff which would soon sort itself out. Uma's mother advised her to return home and contact Krish at the hospital where both of them worked. Uma did not bother to explain that she had already done that many times.

33

Rosie resented returning to her short story, her heart set against it, but apart from her church duties she had little to do in the late evenings and nights, having lost the passion for parish and community work with the same vigour with which she had taken them on. This depression had come about after a long conversation with the mother superior, which, for the first time, had verged towards an argument. Rosie was convinced that the time had come for her to start her one year as a novitiate at the nearby convent where the mother superior served on its committee. If the mother superior supported her application to the convent, it would ease her entry. Rosie was sure the time had come to crystallize her commitment to her faith by taking the next step towards becoming a nun. However, the mother superior was equally convinced that Rosie needed to wait until the call became totally pure. To Rosie, this was just another repeat of the same song the mother superior had been singing, and she began to harbour a grudge against her. Restless and reluctant, Rosie had to turn to writing for comfort and solace. She typed away slowly, plodding with one good hand and the almost useless other one. 'Each pebble made a circle in the pond,' she typed and then stopped, totally lost in distant thoughts.

Away from Panjim, in what used to be the garden city of Bangalore and before that, a pensioner's paradise, supposedly, a decrepit pond reflected a few trees. Uma tossed a pebble into it as if to energize and awaken it. All the same, the lifeless pebble created a widening circle and another concentric one within it. Shivani did the same, rippling the inverted reflection of tall trees and blue skies. The same bench that Uma and Krish had often sat on seemed harder than ever and an unforgiving reminder of good times gone by. A steady breeze teased the silence between Uma and Shivani, ruffling their unkempt hair. Uma had stopped sobbing.

'Krish will be back. He'll be back.'

Shivani wasn't so sure.

'The sooner you accept it, the better. You don't even know where he is or what he's up to.'

'I don't know what to do. Where is he? Where is Krishnan, my little boy? I've tried everywhere.'

'You'll be divorced in a blink, like me. We're both seeing the same shrink, Dr Shah, he of the collective delusional mania, remember? Open and shut case, Umi. Unreasonable behaviour. What have we got left? My body is rotting by the day. I've stopped the booze but it might be too late. Your dreams are disappearing just like Krish and your little boy did. You're pregnant with the second one but you still smoke like a chimney. No, this can't go on. We've got to get out of this mess. But how?'

Uma was on the verge of tears yet again, and choking.

'I want to make it up to my son and my husband. I want to look after my new baby. I will. I must.'

With trembling hands, she extracted a long cigarette, put it to her lips and then spat it out. She got up and started to walk. Shivani caught up with her and put an arm around her as they walked towards the desolate house. Uma put an imaginary gun to her temple and fired, worrying Shivani, although there wasn't anything like the bang of a real gunshot to be heard anywhere.

~

Uneasy days lay ahead. The passage of time either destroys and wounds or creates and heals. Yet its vagary is such that it may, unexpectedly, regress or progress from one to the other. In Uma and Shivani's case, it progressed from destruction to healing in a totally unexpected and sudden turnaround. Whether such fates and their speeds are decreed by some higher power or whether they are under human control becomes irrelevant in the face of the fantastic results of dramatic turnarounds. After plumbing the lowest depths, where Uma wished death upon herself and Shivani was well on her way to it, a strange calm had descended upon them. Uma had accepted Krish's absence, believing it to be temporary as no legal papers for a divorce had arrived. Every day, she immersed herself in work at the hospital, even on weekends, taking on as many shifts as she could. She missed Krishnan but the crying had stopped. It was as if the sad and tragic chapters of the story had given way to neutral ones, which were gradually heading towards calmer waters. The human spirit was indomitable, capable of accepting and living with the worst in the interests of self-preservation and the welfare of loved ones. If the sudden calm that suddenly descended on Uma wasn't example enough, Shivani's turnaround was proof of this indomitability. From being a chronic alcoholic rapidly spiralling downwards, she seemed to be cured. Within a week, the colour had returned to her face, the steadiness of old was back, and best of all, the passion for life and living was reborn. The pain in her stomach was nowhere as severe as it used to be. She knew full well the liver's regenerative prowess when its abuse has stopped. Uma and Shivani had energized themselves to new levels and with much resolve. The two had shared and supported each other through the most difficult stretch of days in their lives. Shivani had been fired from the hospital in Mysore so she applied for a post at Uma's hospital and was accepted, as RAMS graduates were more than welcome there. Without knowing it, the two were fulfilling a simple truism: To be able to save and prolong lives, they had to start with their own.

Shivani phoned Rosie to give her the good news about working with Uma and also to discuss the spate of group e-mails they had been receiving from Kamal and Sanjay. She found a despondent Rosie at the other end of the line, hesitant and unsure. She assumed that Rosie was rattled by the same pestering e-mails that mocked their lack of response where hitting back was concerned. These e-mails threatened 'further action' and Uma and Shivani had decided to ignore them at first, but then came to a decision as the inflow of e-mails continued. It turned out Rosie had indeed been rattled but not by the e-mails. Talking to Shivani, she was relieved to be able to speak of her desolation. Shivani recounted to Uma what had transpired between Rosie and her mother superior, after which Rosie had become a recluse.

Vagaries being what they are, the reverse had been the case with Rosie compared to Uma and Shivani. She had regressed from her previous calm and contentment to deathly impatience and an intense internal turmoil raged within her, all of this being the result of the quarrel with the mother superior. After that, Rosie despised her life as a sister, from which she no longer derived any succour or sustenance. The conversations with the mother superior had ceased and an unlikely animosity had crept in, inch by inch, like an erratically built web, going haywire. Rosie's spirituality, born and honed in this church, had taken a big hit – the kind that is difficult to recover from, rocking both the mind and the heart. She had confirmed over and over in her mind that her decision to become a nun was the correct one and it was time for her to attain what she had been yearning for. She knew the mother superior still thought that she had to wait more, forever if necessary, she had said, but Rosie could not wait another day. If the mother superior refused again, Rosie would leave the church and seek to novitiate at a convent elsewhere. When it happened, not only had the mother superior refused but in a raised voice, had reprimanded Rosie. For the mother superior, nothing could be worse than a nun who had taken the deeper vows only to abandon them later. This was tantamount to a sin, one that she would not permit. The call to become a nun was unmistakable and Rosie had to wait for it. Those who craved for the call did so for the sake of something else, not the call itself. A woman becomes a nun and a man a monk only if the Almighty wants it to be so. Rosie could only interject briefly, her voice also raised, which would have shocked her had she been aware of it. Her protests that she was the best person to gauge her own faith were of no avail.

Confused and dejected, Rosie had returned to her room, and for days could not decide whether to leave her church as she had planned or to accept the mother superior's rebuke. She had known the mother superior since she was six years old, and later, when Rosie was orphaned, she had become everything and more to her. Rosie was unable to contemplate leaving and therein was the dilemma. She could walk away from the church but not away from herself.

Shivani had listened to Rosie and comforted her as much as she could but felt unable to be of any practical use, being a complete stranger to matters of faith. Half an hour later, Uma phoned Rosie, having been apprised of her quandary. Uma knew what the church meant to Rosie and advised her not to leave. Rosie had decided as much in any case, which returned some calm to her. Their conversation turned to how Shivani and Uma were faring. Uma's threatened divorce had remained just that, and as each day went by, her confidence that her husband and little boy would return, grew. The two were also positive about Shivani, who had finally put paid to her alcohol dependency and was well on the way to full recovery. Furthermore, the two of them spent as much time together as possible since they worked together, which helped them both on the road to normalcy. It was during the spirit-restoring calm of these days that Shivani and Uma decided what they were going to do about Kamal and Sanjay.

'It's the obvious thing to do, Rosie sweetheart. We've invited them both to meet us, and we'll tell them about how they and their stupid pranks devastated our lives. They know about your hand but nothing of my, shattered marriage, with Krish walking out on me and what with me putting my pregnancy at risk. They don't know about Shivani nearly drinking herself to death, getting fired from job after job.

Mercifully, all these will be painful jolts of the past but they should know what they caused, don't you think, Rosie?'

Rosie did not want to be reminded of any of this so soon after her painful encounter with the mother superior but she wanted to encourage and soothe her friend.

'Very much so, Umi. Don't spare any details. Make them feel shame. Tell them that in spite of everything, you forgive them because they didn't know what they were doing. You see, Uma, forgiveness has power beyond our understanding. From schoolyard bullies to the worst tyrants, it can bring them to their knees, making them see the folly of their ways. I wish I could join you so I could really ram that into Kamal and Sanjay's heads, but, honestly Umi, I don't want to be reminded of the past. Besides, I have to mend my fences with dear Mother Superior. So I'll leave it to you and Shivani. They're coming are they, knowing what's in store for them?'

'We had to be a little clever there, I'm afraid. We knew they had to be enticed so we told them we have a plan to hit back, which is what they've been goading us to do. It's exactly a week from today, same time, same place. You don't have to be there, Rosie. It's going to be an honest, heartfelt plea from us after we've told them what we've been through. We will just have to accept that they won and we lost. It's the only language they understand. We will just have to grovel and ask, beg, whatever, that they stop this nonsense once and for all. Enough is enough, Rosie. Whatever it takes, we'll do it. We just want them to stop. So, it's better if you're not there. There's absolutely no need for you to grovel to them. The last time I met you at your church you did tell me things got as far as they did at RAMS because of me and I have to admit to that, now. I was an arrogant, stubborn hothead and I would never back off or concede, while you were kind, gentle, and never dug your heels in like I did. You've already paid a high price. If I had not driven Kamal to what he did, your hand wouldn't have been damaged. I have to live with that. If anybody deserves to grovel, it is I.'

There was an eerie silence for a while except for reciprocated sighs at both ends of the phone line. Rosie was saddened by Uma's plight but she was also pleased that Uma had changed and was finally doing right by attempting to banish the sickly obsession with retaliation. Rosie wanted to encourage and motivate her.

'Umi dearest, whatever the three of us have gone through in the past can't be removed or reversed but if any good can come of it, it will be slightly more bearable. I will pray for Krish and your son to return home to you and for Shivani to regain her health. I want both of you to be fulfilled and happy. I won't be there but feel sure you both will be successful. Those two will see the light. No one but no one is beyond redemption.'

34

Every light inside and outside the house was on. The red Mercedes with its damaged front fender and broken lights was at its usual place in the long driveway. When Uma had seen the car in the driveway earlier in the day, her heart had leapt with joy. Krish and Krishnan had returned! She had hoped and prayed for this. It turned out not to be so. Perhaps it was because of the damaged front that Krish had returned the car he had once loved so much. Uma had been using her old Maruti, which had been revived out of necessity after years of inactivity. With a new battery, some repairs, and a major servicing job, the car behaved as it always did; and apart from a few rusty patches it coped well with its owner, who no longer trashed it unlike years ago. What was more, after so many years of being covered with dust, it had finally been cleaned. The keys of the Mercedes were found in the hallway. Apart from these there was no other sign of Krish or Krishnan in or out of the house, although Krish still had his house keys. Uma felt she had been dumped with as much lack of ceremony as the damaged Mercedes. She too was damaged, a result of accidents, some her own doing and some done by others.

It had been three weeks since Uma had last seen her husband or son. Neither she nor Krish attended the same hospital anymore. He had changed his mobile numbers, and after days of agony, Uma had accepted that a separation had happened, but as long as the divorce petition didn't arrive, there was still a crumb of hope. All this changed the day after the return of the Mercedes.

Uma had returned from work after dropping Shivani at her flat, turning down her offer of tea. Shivani had sensed Uma's disquiet at work, and over a hasty lunch, the two had speculated about the return of the damaged car and Krish's possible location and intentions. Uma had more on her mind than the returned car, which had turned her disquiet into a fear that she could not understand. Shivani, ever watchful for any distress in her friend, tried to comfort her, putting down the return of the car as a needless reminder of the recent harrowing events they had been through.

∽

As soon as Uma had seen the large white envelope lying on the hallway carpet, she knew what it contained. She reached for it with trembling hands and fumbled, unable to open it. In the lounge, the offensive envelope was perched on her lap with all the innocence of a wronged, stuffed bird. She resisted her first urge, which was to have a stiff drink to calm her jangled nerves. This was just as well as there hadn't been any alcohol in the house for weeks, Uma having disposed them for the sake of her unborn child. The second urge she could not resist as she knew there was an abandoned packet of cigarettes in a drawer at home. Frenzied, she strode to the antique dresser by the wall and within seconds had a lit cigarette clenched in her mouth, the wispy curls of blue smoke rising to the ceiling from its tip and the stem of white ash lengthening till it fell into her lap. From her nostrils rose out widening shafts of smoke not unlike the fire breathed out by fabled angry dragons. The first hit of nicotine after so many days spun her head and addled her brain, being the stimulant that it was. She sprang up, staggered to the kitchen and discarded the offending cigarette, killing it with a splash of water. Back in the lounge she avoided looking at the envelope as she phoned Shivani.

On her way to Shivani's small flat, in the damaged Mercedes, the tears started and wouldn't stop. At times, Uma sobbed and wept but mostly the whimpering was controlled and the tears silent. The cause of her plight, the envelope, lay by her side on the passenger seat where she used to sit next to Krish during better days, when she used to turn to check on little Krishnan, who would invariably be fast asleep, strapped in his safety seat at the back.

∽

At her flat, Shivani opened the envelope and read the first two pages of the neatly set computer script. She gave Uma the dreaded news, which turned out to be worse than expected.

'Uma, it's an open and shut case like mine. I told you it was going to happen. It's exactly as I thought. Remember that day we were sitting by the pond near your house?'

Shivani decided it would be better for Uma to realize and accept what was happening. She read from one of the pages.

'...mental cruelty due to deep psychological imbalance induced by regular and excessive alcohol, unreasonable behaviour of the highest order, unwonted destruction of property, gross neglect of one-year-old minor of the marriage, total apathy to current four-month pregnancy...'

Uma began to sob, but now that it had happened, Shivani wanted reality to be denuded and Uma brought face to face with it, no matter how cruel it was. Facts were difficult to digest whereas fantasy just passed through, reality was more unforgiving than imagination. She turned to the next page.

'...total disregard of professional etiquette, total neglect of marital and domestic responsibilities, refusal to seek medical and psychiatric treatment... Says here in brackets, "Given medical ethics and patient privacy, a verbal report from our client, the Deponent, will be made available if required. Further, our client..." My God. Oh, my God!'

Shivani read on quietly to herself before she looked up at Uma. Her throat had dried, and after many days the urge for alcohol seized her, but this was nothing compared to what brought it on, what she had just read. For a moment, as a concerned and worried friend, she thought of holding back what the divorce petition had further demanded, but as a concerned and worried doctor, thought better of it. Uma was already in a state of acute shock. It was better for her not to be subjected to the same triggers for a second time. Shivani put aside the divorce petition, knelt on the floor beside Uma and put an arm around her.

'Uma, I can't believe this but I have to tell you. Krish has asked for the custody of not only Krishnan but also of the unborn child within twelve hours of the birth.'

Uma sobbed as before. It was as if she hadn't heard Shivani.

'Umi, Krish has...'

Uma burst into uncontrolled wailing, face covered by both hands as if to shield from further bolts of shame, guilt, and regret – which had been striking her relentlessly, all at the same time. Shivani decided enough reality had come out of the darkness. Uma's hysteria knew no bounds and the wailing turned into ferocious shrieks of anguish. Shivani realized that none of the allegations in the divorce petition were fabrications, fantasies or imagined, or simply put, lies. Each one was a fact and did happen at one stage or another to some extent. Despite that, Krish's demand for the custody of the child yet to be born was beyond cruel. But then as a father, Krish was quite rightly concerned for the future of both his children. Shivani's professional instincts took over. If ever she wanted to save and prolong one life, it was Uma's. Shivani knew her friend needed immediate sedation and was about to reach for her phone to call an ambulance when there was a sharp knock on the door. It was her neighbour, who was alarmed at the wailing. Shivani explained the situation quickly and scribbled out a note for the neighbourhood pharmacy she knew well through her own heavy use of it.

Late into the night, Shivani was nursing a mug of hot chocolate for Uma, who had fallen asleep within minutes of the tranquillizer dose being injected into her. As Shivani heard her friend's heavy breathing, her mind trundled back to the pharmacology lectures at RAMS all those years ago, which covered the very substance of nightmares and within that, the sedation tendencies of both manufactured chemicals and natural nutrients. The memory was enough to bring about a whirlwind in her mind. The havoc of destruction caused by Kamal and Sanjay was continuing like a tsunami that would only rest after there was nothing left for it to destroy. There was one pathetic comfort for Shivani. At least she was on the road to recovery, while Uma's life was crumbling by the day. It would be up to her to be by her friend's side forever and always. The meeting with Kamal and Sanjay was only four days away. She would have to deal with it herself if Uma did not recover sufficiently. Even if she did recover, would she still be in the submissive state of surrender and pleading they had planned? Shivani's mind ticked and whirred erratically, like a clock whose batteries were on the wane. On her own, what would she tell them? What would she do to them? She was distracted as Uma stirred. What was Shivani going to do when the large dose of the tranquillizer wore off as it was bound to? All Shivani could tell herself was to wait and see, just as she used to when awaiting exam results at RAMS.

Uma spent the next two days in Shivani's small flat, which became more of a home to her than her large but soulless house. By the hour, her body pushed itself to some semblance of its former self, driven by the age-old 'survival of the fittest' decree. This involved the shedding of copious tears, cursing her mother-in-law and swearing boldly at Krish, for whom her once unquestionable love had turned into intense hatred. He had not only deserted her but had filed for a divorce, robbing her of everything that she held as life's gifts. In between, she heaped obscene insults on Kamal and Sanjay, to the extent of worrying Shivani about her friend's sanity. Compounded to this were the fast-tracked summons for an imminent court hearing for the divorce, which was arranged through Krish's family contacts. Drawing on unknown forces, Uma sprang up like a wounded lioness. Where the physical recovery came from was the least of her concerns, though as a doctor she ought to have been intrigued by it. Despite Shivani's counsel that contesting the divorce petition would only add to her destruction, Uma sought the opinions of two leading solicitors in Bangalore in the time available to her. She was no longer interested in saving her marriage but wanted to fight tooth and nail for the custody of her children.

A day before the meeting with Kamal and Sanjay, Uma got the expert opinions she was after. Devastated, she hurried to the small flat, from where she would relay her situation to Shivani by phone or wait till she got back from work. Shivani was right. According to both the solicitors she consulted, Krish was going to get what he wanted, not only due to the formal evidence available to him but also because of his family wealth and influence. What was she to do? Her house, her one-year-old son and most of all, her unborn child, were not going to be hers anymore. Her steps faltered outside the wine shop on the way to the flat, to which Shivani had been such a lucrative and loyal customer only weeks ago. Uma was tempted to buy a bottle of vodka and a couple of packets of cigarettes but immediately banished the thought for Shivani and her unborn child's sakes. Although she had two hours of waiting before Shivani returned, she did not want her to come back to the smell of stale smoke and to herself tipsy with a drink. While her own life wasn't worth the breaths she took or the space she occupied, Shivani had fought and won a major battle and had the rest of her life ahead. Similarly, even if her unborn child was to be taken away from her, it still had a right to the world. Chiding herself and forgetting the vodka and cigarettes, Uma quickened her pace and hurried to the flat where another shock awaited her.

Shivani was sprawled on the sofa, a half-empty bottle of whisky on the floor beside her dangling hand. She blinked at the open-mouthed Uma standing above her. Uma reached down and took the three pages clutched in Shivani's other hand. Being more than familiar with medical reports she immediately knew what it was. What was thought to have been a dormant if not receding condition, was anything but. The hospital advised transplant procedures to be set in motion immediately and offered the services of its transplant unit. Shivani's liver had revolted and the cirrhosis was evident. This explained the traces of black vomit Uma had seen in the toilet on some days. Shivani had suffered in silence but she had also been drinking in secret, as she admitted. Uma's hand crept to the base of her belly and rested there as if to test her baby's well-being. It frightened her that she might have already harmed it by her own heavy drinking in the past. She bent down and kissed Shivani lightly on the cheek and then took the bottle of whisky and poured it down the kitchen sink. Back in the lounge, Uma reached for her phone to call her hospital. She was going to start the search for a suitable donor liver immediately, on a red alert basis using her full medical credentials. From the hospital, she obtained the numbers of all the major hospitals in Bangalore and called them one after the other. All the while, Shivani had been shaking her head slowly, unnoticed. Calls made, Uma sat on the edge of the sofa Shivani was sprawled on and held her hand. She had counted on Shivani looking after her and to help her mend her shattered heart. Together, the two of them were to return to a semblance of normal life. As matters stood now, it was Uma who would have to look after Shivani, starting with the search for a liver. The very next day, she would return to her hospital and widen the search to the rest of the country. If there was one life she wanted to save and prolong, it was Shivani's.

Uma's thoughts turned to what else was awaiting her the rest of tomorrow. Her divorce hearing was in the morning. As far as Uma was concerned, Krish and his family were welcome to it as she had already decided not to turn up for it. The meeting with Kamal and Sanjay was at seven in the evening and turning up for it was totally out of the question. There were better things to arrange and do than entertain the two lunatics who had caused all the mayhem to Shivani, Rosie, and her. For now, she would take charge of Shivani both as her friend and her doctor. The first thing she needed was her medical bag. Shivani had hers in the flat with her but Uma preferred her own. To a doctor, a medical bag was what a palette was to a painter, the choice of colours, their mix and arrangement just so. Her new patient's next requirement would be the right medication at the right time with the right dose, none of which was going to tax Uma. After that and equally important was her patient's diet.

'Shivo, I'm going out to get my bag and a few things for you. I'll be back in ten minutes at the most. You stay as you are.'

Shivani nodded as Uma straightened her legs and brought in a pillow and a blanket. She propped Shivani up, covered her, and was about to leave when her phone rang. It was an ex-colleague who called to wish her and Krish well for their new posting in the United States. A stunned Uma sank into a chair, trying to comprehend what was happening. Was Krish planning to emigrate and take little Krishnan with him and was he going to come back for the child yet to be born?

Would her little boy ever remember her? Why give birth only for the baby to be snatched from her? Would she ever see her children again? Uma began to cry, bent double with her face hidden in her hands on her lap. Shivani sat up.

'Umi? Umi, what is it? Who was it? Krish, the bastard?'

The crying intensified and the slouched shoulders heaved. Shivani pulled aside the blanket, got up and reached Uma. She put an arm around her.

'Umi, what's happened? Tell me.'

Uma stopped crying. She had to be strong for the both of them. She looked at the phone still in her hand. Like her old Maruti, it was an older, spare one, as she had smashed up the new one.

'Nothing, Shivo. Nothing worse can happen than what's already happened. I'm past caring.'

'Tell me, Uma. Tell me. We've shared and shared alike. You must tell me.'

Uma got up, wiping her tears and drying her face.

'I'll tell you, Shivo. I will when I get back. I must get some urgent stuff for us.'

She walked to the door making a mental note of the exact medication that Shivani would need for a good night's sleep and to keep her functional for the coming days. For herself too, she knew exactly which sedatives would see her through for the next few days. At the door, Uma turned to see if Shivani had settled back on the sofa, but Shivani was sitting upright. Uma could not decide if she was smiling or grimacing. It must be a grimace of pain, Uma thought, and hurried out for the medicines. She was wrong. Shivani sat there, smiling.

The next day, Uma awoke at eleven in the morning and immediately got worried about Shivani, but she need not have because the latter was still fast asleep. Uma felt her forehead and was relieved. More so when she checked the bucket by the bedside, which had remained unused. She listened closely and found Shivani's breathing to be regular and normal. The cocktail of medicines she had administered to Shivani the previous evening had done its job as had the sedative she had taken herself.

Over a cup of tea, Uma pondered over the day to come. It was marked to be a hectic and a life-changing one with the divorce hearing in the morning and the meeting with Kamal and Sanjay in the evening. She was determined for the day to be nothing like it had been marked to be. The uncontested divorce hearing must have been over by now. There was nothing she could have done to change its outcome so she had done nothing. As for the meeting in the evening, Kamal and Sanjay could head back to their beloved Chandigarh. She and Shivani would have nothing to do with them. That left only two things to be achieved for the day. First and foremost, she needed to spend a couple of hours in her office to organize the search for a donor liver for Shivani and she knew exactly how to do that. Secondly, she needed to get their phone numbers cancelled and obtain new ones. She would wait for Shivani to get up, make breakfast, and then give her a thorough check-up. After organizing her medication for the day she would head to her office at the hospital. It was going to be a simple day unless something unexpected happened or turned up.

Shivani woke up feeling hungry and chirpy which Uma thought were good signs. Shivani answered Uma's diagnostic questions with good humour, smiling often. While checking Shivani's blood pressure, heart rate, temperature, and feeling for any telltale swelling, Uma had outlined for Shivani the campaign to track down a suitable donor liver for her. Uma was as encouraging and positive as she could be but the effect on Shivani was a strange one. She seemed not to be listening as she looked past Uma and out of a window. The smiles and chirpy jokes of a few minutes ago were gone. She had stopped answering Uma's questions as the check-up was completed.

An hour later, Uma had completed all she needed to in the small flat. She was about to leave for her office when she was interrupted by her phone. Apart from the initial 'hello', Uma said nothing and listened on before abruptly cutting the call. Her legs were shaking and she had to sit down, determined not to cry. Her lower lip quivered and she put her hand to her forehead. Shivani was worried and whatever had bothered her before was put aside.

'Was that Krish? Uma, what did he say? Can't the bastard leave you alone? Uma, what's going on?'

Uma was trembling.

'Not Krish. HR from the hospital. Krish has resigned. Emigrating to the States. They want to know when I'm resigning.'

Uma fumbled in her handbag and extracted a small bottle of tablets. Her hands were shaking so much that Shivani had to open the bottle and fetch some water. The previous call from an ex-colleague let her know that Krish was planning to emigrate. Now, HR had confirmed it. Uma's mind was struggling with the demands being made of it. She wanted to get to her office to get the search for the liver underway, but every other second the thought that she might never see her children again was stabbing at her. Shivani was quietly swearing at Krish. All those years ago at RAMS she had kept her distance from him and his airs, and now, she hated him. Uma made an effort and got up. She needed to be busy. She needed to keep her mind occupied. She needed to get to her office for her sake as much as Shivani's.

All of a sudden, she sprang to her feet and locked herself in the bathroom. Shivani waited for a while and then panicked. She tried the bathroom door even though she knew it was locked. She was about to hammer on it when it opened and Uma stepped out, face washed and dried, eyes puffy. She reached for her handbag.

'I'm going to the office for two hours, Shivani.'

Shivani barred her way and held her by both shoulders, looking her straight in the eyes.

'No, Uma you're going to listen to me first.'

~

Uma was on the first of the two errands she had set for herself. After Shivani had finished talking to her, which took the better part of two hours, she had showered and freshened up and then set out in the Mercedes. Although Shivani had done most of the talking, just listening had tired Uma. She was at her house going from one room to another, switching on every light she came across although it was still daylight. In every room, she looked up from the floor at the walls and at the ceiling, taking in as much as she could of the photos, posters, and paintings. In Krishnan's room she felt she was about to cry but there were no more tears left. Instead, a strange calm had descended on her. She was about to pick up a teddy bear to take with her but decided against it. In her bedroom, with the red decor she had chosen, she collected a few clothes from the wardrobe including her black tuxedo and a few other objects from deep within it. Back in the lounge, she looked at the dent on the carpet where the home theatre used to stand. Having collected everything she needed, Uma cast a last look around. She left all the lights on and the front door ajar. Outside, she had a final look at her house from top to bottom. It wasn't going to be hers for much longer.

Her second errand was to go to her parents house, where she had grown up. After exchanging superficial pleasantries with her mother, she went upstairs to meet her father and found him asleep on his favourite leather sofa in the library. Uma watched him for a long moment and decided not to wake him. Looking around the library, she selected the book she wanted and left quietly with it to her old bedroom. She did this every time she visited her parents, but lately it had become frequent. The room was always exactly the same as the last time. Uma didn't linger but left quickly.

Driving back to Shivani's small flat, Uma passed the spot where she thought she had seen Kamal and where the red Mercedes she was driving was damaged. Kamal had admitted that it really was him made up to look slightly different. Uma's thoughts drifted to her and Shivani's present plight. How could one mend a heart broken beyond repair and find a healthy liver before it was too late? The first burnt holes in the mind and the lack of the second rotted the body bit by bit. Just the thought of this situation should have been frightening let alone the reality of it. Yet it didn't perturb Uma one bit and at the end of her long talk, Shivani was able to laugh at it while she searched for her own black tuxedo.

35

The conference room was as dimly lit as before, wall-hugging paintings and prints in gilded frames vying for space, light, and lost attention. One end of the long table was set for four people. Missing were the usual liquor bottles and the plethora of glassware. Seated, Uma sipped ice water and waited, tapping her slender fingers with their crimson coloured nails on the linen-topped table. There were artificial flowers splayed all around. She was wearing the black tuxedo she had fetched from her house a few hours before. Seated next to her, attired exactly the same, if a bit more crumpled, Shivani was also tapping her fingers on the table. She was well-fortified with the medication Uma had prescribed. For her part, Uma was equally calm, thanks to the sedatives. This was solidarity personified. The conversation was sparse, almost non-existent. They had hugged on leaving Shivani's small flat, admired each other and expressed relief that finally the moment was upon them and even more so that Rosie was not present. This would make their mission that much easier and comfortable. The finger-tapping continued until the door was flung open without as much as a knock. The stocky figure of Rosie Braganza marched in, dressed in her usual frumpy frock. In the states of mind Uma and Shivani were in, nothing could startle them, but Rosie's entrance shook them and left them looking at each other, eyes wide open, anticipating unexpected complications. Uma, as always, was the first to regain some composure.

'Rosie! Goodness! What on earth!'

Rosie snatched a chair.

'Goodness on earth, indeed, Uma darling. The saviour cometh. Cometh the hour, cometh the saved woman who is parched beyond belief. Fruit juice! Fruit juice! My kingdom for fruit juice!'

Uma was stunned, numb and speechless, which was unusual for her. Shivani was equally surprised but recovered quickly.

'Rosie! What...what are you doing here?'

Rosie pulled up the chair she had snatched and flopped into it.

'What's this I see? You two drinking water? I say, miracles do happen. You'll be joining the church next. Where's the lobster? Starving, I am. Where's all your booze and all. Party, no?'

Uma leaned forward.

'Why are you here, Rosie?'

'What do you mean why am I here? Same reason as you two. I talked a whole lot with Mother Superior, told her everything, every detail and I thought a lot. It's all sorted. To the nunnery with thee! Not yet, not yet baby. Let's cut to the chase. You were both right. It's time to grow up. There are more pressing and worthwhile things to do on this blessed earth than to thirst after senseless revenge. Omelette, sorry Helmet, sorry, Hamlet. What the hell! Food for thought... eggs, ham, no! What the hell! He said, said, there are more stars in heaven than we dream of. Something like that. What more can I say? I've come to thank you for accepting my little sermon on forgiveness. You two have decided to forgive even if you won't forget. What greater sacrifice than that! You've listened to fatso Rosie. Forgive! Forgive! The two lost souls, Kamal and Sanjay, will be redeemed. Oh, and why are you both dressed up like penguins, might one ask? What's so special?'

Uma and Shivani stared at each other, more concerned than ever. Uma's mind had blanked out. Sensing it, Shivani took charge.

'There's going to be no booze or lobster, Rosie. We will handle this on our own. You should leave now, for your own good.'

Rosie was aghast.

'What? Did I hear you right! I'm with you guys. I'll do as you say. I'll lick the floor and congratulate Kamal on pulling off the prank of the century, which, let's face it, it was. Then tell him and Sanjay we're out of it for good. God has given me a second chance. I'm back in the fold. I've seen the light. Sister Rosie is back. Miracles do happen. Those two will learn.'

Uma lost her patience and almost shouted.

'Rosie, you better leave right now! We don't want you involved in this. Leave, now.'

Uma pushed her chair back and marched to the door to open it but before she reached it, it was flung open, almost in her face. Kamal strode in, followed by Sanjay. Both were also attired in shiny black tuxedos, black bowties and glossy black shoes. Kamal sported a large diamond brooch on the front of his immaculate black turban. They were followed by a waiter carrying five expensively packaged rectangular presents, with frills and ribbons atop each. Kamal took charge immediately in an exaggerated theatrical manner as was his wont.

'So wonderful to see you all. Loved it so, so much, last time we were here, darlings. We come bearing gifts and we come in peace, me and my buddy Sanj. We're all agog, all ears as we hear you have something for us at long last. How exciting! Let the show begin.'

Uma and Shivani exchanged long looks while Rosie's gaze shifted from one person to the other. She was anxious to please the boys before they found out what was in store for them. After Uma and Shivani told them what their pranks had done to them, she would launch into her sermon on forgiveness, which she had prepared specially, and she would parade her damaged hand in their faces.

'Welcome, welcome Kamal, Sanjay. It's good to...'

Still standing at the door and holding it open, Uma snapped at Rosie.

'Shut up, Rosie! You better leave as you are not required here. Leave now.'

Shocked and stunned by Uma's forthright and rude manner, which was totally unexpected, Rosie was silenced, prompting Sanjay to come to her aid.

'Hey, hey, girls. Now, now. What's transpired between you all we do not know, but relax, take it easy and enjoy what's to follow. Right, Kam?'

'Right on, Sanj. Let us begin. First a small gift for you all. The finest malt whisky money can buy, matured for eighty years, craving your indulgence.'

Kamal snapped his fingers at the waiter, who obliged promptly, placing the three rectangular presents in front of the three women and the remaining two presents in the middle of the table. Sanjay was enjoying the moment.

'I know what you're all thinking. Let us assure you this is not a prank. Remember, no messing about with food or drink. To make up for everything. And there's more, right, Kam?'

Kamal fished out three small transparent boxes from his pockets.

'Diamond earrings. Genuine and authenticated. From us to you for old times' sake, to show there's no bad blood between us. No hard feelings. Only games between friends.'

In deathly silence, Kamal placed one small box each in front of the three. Rosie was beginning to enjoy herself immensely, settling down and looking forward to the festivities surely waiting to begin. She was staying and happy as matters were out of Uma's hands and very much in Kamal and Sanjay's. She would wait for the right moment to launch into her sermon. In the meantime, she studied the small box in front of her, which contained a pair of the brightest red diamond earrings she had ever seen. She was a little perplexed as to why, all of a sudden, her best friends wanted her to leave but it mattered little. Rosie looked from one to the other, eyes sparkling, but the silence was eerie. She decided to break it.

'Well! Are we in mourning or what? Like someone died! Girls, let's get the party going.'

Rosie clapped her hands in anticipation and looked to Uma to take charge and order food and drinks. Uma did take charge but instead of the anticipated jollifications, ordered the waiter away in such solemnity that even Shivani was impressed. As the waiter left, Uma closed the door after him and locked the door, pocketing the key. She walked to Shivani in short, measured steps. Shivani got out of her chair and both gave each other a deep, intimate hug, surprising Kamal and Sanjay and puzzling the already perplexed Rosie, whose eyes could not stay steady. Breaking away from Shivani and adjusting her tuxedo, Uma drank water and smashed the empty glass into a painting, which sprang a protest as shards of glass cluttered beneath it. Uma was in awesome control of the conference room and all those in it. She was so calm, even the paintings and prints on the forlorn walls were silenced, to say nothing of the dim lights.

'Sorry, old habit. I like smashing things, eh, Shivo.'

Uma pulled out a small golden pistol that looked like a cigarette lighter, which was what Rosie had thought all those years ago in her study bedroom in RAMS. The retired General's birthday gift to his daughter. Lady guns, he had said. Shivani had the other half of the twin pistols in her hand, the ivory of its handle against her moist palm. She was pointing it at Sanjay's head while Uma had aimed hers at Kamal's turbaned and bejewelled head. Rosie started laughing till Uma silenced her.

'Shut it, Rosie. Too late, you're going to have to watch this, whether you like it or not. You, Kamal and Sanjay, move it, over there by the wall. Move!'

Kamal started to laugh as did Sanjay. The laughter turned to guffaws, both holding their sides, struggling to contain themselves. Kamal recovered first.

'Is this it? You think I was born yesterday, Uma dear. Damn smart toys, though. You look convincing, too. Come on! This is pathetic! Let's sample the malt, shall we? It has already waited eighty long years.'

Kamal stepped towards the table to reach for one of the gift-wrapped bottles. Uma swung her pistol, holding it with both hands; aimed at the bottle, and fired. Shivani seemed to be in a trance and Rosie could not contain her excitement. A dull cracking sound, a small tongue of red and the bullet spat from the pistol and burst the bottle like a melon, drenching Rosie with whisky. Uma aimed the pistol back at Kamal's head but it was Sanjay who squeaked first, as frightened as Kamal was when he was feeding a sweet to a cadaver all that time ago. Sanjay was shaking.

'Man! Man! That is real.'

Kamal was unperturbed enough to smile but Rosie was stunned.

'Uma! What the hell! You did not tell me about this! What is this?'

Uma and Shivani nodded at each other. Both were supremely confident. Both ignored Rosie as if she weren't there. A nervous tick flew across Sanjay's face as he looked at Kamal for help, which wasn't forthcoming. Kamal's smile had evaporated but he was still his old cocky self.

'So, this is it. This is your so-called hitting back. Not bad. Not bad. Next one's blank, right? Best you can do is to keep us guessing, give us a fright. Go on, get on with it. Next one's a blank, right? I'll bet anything on that. Hit me right there, baby. Only make sure you've got the sequence right.'

Kamal pointed to the diamond in his turban. Uma smiled at him.

'I can't get it wrong, Kam. They're all the same. Both of you, to the wall. Now.'

Rosie laughed out loud, almost hysterically. Uma and Shivani ignored her, their pistols trained on Kamal and

Sanjay's heads. Both of them looked at Rosie, nervous and pleading, inching backwards towards the wall. Rosie recovered, wiping away tears.

'I got it! I got it! The four of you planned this together. Nice one, nice one, guys. You're pranking me, all of you ganged up on me, yea? That's why you're all dressed up like stupid penguins, all of you. Team identity, right? Hey, it nearly worked...gave me a damn fright! But I will have the last laugh. You guys carry on but the very last prank will be mine. Bet on that! I'll get you all! Now...'

Shivani lost her calm.

'Shut up, fatso. Just watch this, since you're here. This is as much for you as us. Ready, Umi? Countdown?'

The count began. Three, two...

At 'one', both tiny pistols spat out their leaden weights. Such toy-like playthings had their purposes, designed by someone, somewhere. Kamal and Sanjay's heads rocked backwards, after which they collapsed like overloaded sacks. Their brains, once so vibrantly alive with synaptic hyperactivity, were splattered on the wall behind, abstract paintings outshining others with their indifference. Two brilliant lives, bodies and brains, were smashed up – decorating walls that had adornments which did not welcome newcomers, no matter how spectacular. Rosie jumped to her feet, screaming and flapping her arms like a windmill gone berserk.

'You bloody mad fools! For God's sake! Uma, what the hell...this is not happening, is it? Tell me! Tell me!'

With the supreme clarity of mind that only happens once in a lifetime, Uma began another countdown as she pointed her pistol at her dearest friend, Shivani, whose own little pistol was pointed squarely at her. They walked to each other, pistols pointed at each others' heads and at the brains embedded within. Rosie started to scream but to no avail. After another countdown, the pistols fired at exactly the same time. Two more bright brains were spilled and blood splashed its red glory all over. Five spirits must have flown free if one believed in them, and if an unborn child also had a spirit. Rosie screamed and cried.

'Oh God! Oh God!'

36

The scream, 'Oh God! Oh God' rang inside and around the church and in Rosie's head, which she held in her hands. The screen of her laptop had gone mad with the screen saver of balloons swirling around, reflecting the state of her mind. 'My God! My God!' was circling in her head but the computer demanded attention like a pet yearns for it, yapping and blackmailing. The damaged matchstick model, her real pet, seemed to conspire with the computer, shaking Rosie out of her apathy. She attacked the keyboard with a vengeance she was only too familiar with, making her damaged right hand work harder than ever, thrashing and punishing it.

The Times of India, Bangalore edition, front page, screamed headlines and sad pictures of four young faces. 'Pact killings. Four young doctors dead. Police at total loss.' In a different part of Bangalore, Professor Verma pushed aside the newspaper he could not live without, being a print addict. There was not much for him to live for or be addicted to anymore. Four of his best students had gone to waste. From the apex of life and life-saving to the dustbin of death and destruction. Brilliance tarnished. Diamonds burnt. He extracted a syringe from the top drawer of his antique desk and raised it to eye level. He was happy with it and smiled, scratching his full white beard. He knew where to find the obliging vein in his arm, and injected into it, feeding it what it did not need. He stretched back into his chair and faced his desk and the landscape paintings surrounding it, taking a final look out of his window at the garden he was eternally thankful for. He closed his eyes.

'Professor Verma was blissfully asleep within seconds but he was never going to wake up,' typed wobbly fingers, the ones on the right hand struggling with a familiar tremor that barely mattered anymore.

There was a sensation in the publishing world, the like of which was as rare as gold-dusted nimble fairies which 'fatso' Rosie Braganza was far from. Her debut novel, *PRANKZzz*, as she titled it, sold and sold. On its cover was a creamy skeleton hanging from a black roof with a cigarette dangling from its jaws. Word spread quickly, especially among the urban youth, not unlike kisses that never happened but were imagined enough to be soul-destroying, like her book. Newspapers vied to bestow kudos and praise on what was described as a riveting debut novel written by a failed medical student, based on her experiences. Rosie plummeted into a world which was very different from the one she once aspired to be in. Not the best neurosurgeon of her generation but a wordsmith of sorts, who used to write short stories that no one knew about.

PART THREE

37

The house as described in Rosie's book only existed in her mind but was based on a real one she had been to once, many years ago. With the passage of time, her memory of it had faded and the real house differed from the imagined one in some minor aspects. It was in Koramangla, one of the better and plusher parts of Bangalore, which was unchanged except a few more trees had been chopped down while concrete and glass had risen upwards, and the Metro construction was snaking through it all at the pace of a worm.

A sleek blue Mercedes, not a red one, without a hint of a scratch or any damage on it anywhere, purred along the drive of the house and came to a halt. A power dressed woman, a peach of a dream for many men, stepped out of it and strode into her house, removing her dark glasses with an accomplished and practised flourish, clutching her D&G handbag and her laptop case. This doctor had a busy day as always.

∽

Away from the bustle of Bangalore, fourteen hours by land and two by air, the church that was once a matchstick model stood stern in the afternoon Goan sun, that was as benign as it was unrelenting, duality being its privilege. A brand new BMW saloon, which seemed like an unidentified flying object, perched on the car park, beckoning its owner, one Ms Rosie Braganza, who was to board a flight from Dabolim airport not too far away.

Her book had become a juggernaut of interest; and being the sensation of the publishing world, everyone wanted to be associated with her. Two trends in the news media had been pushed aside with some vigour. For the first time, the publication, release, and subsequent sales of a novel became news items in prime-time TV. Also for the first time, art editors of national TV networks fell over each other to feature the young author, offering hour-long interview slots, even with appearance fees which the new author hardly needed. Taking the advice of her publishers and newly acquired manager, Rosie only selected those channels and art editors who were a shade more cultured than their counterparts.

With a choice of designer spectacle frames and a specially fashioned wardrobe and hair designs to match, Rosie stood on the studio floor of a renowned national TV channel, having flown into Delhi at their expense. She had been well-feted and fed in the green room by the producer of the show and his art editor. Even the bearded CEO of the channel had dropped by for a few minutes to down a glass of wine with Rosie. This was a world that could not be more different for her. Her once intended world of performing life-saving miracles of neurosurgery in rural India was all but forgotten as was the right hand with the tremor which refused to take leave. Or was that so? Was there no longer any regret about her hand and her shattered dreams?

The red studio light 'On Air' came to life and the suave and smooth host of the show waited for the cued applause to ebb, which it did. The host held up a book to face camera B, which was primed for the required close-up of the front cover. The host smiled at Camera A, directly in front of him.

'Yes, indeed, this is the book that is causing a sensational stir right now, and that is putting it very mildly. Please, will you welcome the author of this astonishing work – Ms Rosie Braganza!'

The floor manager cued in more applause from the studio audience and the book cover went full screen, depicting the creamy skeleton dangling from the ceiling in the black room, with a lit cigarette clenched in its jaws, clasping a glass in one set of bony metacarpals. The studio audience obliged with the applause, most of it genuinely meant. Camera C took it in while camera A pulled out to a two shot of the host and Rosie. The host turned his attention to Rosie.

'You've made publication history, hardly ever achieved in this country. I'm told copies are changing hands at three times the cover price. Tell me, what is your secret? Between you and me.'

Rosie smiled at the feeble attempt to relax her.

'Well, there is no secret, really. If there was, I wish I knew it. It started as a short story years ago, about six friends who were in the same study group at a medical faculty. In fact it was called "The Six Friends" at that time but it kind of just grew and grew. Really, it was just to pass time as a kind of hobby. You know, just to take a break from very hard studies.'

The host tapped the book cradled in his manicured hand.

'Yes. It says here at the back that it's based on your college experiences. Facts mixed with fiction. Maybe that's the secret?'

'I don't know about that. But you're right. It's a mixture...'

Many miles away in Koramangla, a bedroom TV set showed Rosie in close-up. The bedroom decor was decidedly blue, with not a hint of red anywhere. 'Uma' was barely awake in the large double-bed after a hard day's work at the hospital. She put away the medical journal she was trying to read and prepared to sleep, saying a silent goodnight to her husband 'Krish', who was working a night shift at the renowned hospital where both of them were employed. On the TV set, Rosie continued...

'...mixture of things, events that did happen. Yea, sure some things did happen as written. Others are totally made up.'

'Uma' tossed the medical journal aside as realization hit her, knocking her out of her sleepy state. She watched the TV, suddenly riveted to it, tossing aside her long silky hair and the sleep out of her eyes. Was she really watching her long-lost friend Rosie Braganza, she of RAMS, on TV? She who had to leave because of her permanently damaged wrist tendons? As she watched, wide awake, 'Uma' became certain, and then even more so. On the TV, the host was still trying to get to the heart of *PRANKZzz* and its writer.

'Let's get this straight. You mean some events you just made up? Total fiction?'

'Yes, some are totally made up. You know? Just pure imagination. Others did happen as written. Some, I changed a little bit here and there. I mean you have to make the plot exciting and believable. You have to grab your reader's attention and keep it. More than that, you have to get your reader involved deeper and deeper...'

'Uma' watched with her mouth as wide open as her newly energized eyes. She snatched her multifaceted mobile phone and shocked it into activity. She punched one key and it connected her to 'Krish', who took the call in his office at the hospital.

In the Delhi TV studio, the interview with Rosie Braganza continued. The camera cluster dallied hither and thither at the whim of a director, who shouted his charges around, while a woman in the control room vision mixed as per the director's instructions. 'A close in. B close-up Rosie. D pull out. Good, good. Cut to A. Cut C. Ready B.' Camera A was on air, its hooded lens piercing at the host of the show.

'So, the intriguing part is trying to work out what happened and what didn't, after having read it. Surely, those horrible pact killings didn't happen, did they? I mean, that would have caught every newspaper headline, surely? And the poor professor who injects himself to a suicidal death?'

Rosie hesitated for a second, which in TV's express virtual reality, is quite an age. Commercial time worth a few lakhs was being wasted. The host was getting stinging, waspish 'zzzes' in his earpiece from his producer. He was about to make an effort, something to justify the large salary he was given, when Rosie smiled at him and continued to speak.

'Best if you decide for yourself. You seem sure none of that happened, all the killings and the professor's suicide. You seem sure of that. Well, you might be right but it is good enough for me that you are uncertain and you pose these questions. Read the book again. A lot of people read it again and again to work out where reality stops and fiction takes over. There are groups of people, mainly young people in colleges all over the country, debating and discussing exactly that. Try reading the book again. That is all I can say.'

The seasoned host rose to the bait.

'Read the book again. I thought you might say something like that. I will do that. Tell me...'

Sitting on the edge of her vast bed, 'Uma' was shouting into her smart phone, not that she needed to.

'Sure, I'm sure it's Rosie! How can I forget her? Hurry up, Kartik! There's a TV in the restroom. Or just fire up your laptop. You won't believe it, Kartik, she's put it all in a book. Listen, listen.'

'Uma' pointed her phone at the TV as if to trap its outpouring. The host was well into the interview, very much in his comfort zone.

'Tell me about yourself. Many deaths in your book, Rosie Braganza. Are you obsessed with death?'

Close-ups cut across from host to guest continuously. The studio audience watched themselves on monitors as the vision mixer punched in reaction shots of them.

'No, I'm not obsessed with death. No more than you are.'

'You became a priest, right? That much is true?'

'No, not a priest. Men become priests. Women become sisters or nuns. I became a sister and still am in real life as well as in the book. So, yes, that much is true. Also, I kept my name in the book but changed all other names. Well, more or less...'

'Why? Why did you give other characters – your fellow students, your friends – different names but not yourself?'

In her bedroom, 'Uma' was so awestruck by what she was watching that she forgot the phone in her hand, still pointing at the TV set.

'Seemed like a natural thing to do. I wanted the book to have an authentic feel to it. When I was writing it, I was writing about the real me. Rosie in the book and I are the same person but sometimes I think she's more real than I am, if you know what I mean. I think she rules me. I'm at her beck and call whether I like it or not.'

'I'm not sure I understand. Let's talk about the ending without giving it away, of course. It is a major twist as they say, but did it happen? Let's just say Sister Rosie in the book, at least, does not fare very well at the end. Endings are crucial, aren't they? The very last line of the book is simply electrifying. I have to tell you, I had goosebumps all over. The last page, specially the very last line? How did you arrive at it?'

'Ah, the ending? You're more than right. Beginnings and endings are crucial. The middle is just a walk down a garden path that you lead your readers up to. It can be pleasant and heavenly or totally crazy. Readers get an idea they are heading towards the end but they don't know what waits there and how to get there. It's expectation mingled with uncertainty. You can make the ending sad and tragic or happy and joyful, or just leave it neutral, but that's a sign of indecision, something readers don't like. Generally they want decisive endings, all loose ends neatly tied up...'

'But why did you choose to end your novel the way you did?'

'Seemed like a natural ending to me. The Rosie in the book has moments of great depression and she is capable...'

'That's the Rosie in the book, as you say. What about the real Rosie, here, sitting by me? The injured right hand, for instance? That happened, right? You've still got the tremor?'

Rosie immediately concealed her right hand under her left one, on her lap, almost as a reflex action. In her ears were blue diamond earrings, not bright red ones. Rosie decided to show her offending 'useless shame of a hand' as she often referred to it. She raised it up.

'This useless shame of a hand is destined to stay as it is, with its ever-present tremor. See, I know a thing or two about nerves and neurons. Enough to know this is beyond cure. Anyway, it's the reason why I'm here and not working as a neurosurgeon.'

Rosie put away the offending hand, hoping that the interview returned to happier matters or better still, ended soon, but the host was as persistent as his job required him to be.

'Would you rather you were the neurosurgeon that you had set your heart on? But then you wouldn't have written this phenomenal book.'

Rosie shuffled uncomfortably, suddenly downcast, looking at the floor.

'I would have preferred to be a neurosurgeon which is what I set out to be. To be the best one, actually, but it was not to be. I try not to think about it and I have learnt to live with it.'

'You don't look it but you must be one happy person, Sister Rosie Braganza. The novel has been translated into umpteen languages, both here and abroad. And a film based on it is being made even as we speak.'

In her bedroom, Urmilla was no longer surprised, but pleased. She smiled, rapt in the interview, and hoped Kartik was also watching it. She began to itch with a yearning to read *PRANKZzz* and vowed to purchase two copies in the morning, on her way to work.

Back at the TV studio, the host had yet more questions.

'Like the book, the film is offered as all fiction?'

'Yes, exactly. It makes sense. There's no other way, anyway. I can't exactly announce in the book or in the film, "this bit happened and this one didn't and this did but not exactly this way." But it can be worked out.'

'I would really love to know which bits were which, which ones happened and which were made up. I think that's the most intriguing aspect of the book. I am going to have to read it again. You're right about that.'

'I'll tell you something right now. There are precise moments in the story when fact changes to fiction and vice versa. Read the book again, watch the film when it comes out. Work it out. Maybe a prize should be offered to anyone who gets it all right.'

'Can I ask you, have you any plans for the next one? Or, maybe you could write a sequel to *PRANKZzz*. You know, bringing your readers up-to-date with the six friends as to what each one is up to? Or maybe write a different one altogether?'

'My publishers are keen for me to start thinking about the next one and your sequel idea is also interesting, but I have to say, at the moment I have not thought of anything. But who knows about the future? It's impossible to predict. I mean, I never dreamt all those years ago that my short story would turn into something so big.'

The host flashed a broad smile, cosmetic and often insincere, as if the predominant purpose was to reveal his expensive and gleaming dentition. This time it seemed to be soundly sincere.

'Finally...must say I'm intrigued about this...the title of your book...*PRANKZzz* is spelt with three "Zs", not a simple "S". Why?'

'The title of a book, like its cover, should hint at the world within it so a potential reader gets some idea about the book and at the same time, for commercial reasons, it has to be eye-catching. And yes, copyright reasons too. You never know – some idiot somewhere might have or will come up with a somewhat similar title. So, it's best to be different.'

Urmilla smiled to herself as the host rounded up the interview in his usual polished style, thanking his guest. She was prepared to sleep but it was going to be difficult as her mind travelled back to her student days at RAMS, all those years ago.

38

Over the years, the academy, RAMS, as it was known, in the northern fringes of Bangalore, had changed little except for losing a lot of trees. Accommodation block 'A' had been demolished and a new one built where the old one was. Some of the teaching staff had moved on and the academy had started to accept more foreign students. The corridor of the administration block still boasted various posters and photographs. The name on the dean's office did not read 'PROF VERMA' nor was it in gold lettering as described in Rosie's recently published fiction. In fact, the name on the door read 'PROF SHARMA' and it was in blue lettering, not gold.

Inside Professor Sharma's office, the paintings adorning the walls were not classic landscapes but modernist abstracts. 'Prof V' sat behind a large modern desk made of glass, which was hardly an antique, chuckling to himself as he finished reading the very last page of *PRANKZzz*, shaking his head in amazement. He wasn't as old as Prof V was described in the novel, and had a small goatee beard instead of the flowing white one given to him in Rosie's novel. He thought aloud to himself.

'So Sharma becomes Verma. Not bad, not bad, Rosie Braganza.'

'Prof V', actually Prof Sharma, flipped through the novel, snapped it shut and put it aside, still smiling.

~

In another part of Bangalore, one of Professor Sharma's previous students, now a reputed doctor, sat in her consultation room and office, in a hospital of international repute. The doctor's eyes were clear and bright as they scanned the last page of the novel, *PRANKZzz*. The doctor looked as fit and well as she did in her student days at RAMS. She was expensively and elegantly dressed as she sat in one of her easy chairs, absorbed in the book. After a soft knock on the office door, a nurse peeked into the room.

'Dr Shaila, your patients are waiting. The third appointment has just arrived.'

The doctor kept reading. The nurse shook her head.

'Dr Shaila, you're running an hour late. Please.'

The exasperated nurse removed herself, shaking her head. The doctor finished reading the book, sighed heavily and looked up at the ceiling and thought to herself.

'Shivani? Shivo? Me? Alcoholic, to boot! Oh, Rosie, Rosie. Only once did I touch a drop in Urmilla's room and it nearly choked me.'

Dr Shaila tossed the book on to her desk and sighed again after which she permitted herself a smile.

~

The oars were idle, the fishing rods lay ignored. The small wooden boat was drifting calmly on a placid lake. 'Sanjay' and 'Kamal' sat at opposite ends, facing each other, heads down, eyes running across the last page of *PRANKZzz*. Both finished reading almost at the same time.

'Unbelievable! Astonishing! I am impressed. Don't like the name "Kamal", though. Wonder where she got it from. Yours isn't too bad, Suresh. "Sanjay" is better than Suresh.'

'I had no idea Rosie became a writer. We have a famous friend, Karan. Let's invite her over. For old times' sake. Just wish we were as well off as she's made us out to be, to own chunks of Chandigarh! Whatever gave her that idea?'

'I like the idea of you bringing back my dead body back like the true friend that you are. Good dramatic stuff. Ending's a bit disturbing. Not like Rosie.'

'And me not returning to RAMS! What imagination! Yea, the ending's a bit strange. Bit on the dark side. That very last line of the book...'

Both turned quickly to the last page again. One of the fishing rods jerked into life and the line began to run but neither of the two jumped to it.

~

In the main bedroom of the real house in Koramangla, the two doctors, husband and wife, were in bed. Kartik had a copy of *PRANKZzz* resting on his chest. He had just finished reading it and was waiting for Urmilla to finish reading her copy. Kartik had no grey hair and neither did he wear spectacles. He stared ahead, deep in thought. Finally, Urmilla finished reading. She was excited but thoughtful at the same time. She remembered Rosie's TV interview and Kartik had only missed the beginning of it at work. Both had followed the media coverage thereafter. 'Wow, killer punch at the end. And that's not all. We have one kid and another one on the way and you walk out on me! I'm a right bitch and smoke like a chimney and play with a gun. Me! Me! I've never touched a cigarette and I wouldn't know one end of a gun from the other! So, Shaila becomes Shivani, Karan becomes Kamal...'

'And the rest of it...I know. I know. Just read it. Prof Sharma becomes Prof Verma and so on. Remember she came to see us just after we'd moved into this house. It's been a long time but she's remembered bits. She's given us a red Merc. Must have forgotten it's blue. Let's invite her for the weekend and talk about the book and the old days.'

'I used to tell her I could read her like an open textbook with big diagrams in it. She's put that in the book. It must have stuck in her mind. I'm still wondering about the ending, though. The very last line.'

Both became thoughtful. Kartik had read the last line in the novel several times and recalled its discussion during the TV interview, with the host saying it had given him goosebumps. Kartik began to feel uneasy. 'When is Rosie's birthday, can you remember, Urmi? We used to go for drinks on everyone's birthday.'

'Rosie's birthday? What about it? I must have it written somewhere. Why?'

'Just wondered. The last line is a bit shocking.'

'It comes as a bit of a shock, I must admit.'

Both picked up their copies and sought out the last sentence again. Kartik looked at Urmilla.

'No. She wouldn't.'

'Are you thinking what I'm thinking, Kartik? Surely not. It's not like Rosie. I need to talk to Shaila and Karan and Suresh.'

After that, there were a frenzy of phone calls. Shaila got through to Urmilla just as her number was being punched in. All the way up north, in Chandigarh, Karan got through to Suresh straight away after which Suresh managed to get through to Urmilla. Everyone had the same questions and concerns about the very last line of *PRANKZzz*. What was to be made of it?

~

In her church office, the mother superior was reading the last page of *PRANKZzz* and quietly smiling to herself. She finished reading it and snapped the book shut, looking up, still smiling at her protégé's exceptional and unexpectedly creative work. The smile vanished suddenly as she reached for the book again and read the last line, loudly to herself.

'Finally and forever, on this the day of her birth, the ever-trembling, ever so useless shame of a hand was still, as still as it was ever going to be... That too, of its own volition.'

The mother superior shut the book in a snappy manner that she would never even think of while closing her bible, which, in contrast, was like putting an angel to sleep. She got to her feet as quickly as she could when she realized she had not seen or heard from Rosie for at least the last four days. Gathering her cassock around her, she rushed out of her office. It took her all of ten minutes to hurry across to the other end of the church and up the stairs to Rosie's small living quarters. She prayed that the door would not be locked and that Rosie would be quietly tapping away at her laptop as she had been doing for long hours only a few months ago. Without knocking, the mother superior tried the door handle and found it to be unlocked. She rushed in and looked around. Rosie's room was neat and tidy, with everything in its right place. The printer and laptop positioned next to each other, all books neatly arranged in the one bookshelf, magazines neatly stacked on the desk, and her collection of old-fashioned vinyl LP's in their rack on the floor. The mother superior extracted her mobile phone from somewhere within the folds of her cassock and called Rosie's number. There was no response, not even the standard service provider message. She closed the door behind her and continued trying Rosie's number as she walked back to her office, wondering why there was no response, which was very unlike Rosie. On reaching her office, the mother superior checked if there was an e-mail to her from Rosie. There wasn't. Instead, amongst the few new ones was one from someone she had no knowledge of – Urmillamedico@hotmail.com. The mother superior was weary of opening e-mails from unknown people, institutions, and organizations ever since she had opened one which promised the 'hottest ever times in the tropics', only to have her computer plagued with pornography. At that time, some years back, Rosie had reset her computer back to its better behaviour after chuckling at the irony of the mishap. Rosie had also explained how malicious 'bugs' could make computers sick but it only managed to baffle the mother superior even more.

Down south in Bangalore, the sender of the unopened e-mail, Urmilla, was sharing a bottle of red wine with Kartik and her best friend Shaila, but each one was subdued with worry about the last line in Rosie's book. Urmilla had the book on her lap. Reluctantly, she picked it up again and read aloud the last line, much slower this time.

'Finally and forever, on this the day of her birth, the ever-trembling, ever so useless shame of a hand was still, as still as it was ever going to be... That too, of its own volition.'

Rosie had revealed in the full glare of the media that her book was made up of facts intertwined with fiction. The worry the three had was shared by Karan and Suresh as well. Was there even a remote possibility that Rosie might turn the fiction of the dreaded last paragraph and line into an unforgiving fact? She had threatened to have the last laugh a number of times while at RAMS, when the others in her study group had teased her and played harmless pranks on each other and on her. These empty threats were in a light vein and in good humour, more an attempt by Rosie to be in her friends' good books, a way of demonstrating solidarity and nothing more. This had changed dramatically after Rosie's wrist was permanently damaged during an outrageous prank, of a fake suicide by hanging, that Karan and Suresh had planned and executed. After the disastrous consequence of this prank, Rosie had to leave RAMS, while the other five in the study group vowed to stop all pranks, harmless fun or not. They continued with their studies at RAMS and went on to bright and brilliant futures, just as their mentor and guru at RAMS, Professor Sharma, had predicted.

Rosie's dream to be the best neurosurgeon of her generation had been shattered. Subsequently, she had sought sanctuary at her church, where her parents had died in tragic circumstances as in the novel. She had plunged herself into worship, community and parish work, but could not keep at bay the increasing rage and depression which was threatening to become clinical. All of this had emerged bit by bit during the weekend Rosie had spent with Urmilla and Kartik, when they had moved into their present house. Urmilla recounted this as Kartik uncorked the second bottle of red wine. Instead of good cheer, the wine only made the three more sombre and the second bottle was destined to do even more so. More so because Urmilla had managed to trace Rosie's birth date from an old diary of hers. This added to their worry as 'the day of her birth' as it was described in the last line, was only thirteen days away. The speculation as to the remote possibility becoming real trundled on. Finally, a consensus was reached, which made them feel slightly better. The line, 'That too, of its own volition', was hardly indicative of suicide. This last line could even be hinting or wishing for entirely the opposite. It could well mean that the hand had stopped its tremor by its own wish, that it had willed itself well, that it had become still at its own behest at long last. Medically, this was far from possible as the three knew only too well. Tendons and nerves wasted and withered over years were as likely to regenerate as dried and shrivelled weeds were to sprout to new life.

Based on the opinions and observations the three had about Rosie and her personality, each felt instinctively that Rosie could not, possibly, do what she had threatened in the last paragraph, if the more drastic interpretation of it was to be taken. With the hugely spectacular success of her book, she had too much to live for. What she had not achieved or wasn't going to achieve in the field of neurosurgery, she had achieved in another sphere. Shaila felt that if she was in such a position, with all that acclaim, not to mention the untold riches and more to come, she would not complain, let alone wish death upon herself. Kartik was more cautious as he reminded himself and the others that such spectacular success could also bring its own problems. Urmilla had stopped fretting and fidgeting, which she had been doing all evening. She wanted to compare notes with Karan and Suresh. Sure enough, Karan and Suresh had speculated similarly and had come to the same conclusion that Rosie would never do what the line in the last paragraph suggested. The ending of the book was as she saw fit as a writer, whatever she meant by it. It seemed right to her. Only a few days ago she had said, so herself during a TV interview. No, Rosie had no death wish for herself nor would she ever. Feeling even better, Urmilla called Rosie on her mobile yet again. There was still no reply, just as the other four friends had found every time they tried to reach Rosie.

∽

Late at night, in the church office, the mother superior was speculating along a different line after failing to contact Rosie despite many attempts. Having kept up with the media frenzy about Rosie and her book, especially after watching the TV interview, the mother superior had convinced herself that Rosie had no further need for her church, possibly even her faith. With the fame and wealth she had acquired and with much more to come, she could buy a palatial manor with servants, drivers, cooks, and gardeners at the snap of her fingers. The process had already begun as a sparkling car had arrived a week ago, turning out to be Rosie's purchase, and that very evening a uniformed chauffeur had arrived to take charge of it. The mother superior had known Rosie since the time the latter was six years old, when her parents had moved to this poor part of Panjim from Londa in search of better prospects. By the age of sixteen, Rosie had lost both her parents through no fault of hers. With the grace of this church, several NGOs and herself, the mother superior thought, Rosie had more than evened the odds stacked against her. Having grown up with dispossession and poverty, the grown-up Rosie was going to revel in her new wealth, forgetting her past, her God, her church, and her guardian. The mother superior summed up her thoughts and ended up by not blaming Rosie one bit, even if she had abandoned God. The one comforting thought was that she had correctly adjudged that Rosie's call to be a nun was not firmly rooted or steadfast. She had stopped Rosie from taking the route she was not meant to take. Regardless, she would continue to pray for her hand to be healed as she did twice each day, and also for Rosie to return back to God's fold. Just as the mother superior's thoughts turned to the next day's promises, hopes and sleep for the night, she heard the heavy bolt of the church's vaulted front entrance. It could only be Rosie as no one else had the key for that ancient lock. The mother superior heard the familiar heavy footsteps heading toward her office instead of receding towards the further end of the church. She waited and then opened the door to a very tired Rosie to receive an instant hug.

Greetings mingled with apologies from Rosie and exclamations of relief from the mother superior were exchanged. Soon the two were ensconced in deep chairs, clasping mugs of hot chocolate. Rosie explained that she had to switch off her phone due to continued interruptions from the media. Their discussion turned to the unbelievable success of Rosie's book and the implications of it. Rosie assured her guardian of her intention never to abandon her church and her God. After that, the discussion had turned to

PRANKZzz and its last paragraph, in particular the last line. It came under much scrutiny, with much mysterious mirth, especially from Rosie, who had every reason to live and enjoy life to the hilt. There was another reason Rosie had switched off her phone. She did not want the five friends of the RAMS days to reach her; not yet. She had plans for them and it was this that was the cause of the ensuing mirth between the two. Rosie had never felt happier and the mother superior could not help but be part of it. It was way past their bedtime and most people across the vast land were fast asleep. The mother superior decided to retire for the night and Rosie took her leave, looking forward to her own small bedroom, which she had not seen and slept in for a few nights.

∽

A full moon cast a chink of its charm through a small parting in the curtains, which were as still as silent sentinels. The rope dangling from the high rafters was lit in a chiaroscuro of soothing blue and Rosie was suspended by the neck at the end of it. Her hands were hanging limp by her sides, still, very still, shamelessly so forever.

In the master bedroom of the house in Koramangala, Urmilla woke up with a scream and sat upright in the darkness. Next to her, Kartik fumbled for the light and switched it on. In the eye-numbing brightness he saw his wife sitting, perspiring, and breathing heavily. He pulled himself up to sit by her and put an arm around her.

'You okay, darling? What's the matter?'

Urmilla muttered vaguely.

'Rosie. Rosie. I saw Rosie...'

'You had a dream, sweetheart, a nightmare. What about Rosie? What happened?'

Urmilla spluttered.

'Hanging by a rope. She's hung herself!'

Kartik rubbed her shoulders.

'Just a bad dream. Only a nightmare, Urmi. It's not like you, having nightmares. I'll get you some water. Come on, lie down.'

Kartik slid out of the bed and left Urmilla, who was shivering despite the humidity, her mind racing. By the time Kartik returned with two tumblers of filtered water laced with brandy, Urmilla was convinced that Rosie would carry out the intention stated in the last line, if she had not already done so. Kartik gently dismissed Urmilla's foreboding. She wasn't totally convinced because of the unanswered calls and the unanswered e-mail she had sent to the mother superior. However, for the moment, the brandy-tinged water was beginning to work wonders and she was fast asleep within minutes. A relieved Kartik shut the lights. For him, sleep was more elusive as he started wondering what exactly Rosie meant by the very last line in her book. Random images of Rosie and the others during their days at RAMS floated in his head – the good moments and the bad ones – and of the silly pranks and games they had played on each other. He had played his part in a prank or two but had always intervened when matters seemed to get out of hand. Except once when Karan and Suresh had faked that stupid suicide by hanging. If only he had known what they were up to. If only Rosie had not hurt her hand. If only... It was nearly an hour before he drifted into sleep, thoughts ebbing away like reluctant waves.

∽

Over the next few days, Urmilla, Kartik, and Shaila all but forgot the momentary ado caused in their busy lives by the release of Rosie's book and its subsequent media saturation. Up north in much colder Chandigarh, the same applied to Karan and Suresh. All of them, whether north or south, had in common the passion to save, prolong, and improve lives through their medical skills, honed at RAMS and later affirmed by long hours of work at their respective hospitals. The zeal and compassion inculcated into them by their dean, Professor Sharma, was beginning to pay dividends. Ward rounds were made, case meetings attended, symptoms analysed, diagnoses made, treatment decided on and administered, progress monitored, and happier patients discharged. At home, at any available hour, journals were read, the internet scoured for the latest medical developments, and notes made.

Of the six friends, only Rosie had no part in the exciting hustle and bustle of the practice of modern medicine. Her days had increasingly become less exciting and the hours seemed like weeks that were reluctant even to drag themselves by. She had tried to get back into the thick of her devotional work at the church after the whirlwind of lavish high-octane book launches, interviews, and receptions, which she had thoroughly enjoyed while they were happening. Then, fewer and fewer of these happened before coming to a stop. Rosie could not decide whether this was good and peaceful or bad and disturbing, as she put it to herself. She was left with her increasingly impatient publishers, who chased her to begin work on her next book, while her manager, her chauffeur and the car, became increasingly redundant, not that they complained, till they were dismissed. Having tasted life on the crest of high waves that she had conquered and ruled for a short while, she was, now, beached on debris-strewn shallows in which she was doomed to drown forever, it seemed to her. Then, she lifted herself out of the shallows, remembered her faith, remembered the mother superior's guiding hand, and foremost, remembered her own shame of a useless right hand. Rosie's phone remained switched off but it was time to reacquaint herself with her laptop and to cheer herself by sending the group e-mail she had planned. It was time to make use of the final paragraph of her book and pray for the best for everyone, not least for her blighted hand.

∽

Dr Suresh Dutt hated checking his e-mails, especially as most of them were unwanted and useless. Whenever he could bring himself to do so, regardless of the time or the place, it felt like opening his front door to a crowd, only to recognize a face here and there. The first chaotic step he took was to delete unopened, unwanted, and unknown e-mails. It gave him a tinge of gleeful satisfaction, the same as from swatting irritating mosquitoes and flies. This was almost the same as turning away the myriad marriage proposals that were knocking on his door every now and then, much to his parents' satisfaction and his consternation. When he reached an e-mail from a name he recognized instantly, his finger hovered and waited in suspicion. The e-mail was from someone he knew from his RAMS days, he recalled. Only recently he had come head to head with her potential as a writer of fiction mixed with facts. Rosie Braganza, who wrote from RosettaBrz@hotmail.com. Not much given to reading anything but medical journals, Dr Dutt had already read Rosie's book twice and now he had an e-mail from her.

∽

Chote Sardarjee, Dr Karan Singh Virdee, still lived in the huge, old ancestral house, only minutes away from his childhood friend Suresh Dutt. The little spare time he had on his hands he spent on his small rickety boat, fishing on an artificial lake on the outskirts of the city, very often with Suresh, catching small, sullen and sad fish and tossing them back into the lake. What was the excitement of hooking small fish, only to release them back into the lake? A small thrill, was his answer, if he was ever asked. Ever the family man, he loved his grandmother most of all in the huge extended family of uncles, aunties, nieces, nephews and all. Only his grandmother knew of his failing romance with a nurse at his workplace and Nani kept her secret. As for e-mails, Karan was religious and methodical. Every night, before he tumbled into bed he questioned his computer, resisting surfing the net and getting straight to the business of answering e-mails. This night he came across an e-mail from someone he knew years ago, that someone whom he had seen recently on TV and read about. Someone who had gained much more than her fifteen minutes of fame, much deserved, though, he thought.

∽

Dr Shaila Sirinavasan was as serene as ever and still single despite a swarm of admiring wasps around her, mostly from the medical world. She resisted each one. Her 'Mr Right' had not yet materialized, though she did have love pangs years ago for a hunk of a fellow student at RAMS, one Suresh Dutt, who was in her study group. She had often wondered about him and had spoken to him several times lately, after years of not being in contact. The subject of their conversations had been Rosetta Braganza, or Rosie, or 'Fatso', as the slightly overweight student was often teasingly called while they were all students at RAMS; until 'Fatso' had to leave because of very unfortunate and unexpected circumstances, for which Suresh was partly to blame. As for e-mails, Shaila was totally methodical and rigid and prowled through them at each and every opportunity, whether at home in her bijou flat or during very rare slack periods at work. Relaxing after a thorough workout at her local gym, she came across an e-mail she was intrigued about. It was from RosettaBrz@hotmail.com.

~

Spent and tired, but happy, the newly married Subramaniams were enjoying a well-deserved rest. The squash game they had played had not tired but energized them. It was the subsequent lovemaking that had left a glow on both their faces and tired them pleasantly. Not yet parents themselves, they had spent a precious free weekend hosting their two sets of parents. Urmilla's father, a retired banker, and his gentle wife, had Saturday evening with their daughter and son-in-law while Sunday afternoon and evening were devoted to Kartik's parents, both wisely-aged and full of advice. Urmilla had taken heed of several comments, jibes, and hints about the patter of small feet. Both sets of parents were awaiting the arrival of their first grandchild. Urmilla was warming up to the idea but was not totally hot about it, as she checked her e-mail before retiring to bed. Before any others, she clicked on the one she thought might be most interesting. It was a group e-mail sent to five people, Urmilla and Kartik being two of them. The others were the same as the old study group at RAMS: Suresh, Karan, and Shaila. Urmilla scanned the e-mail and read it again, slowly this time, trying to make sense of it. It was typical of Rosie. Like the last paragraph of her book, it was puzzling and needed deciphering. What was Rosie up to?

Hi guys and gals,

Fatso calling. Hope you're all well. I am well. Another day in paradise. Long time, no? This is mainly to apologise for you know what. You all might or might not have read the blasted book or might have heard of it. Come on, you must have, given all the hoo-ha. Sorry, used some shared experiences and used you guys in the book, giving you different names and some bad habits! I did it because the story had to be masalafied, so to speak. Sorry for giving bad characteristics to good guys but there were many times you guys were rotten to me too. Anyway, I only did that to add excitement to the story. The real reason for my writing to you all is to apologize and invite, no, force you to come for a celebration. My birthday. We used to celebrate each others' birthdays, remember? So, why make an exception this time? Also, the success of my book calls for celebration. You will surely see me via the media but only meet me after a long time, as I am a very busy person, all of a sudden. Mama (Big Mother Superior) will get in touch with you all and give you a date to keep free, please. You must attend, as every time people meet, it might be for the last time. Look forward to it. I only look backwards. Looking forward is not interesting, what with my useless and wasted shame of a hand. Be there, for old times' sake! It's only harmless fun. Come and see me as never before. It might be your last chance as I will be starting my journey for eternal peace on the day of my birth.

Yours with love and mirth,
Rosie the fatso, good for nothing and nothing.

This e-mail had more questions than answers, quite literally like the last paragraph of her book. It was puzzling and needed even more urgent interpretation. What did Rosie mean? It was perplexing enough to set off a flurry of frantic telephone calls, yet again. Urmilla, Shaila, Kartik, Karan, and Suresh, were filled with speculation, this time with a tinge of remorse and much panic. A consensus was finally reached. Rosie had to be reached; the suicide she was planning had to be stopped at any cost. She was much too nice a person to be lost in such horrid circumstances, especially as, in varying degrees, each one of the five friends were responsible for her plight. Phone calls to Rosie were made but remained unanswered, as were the e-mails sent to her and to the mother superior. The five debated and discussed what to do. Rosie's birthday was less than a week away. The best way possible was to get to Rosie at her church, before her birthday, to make absolutely sure she had no plans or intentions to end her life on that day. Four of the five favoured and wanted this and were prepared to fly to Goa and get to Rosie's church, none of them having ever been there before. They were only as familiar with the church as the matchstick model of it, which Karan had sliced to bits with a surgical knife to avenge a prank when his coffee had been laced with a laxative. The only restraining and cautionary, but muted voice, was that of Kartik, as usual. He was the one who always brokered peace and invited sense when pranks and ensuing matters used to cross safe limits at RAMS all those years ago. The other five had always been thankful to him for his counsel and decisiveness, often without acknowledging it. Kartik suggested that to await communication from the mother superior would be better than rushing to Rosie at her church. Judging by the media coverage, for all they knew she might not even be there, given her newly acquired fame and wealth. All agreed to wait for the mother superior to tell them where to meet Rosie and when.

Another group e-mail vaporized into ether and condensed into five computers, waiting to be energized. It was surprising, pleasant, and confusing, all at the same time, even to Dr Shaila Sirinivasan's mind, which was otherwise as clear as a bright and sunny day. Yet another flurry of phone calls between the five recipients of the enigmatic e-mail followed, as it contained a surprise. The birthday or whatever Rosie had in her mind, was to be celebrated not in Panjim but in Bangalore, in a conference room which none of them had ever been in or heard of. Except Kartik and Urmilla, who had hosted a dinner for Rosie at this hotel one evening just after they had moved into their new house in Koramangla. On her way to the ladies toilet, Rosie had wandered into the semi-darkness of the huge conference room and its spooky gloom had stayed in her mind. She had set many a scene there in her mind and in her book, but now, with the help of Mother Superior, she was going to stage the finale of her life there, as real as flesh and blood. The e-mail from the mother superior to the five was to be pivotal but organizing the party was a logistical nightmare that wasn't beyond the combined talents of the two women of cloth, one more superior than the other in matters of godliness.

Dr Karan Singh Virdee read the e-mail again and again as did his four friends.

> *Dear friends of Rosetta and therefore also mine, blessings of the Almighty be upon you. Rosie talked much about you all but I have not had the pleasure of meeting any of you, which I hope will change soon. You were all a great inspiration for Rosie and she wanted me to convey her gratitude. You will have received an e-mail from her apologizing about the way she based her story on some of your shared experiences. Rosie felt indebted to all of you and charged me to arrange her heartfelt thanks at her birthday get-together, where you might see her. Details of the venue, date, time, etc., are attached. There will be several of your and Rosie's friends and acquaintances there, hopefully, but you five will be privileged guests of honour. Your presence will be greatly valued at Rosie's birthday and prayer meeting. Presents are not necessary or needed.*
> *I look forward to our meeting.*
> *Trust in God and all will be well.*
>
> *Yours,*
> *Mother Superior Henrietta Lall*

There was no choice. Each of the five talked to each other and agreed to attend, even if surprised at the content and intention of the e-mail. What was it an invitation to, exactly? A birthday celebration? A book publicity stunt, not that it was needed. A funeral? All of these? There was only one way to find out and that was to turn up with birthday presents for Rosie at the appointed place, which Urmilla and Kartik knew about. The others, they decided, would have to find their own ways to the venue. The five ended up feeling the same. Whatever it was that the mother superior was inviting them to as privileged guests of honour, Rosie owed them an explanation when they got to her.

That very night, Rosie was restless, having achieved what she wanted to. Her plan was proceeding well and there wasn't much left for her to do. She had more than mended her fences with the mother superior and finally had accepted totally that, for whatever reason, the call to become a nun was yet to be heard or felt, however it announced itself. She would happily remain 'Sister Rosie' till it happened. Until then she would wait; but waiting made her restless. The hullabaloo about *PRANKZzz* had died down, about which she was pleased, but it left her with nothing much to do. She toyed with the idea of starting another short story and see where it took her but could not think what it was to be or where to begin. Sleep eluded her and it was nearly dawn. On impulse, Rosie switched on her bedside lamp, got out of bed and rummaged in her waste-paper basket, which was always full to the brim. She switched on the main light in her room and soon had the pieces of her broken matchstick model on her desk. What made her turn to the model of her church did not matter to her. For years, she had tried to repair it to completion and failed. What was the point of trying yet again? It was something to do, she convinced herself, regardless of what made her pick the pieces she had discarded. So far, after so many years, she had only managed to glue three of the pieces together. She glued a fourth piece and stuck it in place. Then the fifth one and the sixth one and the seventh one...

39

The five had decided to meet for a drink at another expensive hotel before attending Rosie's birthday celebrations, if that was what the occasion was going to be. The chilled Chablis was more than agreeable and the accompanying olives and cubes of cheddar were even more so. The conversation was pithy and mainly hovered around the book, which events within it happened and which didn't, and which ones had been tampered with. The names given to them in the book became a topical relief and the butt of many a jibe and joke. Memories and reminiscences bounced forth and then homed in to the here and now. Present posts, researches and work notes were exchanged and finally Rosie was mentioned almost offhand, despite her being the main reason for their gathering in Bangalore. Suresh and Shaila exchanged several glances, which became increasingly more meaningful, more so to them and unnoticed by others. Urmilla and Kartik touched toes every now and then and their elbows contacted even more frequently. The stretches of silence were getting longer. Hugely intelligent people, talented, painfully trained and skilled, miles beyond those on the streets that they were destined to look after, had run out of things to talk about. Kartik cleared the bill and led the way to the foyer of the hotel where his pristine blue Mercedes waited for them, to crawl a few hundred yards to the next five star hotel with the conference room, where Rosie awaited them. Or did she?

Greetings, hugs, smiles, and surprises were flying about but not with much abandon. The five friends were immediately taken aback by the gathering in the brightly lit conference room, with a long table laden with food and drinks, and waiters hovering about with proffered trays of this and that. Familiar faces, voices and mannerisms were soon to be spotted. The old caretaker of accommodation block 'A' at RAMS was lapping it up like no one else. With a glass of single malt whisky and certainly without the thick glasses and even more certainly without the *Russell and Whitehead* tome, he was flitting from one person to the other, holding and hugging them. Keeping him company was Girish, not 'Gopal', the manager of the old common room at RAMS, who was slightly portly and older than the young buck described in Rosie's book. The eminent, somewhat bemused, and totally upright Prof Sharma became their friend, at least for the duration of this strange function, and not the feared boss he was. As for the eminent Professor himself, it was a delightful evening away from his normal RAMS existence of teaching, caring and planning bright futures for his students – some of whom he was delighted to meet again, even if in somewhat unwarranted and far from academic circumstances. The place was most unlike the common room at RAMS, with a totally different resonance. Neither a disco nor a club of total disobedience nor a cafeteria for all needs, this was a brightly lit conference room with many paintings adorning the walls. Prof Sharma was particularly pleased, and even excited, at meeting his somewhat subdued number one study group of Urmilla, Kartik, Shaila, Karan, and Suresh, all of whom had more than fulfilled his expectations. He had done his job and was happy about it. There was young Karan, who could diagnose a patient from miles away, as if he had divine powers, and could prescribe the right treatment with equal aplomb. There was the reserved and calm Kartik for whom nothing but nothing was a challenge. Treating his patients and writing prescriptions for them was easy at his magical fingertips. There was his brilliant wife, Urmilla, who was always the topper every year, beating her friend and friendly rival, Karan, each time, even by a mark or so. As for Urmilla, Prof Sharma had no terms of endearment deep enough when he hugged her. Urmilla's research work into the impacts of malnutrition during pregnancy, and its publication in various medical journals of international repute wasn't the proof the professor needed. He just knew it. She had it in her eyes. Was there ever an embodiment of beauty, grace, and such intelligence? Was there a person luckier than Kartik to have married such a one? Then there was Suresh, the plodder of the group, but what a plodder, the best-loved of them all, who had the gift of uplifting and curing by his charm and smiles alone. Patients, young and old, awaited his rounds eagerly, and the nurses ran after him. Then there was Shaila, the quiet and serious one of the group. What little natural talent she lacked was more than made up by long hours of studying. Over five years the carefully selected study group had gone through the rigours of medical study, together, apart from Rosie Braganza, who was the one sad blot on his mind. Rosetta Braganza, the much loved and missed baby mascot of the study group, who had been treated like a stuffed teddy bear by the others, had to leave RAMS despite much promise of rare brilliance. Prof Sharma had etched on his mind the memory of the best 'first incision ritual' he had seen by a new student. The hand was deft and precise and knew what to do and did it unbidden, it seemed. This was talent and ability so vastly scarce, it should have been bottled and preserved for others to see and emulate. Yet, Rosie had to leave without fulfilling that potential, much to his regret and to the country's loss. Like most other and less brilliant students, this study group of his had played their part of pranks, occasionally overstepping the mark, one of which Rosie had to pay for dearly when her right wrist was damaged beyond repair. After this incident, which shocked everyone but which was forgotten weeks after Rosie had left RAMS in a flood of tears, the depleted ace study group of five had given up all pranking for good, and had knuckled down to their studies and all had gone well after that. Romances were usually short-lived as time constraints were aplenty and preparations for exams claimed priority over everything during the five years they spent in RAMS. The togetherness also prompted separation and long lonely hours of studies in quiet study bedrooms. During the fifth and final year, Shaila's interest in Suresh had shifted a gear but she wasn't sure whether he was aware of it or whether he should be made aware of it. Final-year exams had put paid to the small spark of extra interest, whereas in Kartik and Urmilla's case, a rarity, passing glances had turned to hugs and kisses; romance had blossomed to love as they spent long hours of studying together, with a kiss and a cuddle for a break, every now and then, just as other students stopped for a cup of tea or coffee.

Here, at the birthday party of an ex-student which Prof Sharma had made an exception to attend, he kept the small coterie of teaching staff from his beloved faculty enthralled with his easy wit, while keeping a proud eye on the rest of his ex-students. Rarely ever did he have misgivings about his students, but for these six – the best study group he had put together – he had one. Like other students, each one of the six would head their separate ways to plough their own fields. What a pity that would be. Wasn't there some way the six could stay together even if one of them didn't make it? Reluctantly, he dismissed his musing as it was unlikely to happen. Little did he know what was to be.

Prof Sharma returned to the party, which was well and truly underway, with an increasingly loud babble of several conversations competing with each other, now that alcohol – in various forms and versions – was beginning to shed the outer shells of decorum. The conference room was slowly edging towards being like the common room, at least noise-wise, but nobody seemed to be in charge of it. Still, the invitees seemed not to mind as there was much to catch up on and the food and drink was free-flowing. Finally, a microphone was placed on a raised dais at one end of the long room, switched on, and tapped and tested. It was in fine working order and the young waiter, who had placed it in all its solitary and still gloom, stepped away. Apart from the talking, drinking, and eating, nothing was happening and it seemed like this would go on. The study group of five who had remained as one throughout the halfhour that had elapsed, became aware of the increasingly conspicuous absence of their sixth friend, in whose name they were present here. Where was Rosie Braganza and what was happening here? This function was assuming all the makings of an upper-class wake, it occurred to Urmilla. Just as she was about to suggest they make enquiries, the mother superior sauntered to the microphone, and looked around the conference room, in which were present all the guests and also a couple of press photographers and a TV crew. A bronze cross swung suspended from the side of her cassock with its chain tied around her waist. In her hand she held a rosary. Her timid coughs into the microphone failed to silence those present, some of whom had not even noticed her arrival. The mother superior tapped the live microphone with the ring on her right hand and the resulting noises on the PA system produced the desired silence, as the jumble of conversations ebbed slowly to low murmurs before silence ensued. The experienced public speaker that the mother superior was, with many a memorable sermon behind her, she let the silence sink further, which, within seconds, transformed the jovial air of bonhomie in the conference room into that of some sobriety. She knew very little about those gathered apart from some tales of academy life that Rosie used to regale her with.

'Dear friends, may I welcome you all to this function at the behest of Sister Rosie. I am sure she is here with us all in spirit if not in person...'

Urmilla trembled and Shaila gasped audibly. The three men glanced at each other, faces turned to stone in disbelief. Urmilla's hand reached for Kartik's and clasped it hard. With the other hand she reached for Shaila's hand, and Shaila in turn, almost as a reflex action, reached out for Sanjay's. The mother superior continued her address, having gained her stride.

'Lately, Sister Rosie had been very busy. As you all know, the prelaunch of her debut novel, the subsequent launch, and the ensuing aftermath of it took her and others' connected with the book by complete surprise. The pressure to attend all manners of book launches and promotions, I am afraid, took its toll. More than that, as most of you know, and very likely most of you will be aware of, Sister Rosie suffered a tragic setback at the medical academy when her hand was damaged. This led to stretches of depression which got worse...'

Karan noticed his friends were holding hands, so he reached out and held Suresh's hand. What they had speculated about during long phone calls and dismissed as totally unlikely had happened. Rosie had done what she prophesied in the final paragraph of her book. Like the others, he had read it so many times that he knew it almost word by word.

'Finally and forever, on this the day of her birth, the ever-trembling, ever so useless shame of a hand was still, as still as it was ever going to be... That too, of its own volition.'

It was the very last line that was worrying. This was no time to speculate yet again, about what it might mean. Karan wondered how many people present here had read the book and how many within those had puzzled over the last line. He lost the mother superior's address as he could not help but decide that Rosie's 'ever so useless shame of a hand' had finally driven her to suicide and this was either a wake or a funeral or both. What else could the mother superior mean... 'I'm sure she's here in spirit...'? This snapped Karan back to the ongoing address.

'...Sister Rosie had asked me to arrange this function to mark her birthday and she left a list of all those to be invited. I am very pleased to have done that and note that almost everyone invited is here to pay their tribute to Sister Rosie, whose birthday was in fact yesterday. Sister Rosie left a note which I am to read to you...'

Silent tears were rolling down Urmilla's face and Shaila wasn't far behind. The three men of the study group, no longer boys, seemed outwardly stoical but inwardly and secretly, were crumbling. All five of the study group awaited the announcement and revelation of the demise of the sixth member of their study group, and dear friend, Rosie. Each one dealt with his or her own grief and guilt in his or her own way, inwardly or outwardly, eyes firmly fixed on the mother superior, who unfolded a piece of paper and began reading from it.

'Friends, seniors, esteemed professors, and others, especially those more than my friends, those who are responsible for what happened to me and for why I've ended up where I am. This gathering, thanks to Mother Superior, who arranged it on my behalf, is mainly to thank you all, and more so to offer apologies to those of you who I pilfered from to write my book. Urmilla, Kartik, Shaila, Karan, and Suresh, my dear friends, I know you're all there. So are Prof Sharma and Caretaker Uncle. If you liked the characters I based on you all, I will be happy. If you did not, I hope you will forgive me. The reason I am not with you all is...'

There was a stir at the other end of the conference room and the mother superior looked up to see the cause of it, and smiled broadly. She lowered the paper she was reading from.

'Thanks be to Almighty, I don't have to read the rest of this...'

The mother superior stepped away from the microphone. More heads turned toward the entrance. A slightly burly figure attired in designer pink, carrying a matching handbag and wearing the latest in make-up, strode towards the raised dais. Her hair was dyed light brown with blond streaks in it. It took most people a few seconds to realize that Rosie Braganza had arrived. The study group of five, somewhere in the middle section of the conference room, only saw Rosie when she had stepped on to the dais, hugged the mother superior, and turned to her guests. There were sharp intakes of breath from the five friends and huge sighs of relief when they heard Rosie's voice, still familiar even after so many years, boom out from the PA system.

'Hi, everyone. Good to see you all. I just want to say a few words and then we'll let the party take over and I will come around and meet each one of you. First and foremost, I must apologize for arriving late...'

Urmilla's hands flew to her head, holding it lest it dropped out of sheer disbelief, mingled with relief and quickly turning into joyous excitement. Shaila was still shaking her head for the same reasons as her friend next to her, and the three men, not normally given to full displays of emotion, stood with mouths gaping open. All unblinking eyes were locked on Rosie. Yes, it was Rosie behind the microphone.

'Things have been very hectic of late due to my book taking off, in a way I never expected. However, I am more than pleased and relieved to tell you that today's book promotional event in Mumbai was the last one and it delayed my getting here. Anyway, I will not be writing any more books. That decision has been made. If you're wondering why not, despite the phenomenal success of *PRANKZzz*, I will tell you later. Now, to today's business. Mother Superior must have thanked you all, already. All the same, let me add my personal thanks to each one of you. In particular to my study group over there, all of whom are very dear to me, Professor Sharmajee and our Caretaker Unclejee and our common room manager, Girish, over there. This party is for you all. My birthday was just an excuse to get you here. The main reason for the party is also for another, bigger apology. Those of you who have read my book and seen or read all the mad media coverage will know that it is based on some incidents that truly did happen at RAMS, some that I took the liberty of changing a little bit here and there, and others that never happened. To tell this story, I based my characters on real people I had the good fortune to meet at RAMS. For those of you who don't know or didn't realize, let me tell you that my study group and dear friends for ever, Urmilla, Shaila, Kartik, Suresh, and Karan became Uma, Shivani, Krish, Sanjay, and Kamal in the book, and of course Prof Sharma became Prof V. I gave nasty habits to some of these characters and that wasn't a nice thing to do. I am sorry about that, but to make a story interesting and believable you have to invent characters that are perfectly capable of doing what they do, or what you make them do as a writer. I have to say, I enjoyed my time at RAMS even if I was unable to complete the course and fulfil my lifelong ambition to be the best neurosurgeon. About this I want to say some more at the end...'

Rosie's listeners were beginning to relax and smiles reappeared. The study group had finally and fully grasped the reality of Rosie, not only very much alive in front of them but that she seemed to be more full of life than ever before, radiating energy and passion, to boot. They could hardly wait to put their arms around her but for now they continued to listen to her.

'If you're wondering why I chose to write this book and why I chose to write it the way I did, I will tell you. It began as a short story during my first year at RAMS before I had to leave...more about that later. When I returned to my church and became a sister, I immersed myself in church and parish work, but I still had time on my hands, sometimes in the early hours of the morning, and other times late at night. The short story grew and grew. It simply flowed and wrote itself, as they say, until I came to the ending, which I simply could not decide upon. To make it happy or sad, comic or tragic or none of these and leave it open-ended? That was the question. Then, I remembered that Urmilla, Shaila, Karan, and Suresh played pranks on each other and more so, on me, as they saw me as an easy target; but I have to say there was never any malice, implied or meant. Kartik, for his part, largely kept out of these pranks, mainly because he lived off campus and also because he was too busy wooing and trying to impress Urmilla, to whom he's now married, I might add. Whenever anything got out of hand it was Kartik who always brought the rest of us back on track. Yes, there was rivalry between Urmilla and Karan but nothing of the sort as described in the book. It was very much friendly and healthy. As for me, I used to suffer fools gladly because I was only too pleased to be a part of this high-powered study group, as selected by Prof Sharma. All I used to say was that they could prank me as much as they wanted, but when the time came, I would have the last laugh. The time came and I did. This is it. This is my last laugh at my five dear friends. Some of you, maybe most of you, will have realized that the very last paragraph of my book, *PRANKZzz*, implied that the Rosie in the book committed suicide by hanging, if only to make her "useless shame of a hand" be still finally and forever. Well, the real Rosie as you see, is here before you – alive and well – and I have no intention of doing what the book Rosie did at the end. There is the best possible reason for that, which I will tell you shortly. For now, let me tell you that the ending, that last line, was designed by me to have the last laugh at my fellow study group members. You guys, over there, tell me, did I not have the last laugh just now? Did I not get you all worried, thinking I might do away with myself or that I might have already? Did I not make you guys come running to me, as I said I would? Didn't my e-mail make you run around like headless chickens? Didn't Mother Superior's e-mail send you all on a wild goose chase! You guys fell for it! Didn't you, guys, over there?'

Rosie pointed at the five standing next to each other. All of them were sheepish and each one had a wide grin, a sure sign of acquiescence. Karan waved at Rosie in acknowledgement and the other four followed suit. Rosie waved back.

'Don't take it badly, guys. Only harmless fun! I'll see you shortly. Just one last thing to tell you about why I won't be writing any more books and why I won't be doing what the book Rosie did at the end. No, I have the best of reasons to live because I will achieve my lifelong ambition to become the best neurosurgeon of her generation. For that I request Prof Sharmajee to accept me back at RAMS and let me complete my studies and skills under his aegis. Yes, I want to return to RAMS and start where I left off.'

After a collective gasp, a hushed silence filled the conference room. Prof Sharma scratched his goatee, and after exchanging looks with one or two of his junior teaching colleagues, looked back at Rosie. A similar frisson had passed between the five friends, as they, too, exchanged looks. Rosie sensed that her request had baffled most of those present. Even so, she smiled broadly and raised her right hand as high up as she could, while next to her, the mother superior crossed herself. Rosie lowered her hand to eye level and studied the palm before addressing the microphone.

'This right hand of mine is no longer shameful or useless. It will go on to perform surgical miracles. It is cured. It is healed!'

There was a murmur around the conference room which began to rise in volume. Urmilla hugged Shaila and both of them burst into tears but for different reasons this time. Even the mighty Suresh had to wipe away a tear before getting into a clinch with Karan and Kartik. The long-harboured guilt and remorse that had weighed heavy on Karan and Suresh lifted. Someone whistled, someone else clapped, and soon the conference room was reverberating with whistles, clapping, and table thumping. Leading the cheering and almost dancing with joy were the five friends, who had the urge to run to Rosie, and almost did when Rosie raised both hands and requested calm and restraint. While the exuberance became less noisy, Rosie hugged the mother superior before turning to the microphone.

'As a scientist and knowing a little bit about nerves and nerve cells, I have no explanation as to why the damaged tendons and nerves have regenerated after wasting away nearly seven years ago. It just means I don't know as much about nerves and nerve cells that I thought I did. So I need to learn more. One thing I do know is that Mother Superior has been praying each day for the recovery of my hand. Has a miracle happened? The scientist in me tells me to discount this possibility but my faith tells me not to discard it, whether I believe it or not. Tried and tested, my right hand is as good as it used to be, if not better. How it came about I don't know or care. The fact is, it's happened. My hand is cured. Prof Sharmajee, please, I would like to return to RAMS and finish what I started.'

Prof Sharma was standing with his small group of junior teaching staff. Heads turned towards him and all eyes fixed on him. The professor shuffled his feet, took his hands out of his pockets and strode up to the dais; he smiled warmly at Rosie and offered his hand. As they shook hands, Prof Sharma kissed his new student lightly on both cheeks and hugged her. He said something to Rosie which nobody heard and sought her right hand again. He rubbed the palm gently and examined it. While loud applause broke out like a huge number of racing pigeons taking off, Prof Sharma left the dais to rejoin his group. Rosie turned to the microphone and yelled into it.

'Everyone, let's party!'

The music started with a drum roll. Rosie and the mother superior left the dais and walked hand in hand. The main lights dimmed a little and other lights of different colours and hues sprang into life. Rosie saw her five friends hurrying towards her, headlong, and within seconds she was surrounded by them. One by one, hugs were exchanged with each. What they said to each other, not even Prof Sharma, standing next to the six young adults, could hear; but then it hardly mattered. Fingers were wagged at Rosie amidst much cheering, backslapping, and laughter. The professor watched them, smiling. He hoped nobody would notice his misty eyes.

He had done his job and done it well. Also standing close by was the mother superior, smiling broadly as she watched the six. She crossed herself and stepped up to the professor to thank him while the six friends went into a huddle, arms around each other's shoulders. All six of them were clearly overjoyed and living up every moment of the final prank that Rosie had played on them all. She had done what she had said all along and had made them run to her. The huddle broke apart when most of them felt urgent tugs on their backs and elbows. Caretaker Uncle, nothing like he was in Rosie's book, was swaying on his feet. The glass of whisky in his hand was doing a tango on him.

'One of you is not going to make it. Mark my words. One of you is not going to make it. Silly asses and stupid girls, I love you all but one of you is not...'

The six smiled at each other and Rosie put her arm around Caretaker Uncle as much to steady him as to get some sense out of him.

'Uncle, you always said that but we all made it. I'll be a bit late but I'll make it too. I'm coming back to RAMS to give you more trouble.'

'One of you is not going to make it...mark my words...'

Kartik took over as he often used to at RAMS. He turned to a grinning Girish, the common room manager he knew only too well.

'Giri, look after uncle. Get him a seat and get some food down him.'

The six turned to each other and no one thought more about him and his long running prophecy except Rosie. In her mind, his slurred words kept ringing longer than they should have. 'One of you is not going to make it...' Rosie had too much to celebrate, so she dismissed him and his prophecy as a result of too much to drink, which is what most of the six used to do sometimes at RAMS. The huddle formed again.

Epilogue

LIGHTness.

The longest queue wormed past the storefronts in the mall. It seemed everyone wanted to see this film in the largest multiplex at the mall. Predominantly made up of young people, the queue was patient and inched forward slowly. Two policemen strolling casually along the queue had nothing much to do as yet. It was only when the current show ended and another large number of people exited from the cinema, excited and chattering, that the two policemen would need to be more alert. Also idling away the minutes were two press photographers and a young woman fiddling with a small voice recording device, who appeared to be a journalist. The presence of police and media persons was very rare at a cinema unless a celebrity was passing through. All the posters, large and small, showed a human skeleton hanging from a gallows with a lit, smoke-emitting cigarette clamped between tight jaws and a liquor glass clasped in one set of metacarpals. The tag line swirling around the skeleton read – 'From the mega bestselling book by Rosie Braganza... An astonishing story of six friends... Where nothing is as it seems... Where the truth is savage and the lies barefaced...' This was the first showing of the much acclaimed film version of *PRANKZzz,* which was causing as much of a stir as the book had. Rosie had declined to write the first draft screenplay as she had already made the decision not to write any more fiction in any shape or form. The two producers of the film brought in two renowned screenplay writers at the top of their trade. Rosie attended one or two crucial creative meetings with the producers and the screenplay writers and finally agreed that the eleventh draft was the closest to the best, and would be difficult to improve further. All knew that a creative work never ends, and changes for better or worse are made right up to the eleventh hour. Rosie knew this only too well, as had been the case with her short story – which had grown to the length of a novel – while she kept changing this bit and that. The film spoke for itself. The one star of the film was the screenplay as was intended, which turned all the relatively unknown actors into stars as well. After some seven years, during which a short story that began as a respite from studies had evolved into a best-selling book which had then turned from page to screen, the result was there for everyone to see and everyone did want to see it. *PRANKZzz* the film was a massive success and was on its way to be equally so, commercially.

The current show ended and out thronged the well-satisfied crowd. The debates and discussions as to who did what and why in the film had already started. Several wishes to see the film again were expressed and those who had not read the book were going to head for bookstores at the earliest opportunity. Those who had read the book wanted to read it again.

The journalist was scanning the crowd of youngsters, the photographers primed themselves and their cameras, while the two policemen positioned themselves in between the orderly queue and the faster unruly crowd going out. Rosie emerged with Urmilla by her side and Shaila by the other. Behind them were Kartik, Karan, and Suresh, all six of them in deep animated conversation, no doubt about the film, like the youngsters around them were. The journalist stepped forward, raising her voice recorder.

'Ms Braganza, quick word with Metro Radio, please.'

Rosie's way was almost barred. The photographers flashed away. Rosie had to stop, surrounded by her five friends as the rest of the young crowd filed by casting curious glances at her, not knowing who she might be, although her portrait was pasted inside the dust jacket of her book. The journalist continued with her work.

'What did you think of the film of your book?'

Rosie had had enough of media attention, large scale or small, but felt obliged to answer.

'Excellent. Much better than I expected. They've done a good job, especially the actors.'

'What is it like, seeing yourself portrayed on screen? How close is the screen version of yourself to the real you?'

Rosie perked up, her interest revived.

'Good question. It's a very strange feeling. It's seeing an actress trying to be me as written in the screenplay, which is based on what I am like in the book, where I am me as I wrote it. Does that make any sense?'

Rosie started to laugh and her friends joined in. The baffled journalist was trying to think of the next question. The photographers left, having got what they wanted, and as the crowd thinned, the two policemen returned to their casual sauntering.

'Are you working on the next book?'

'No. No time for that. No more stories from me.'

Rosie started to walk away with her friends. Dinner at a well-known seafood restaurant was waiting. The six had much to talk about, not least about the film they had just seen – in which they viewed versions of themselves based on their versions in the screenplay based on Rosie's book based on her RAMS experiences – real, imaginary, or in between. Could life be more complex but as interesting and exhilarating as this?

It could be and was.

Rosie remained true to her word. Despite repeated pleas and offers of massive advances from her publishers and many more from others, she did not write any more fiction, short stories, or long ones. She was back at RAMS, where the years flew by as she completed her training. The six friends remained more than in touch. They held reunions every four months or so, usually in Bangalore, where they stayed with Urmilla and Kartik in their spacious house, and sometimes in Chandigarh, where Karan and Suresh hosted them. The reunion weekends would be spent reminiscing about the past, discussing their present lives, and planning their futures. The latest developments in their chosen world of medicine would be analysed, and future trends and developments would be speculated upon. In between there would be much laughter, fun, food and drinks.

One year before she qualified, Rosie and the five friends embarked upon a joint initiative at her instigation. A stretch of land on the outskirts of Panjim, between Miramar and Dona Paula, was acquired, a renowned architect commissioned and a reliable construction company engaged. Rosie's considerable new wealth with contributions from her five friends, grants from the state government, and loans from financial institutions, enabled the 'Six Friends United Medical and Social Centre' to come into existence. It specialised in neurosurgery and preventive medicine but would also provide full curative health care and much more. The doctors, nurses and others were the best available and proven experts in their chosen fields of medicine; and the facilities were the latest in terms of technology. In many ways it was like RAMS, with the same hive of activity, with some tension-ridden moments and others, more relaxed. The medical centre's one underlying principle was that rich patients subsidized the care of those who could otherwise not afford it. The founders of the centre were jointly and firmly of the belief that no one who genuinely needed medical care and attention would be turned away, regardless of their backgrounds or circumstances. More than appropriately, the foundation stone of the centre was laid jointly by Professor Sharma and the mother superior. Both of them had already laid even deeper and more significant foundations earlier where the six friends and their futures were concerned. The opening ceremony for the centre was performed by the president of the country, no less, since it was the first of its kind – combining social care with medical care, while providing teaching and training facilities of the highest calibre. The patron and mentor of this unique project was none other than Professor Sharma.

The very first Head of Neurosurgery was the newly qualified Dr Rosie Braganza. Amongst the other heads of different departments were her five friends who would now also be colleagues – Urmilla, Shaila, Kartik, Karan, and Suresh – each one having more than readily accepted the offer without a moment's hesitation, despite the changes this would bring to their lives. Only Urmilla, a new mother, would be working on a part-time basis as she had a set of twin boys to look after. When the boys were born, the joke among the six was that Urmilla and Kartik never 'did things by halves'.

The 'Six Friends United Medical and Social Centre' became fully functional within weeks. Under the aegis of Professor Sharma and with advice from the mother superior, and not least with the life-saving and prolonging work of the six heads of department, it wasn't long before it settled into its busy routine. It became more and more like RAMS in its ethos, although the accommodation quarter at the medical centre was very different from the old accommodation block at RAMS. It was a cluster of villas around a swimming pool, and had extensive gardens and a car park, which was host to expensive vehicles unlike the one at RAMS. However, six of the residents of the accommodation wing were the same as at the old block at RAMS.

Urmilla and Kartik had sold their big house in Bangalore and moved in with their twin boys. Sanjay and Kamal relocated from Chandigarh, glad to leave the cold winter months behind. Shaila moved in with her elderly parents, for whom the tranquillity of the new setting was infinitely preferable to the traffic and bustle of Bangalore. It was a small distance for Rosie to move from her church in Panjim, but the journey had been a momentous one. Her heart was still with her church. She had the church repaired and repainted, and she had finally been able to present her completed matchstick model of it to the mother superior. Rosie remained Sister Rosie, and was also a brilliant neurosurgeon well on her way to be one of the best ones of her generation. There was no longer a void in her life and so the call to be a nun was no longer at its centre. Whatever little free time she had between her work at the medical centre and her devotion to her church, she spent in reflection or in the company of her five friends and colleagues, when they would reminisce about their times at RAMS in Bangalore. Sometimes, the six would wonder about Caretaker Uncle of their old accommodation block and his often repeated prophecy that one of them wasn't going to make it. He had said the same at Rosie's party but that was after he had downed a few drinks. When he came to the opening ceremony of the medical centre, he had repeated it in all seriousness and he was stone-cold sober then. Five of the six friends still did not attach any significance to it because they had all more than made it, patently so. Only Rosie often wondered and speculated about it. What if it did come true at some time in the future? It was true enough they had all made it as top-notch professionals, but that was only one aspect of life, and a lot more of it was left to be lived. The more free time Rosie had, the more curious she became about this and as the medical centre became more and more efficient, she did have more time.

One Sunday evening, having returned from the service at her church, Rosie was restless. At least once every month Karan and Suresh went to Chandigarh, and Urmilla and Kartik to Bangalore. This weekend, all four were away at the same time and Shaila had taken her parents for an outing.

Rosie was sitting on the veranda of her spacious villa, and having finished reading a newspaper, it struck her that although more than rewarding, life at the medical centre had become a routine. Perhaps it was time she played a harmless little prank on her friends? Rosie toyed with the idea then chided herself and banished it. That's how it had started, with a harmless prank at RAMS all those years ago and look where it had got to. Next, she thought of taking up matchstick model making again but there was no need for that, as her hands, both of them, were as rock steady as they would ever be; and she was already a top neurosurgeon. Suddenly, it struck her. She would reverse a decision she had made some time back and do what she did at RAMS, and later in her small room at her church. Rosie rushed into her villa and returned with a notebook and a pen. Resuming her comfortable seat, she doodled for a while and came up with a title and wrote out the very first page:

One of You
a short story
by
Rosie Braganza

Rosie thought for a while and then wrote out the very first line:

Located on the coast just outside Panjim, The Friends Medical Centre was reputed to be one of the best two in the whole country...